THE
Canyon House

ISBN: 978-1-68313-002-4

First Edition
Printed and bound in the USA

Cover photos: © : 1stGallery, Varandah
Cover and interior design by Kelsey Rice

THE
Canyon House

BY

JANICE GILBERTSON

𝒫
Pen-L Publishing
Fayetteville, Arkansas
Pen-L.com

Also by Janice Gilbertson

Summer of '58

Acknowledgments

Thank you to those nice people who stumbled through the first (or maybe sixth) draft, and to editors Ken and Betty Rogers, who set me straight when I began writing *The Canyon House*. Ken convinced me to send "Toby" packing, and my story never missed him.

Thank you Kimberley and Duke Pennell for trusting in me again; to Meg Welch Dendler for outstanding editing; and to Kelsey Rice who designed the book inside and out, and did such a great job of it.

I hold enormous gratitude for my readers. It is you who boost me on to do this all again.

Dedication

To my childhood friends,
the Nation and Holeman kids
All six

One

I know it had to be in early June, the day I first saw the canyon house—squatted like a tombstone in shade as dark as Mama's black coffee, all but hidden beneath the colossal Mulberry tree. Summer-dried grass and weeds grew right up tight against the gray stucco walls. My father warned Mama and me to "watch for rattlesnakes" as we high-stepped through the tangle to peer through the windows of the two bedrooms along one side of the house.

The thought made me shiver to the bone for a second or two. My cowboy boots, the ones with the toes nearly worn clear through, and my mother's white Keds stirred weed spores and dust that rose up and tickled our nostrils, causing my mother to break into a sneezing fit. I blessed her, to keep the plague and the devil at bay, and trudged on, eyes down, the snake warning replaying in my head. Which is why I saw that Mama's anklets bristled with foxtails.

"Oh, Mama," I said, pointing to her feet.

"Damn bugs," she said, swatting at the sweltering air and bending at the same time to pick at her socks. "I hate these gnats. They get in your ears, your nose, and everyplace else they can get."

Side by side, me up on tiptoe and Mama bent at her waist, we put our faces near the glass and cupped our hands around our eyes to get a clear look. The rooms were small and lacked any kind of likable character at all. The walls bore no color I could name. The one sign of a previous inhabitant of the tacky room was a pale oval where a picture had hung from a carpenter's nail. The floors were covered with grainy, flower-patterned linoleum. Footfall had worn the swirls of flowers ragged and muddy-looking at the doorway. My interest shifted to the window pane I'd been peering through. It had a long, diagonal crack, and the thin, wavy glass to one side of the flaw captured a dozen clear bubbles. I traced them lightly with one finger.

"Don't do that, Poppy. The glass'll likely fall out of there, and then we'll have us a mess." I noticed Mama's face growing redder, either from the heat or from bending again and again to pick at the foxtails gripping like fishhooks. "Wish he'd told me about these weeds and stickers. I would've worn something else."

I wondered what the something else would have been. She sure didn't have any cowboy boots. I turned away from her look of agitation and made my way around the house and up the front step to inspect the porch.

I heard her say "Dear Lord" as I walked away.

To get to the canyon house, my father had driven us in his faded-green Chevrolet pickup from the valley town we lived in up the El Camino Real. The pickup's cab reeked of cigarette smoke, and the ceiling wore a coat of orangey-brown nicotine. The dashboard was piled with feed store receipts, livestock news reports, and empty cigarette packs twisted into red and white bow shapes. My father's rope lay coiled beneath my mother's feet in the grit and dry cow manure. I knew his .30-30 rifle, slid into its dry, scarred leather scabbard, always lay right behind the seat, tucked beneath his Levi jacket and a small box of miscellaneous cattle-doctoring paraphernalia.

"If the doctorin' don't make 'em better, the gun sure as hell will."

He'd said those words too many times for me. I'd already formed a strong dislike for guns ever since I'd struggled to follow his long stride up a canyon, watched him raise his rifle and shoot a deer. And that wasn't the worst part. He had packed the big, glassy-eyed buck draped over his shoulder back to the pickup, causing the deer to bounce with each long stride he took, and I, trudging along behind and blinded by tears, thought the poor thing still alive. My ears rang with the blast of the shot he'd fired as I trailed back to the pickup. I believe it was after that certain loud noises made me edgy.

In truth, the drive was twelve miles south on the two-lane highway to the canyon road turn-off and then another eight miles west to the new house from where we lived in the valley, but if asked about the first trip there, I would have guessed the trip to be a hundred miles at least. I could tell my mother thought so, too, by the still, thin-lipped look on her face.

"How much farther is this place, Norm? This sure seems like a long ways. It's hotter than blazes." She reached for a tattered, yellowed issue of the *Templeton Livestock News* to fan herself with. She waved the limp pages up in front of her face a few times but gave up right away and put it back on the pile.

"Damn it, Frankie. I told you before it was about eight miles out here. You'll see it's nothin' when you've been up here a few times. You just gotta get used to it."

"Well, I can already tell you I don't want to live clear out here. You may as well just take me back home right now." She'd given her head a little toss of cheekiness.

"I ain't turnin' back now, Francine. We're just about there, anyway. I don't know why the hell you always have to be so disagreeable to anything I try to do. We won't get another chance at a place like this, that's for damn sure."

"Ha!" She let out her favorite snippy little noise. "I swear, sometimes I think you are crazy, Norman. Losing your ever-lovin' mind. Don't you know that valley people say only poor, dirty people live out in this canyon? The place has a reputation."

"That is bull hockey. Who says that? Some of your highfalutin' friends? Since when did you get so high and mighty?"

Mama's lips pressed thinner until they were practically a straight line with the slightest lift at the corners of her mouth. She may as well have just said outright that she knew for sure disaster was on the way, and when it befell her she could say, "See, I knew it." She gripped my bony knee hard with her left hand as we rounded curve after curve along the narrow road. I could tell that the worst part for her struck at the same instant the pickup gave us a good jarring after the road changed from potholed and patched blacktop to gravel and dirt and my father kept right on driving. She turned her face away and looked out the side window, and I saw her right hand grip the armrest, as if she was holding on for dear life.

As we bumped and jiggled over the road, drifts of suffocating dust seeped up through the cracks in the floorboard and the gap around the clutch pedal. I could taste the grit in my mouth and feel the dryness in my nose. I thought about the cowboy movies I'd seen where the stage-coach tilted and heaved across the prairie until a wagon wheel flew off and rolled to the side, letting the axle drag a crooked ditch in the dirt. I wondered if that could happen to our pickup.

My father drove with one hand lying loose and heavy over the steer-ing wheel and the ever-present cigarette between his fingers. His other hand steered nonchalantly from near the bottom of the wheel. As a tire dropped off into a pothole again, I watched as the long ash on his ciga-rette fell to the truck floor into the dirt under his feet. Hunched over the wheel, head moving from side to side in rhythm, he never missed a thing and commented on most of what he saw.

"That fella better staple the wires up to them posts one of these days, or he's gonna lose this whole goddamn fence along here," he pointed out. "Look there. That gate's fallin' off the hinges. They ain't big enough to hold the damn thing up." Cigarette ashes fell again as he gestured.

Because of the dust, when we left the pavement the windows were cranked up and the wind wings pulled in to just a crack—futile, since the powdered dirt sifted in anyway. We all wore a sheen of sweat on our faces. I bent to wipe the dampness away with my shirttail, but my mother pulled the material from my hand. The old pickup's parts rattled like steelies in a coffee can, and the tread on the tires grabbed the graveled dirt and threw it up beneath the big, round fenders, making a terrible clatter. The racket had me putting my fingers in my ears, but I caught a reprimanding glance from my father, so I took them away and folded my hands in my lap. I noticed that his blue eyes, usually pale and opaque, were shiny and clear below the brim of his straw hat. I began to understand that bringing us to this place was important to him, his show, and he would not allow any lack of enthusiasm from my mother or me to ruin it for him.

On the other side of a barbed wire fence snaked a winding arroyo that matched the curves of the road. My father pointed toward that direction with another cigarette between his fingers.

"That's the creek there," he declared, but in places I could get even a glimpse, there were few spots that showed any water. I wished that I was taller or, at least, sitting by the door in my mother's place so I could get a better look. We drove across two short bridges where the creek zigged and zagged under the road. A question burned my insides up.

"If that's a creek, why isn't there any water running? Isn't that what a creek is?"

"Because there ain't no damn rain in May and June," he said like I should have known that.

I sat forward on the edge of the seat and stretched my neck out like a gander so I could see better. I watched as oak trees and fence posts went by in semi slow motion. My father tended to drive so slow it made my mother want to pull her hair out. She and I both started and squealed a little when a deer bounded out into the road right in front of us.

"A deer! Look. A deer!" I yelled

I saw her leap over a fence with graceful ease and melt into the shadows of the low scrub brush growing thick as a hedge on the opposite side of the road. I became so excited I bounced up and down on the edge of the seat.

"That was a nice doe. We'll see a lot of 'em up here," my father said. "She should have a fawn this time a'year. There's a hell of a lotta deer in this country."

Sounded to me like it could have been a sales pitch with cuss words.

In my excitement over the doe, I nearly missed seeing the place opposite, over across the creek,—a curious place, fitted into the bend of the streambed and then sloping up here and there to some old oak trees and running into a cliff of sorts, high and layered with rock and rust-colored dirt.

"Don't know why the hell those people think they can build that place like that." My father motioned across me and out the side window with a nicotine-stained finger.

I leaned into my mother, trying to see what he was talking about. I caught just a glimpse of a low wall made of blocks stacked to make an L shape. I turned backward in the seat and got on my knees so I could see out of the back window. Just before we rounded the curve, I caught sight of a lady with long, dark hair and a girl beside her. A thick stand of creek willows formed a green, leafy curtain so that I couldn't see what lay behind them, but I caught a peek of something blue that glinted in the sunshine. I wished we could stop so I could see. I wished it so hard that, for just a second or two, I thought I could feel the pickup slowing.

"Can we stop and see those people?" I asked, still looking back. For someone as shy as me and withdrawn from strangers, why in the world I wanted to meet those people across the creek was a mystery, even to me.

"We don't know them people, Sis," my father laughed at the ridiculousness of my request.

"Well, we *could* know them. Maybe we can stop on the way back?"

"No. We ain't stopping there. Turn around and sit down."

Harsh. He always spoke so harsh.

Of course, we didn't stop there at all. But the vision of the lady and girl stayed in a corner of my mind. When I recalled the image, their picture sometimes loomed plain as day, just as I'd seen them, but sometimes it came to me faint and ghost-like, as if looking at them through a strip of gauze. I had seen a painting of a lady in a garden once where the artist had blurred all the edges and outlines. That is how I remembered the lady and little girl for a long time.

My mother had begun to fidget and give my father a lot of sideways glances. Her eyes could get small and dark when she became annoyed, and I could see that they were squinting a little bit. I could feel my insides just waiting for her to let go and give my father what for. Another mile and she probably would have lit into him royally.

The canyon had narrowed as we went along so that it spread about a half mile across when I first saw the little house. My father announced it, as if we had discovered the White House.

"Look there! There she is!" He pointed with his cigarette hand again and then, without looking, crushed the butt into the overfilled ashtray in the dashboard. The stench of burnt filters filled the hot cab, making me feel queasy.

My mother and I craned our necks to see across the creek where the drab little house faded into its colorless surroundings. The canyon road passed by the house a short distance before the driveway swung back in a hairpin turn that had to be maneuvered slow and careful to avoid driving off the bank and into the creek. We bumped across a dry, rocky crossing and came to a stop in a parking area a short distance from the house. I could see that there was no yard, no yard fence, only all those tall, dry weeds. Mama's face had grown stiff as starch. My father set the brake with the slam of his foot, same as always, flung his door open, and said, "Come on. Let's go take a look."

The new place and my mother's obvious unhappiness made me feel hesitant about leaving the pickup. I had in mind that I would just sit and wait for them to go look at the house without me. But Mama lifted the chrome handle and gave the door a push with her shoulder. She took a tight hold of my hand and guided me across the seat. I had no choice but to follow her out.

Taking my father's snake warning to heart, we picked our path like we were walking through a patch of stinging nettles. We came to the front porch, two steps high and not quite the width of the front of the house. The tin roof was held up by several four-by-four posts. The front door, paneled from top to bottom with thick, beveled glass panes, reigned center on the front of the house behind a wood framed screen door that wore a coat of peeling white paint. There were small, paned windows on either side—one for the front bedroom, the other for the living room.

On the porch sat two chairs, their red and white paint eaten away with rust. After we'd looked through the bedroom window, I wiggled onto one of the chairs and looked over the weedy ground that spread out toward the pickup and then beyond to the edge of a bank that fell off into the creek. At that exact moment, I felt a small prickle of excitement shiver up the back of my neck. A creek! I could imagine living with my own creek in front of my house. The idea seemed too good to be true.

I could hear my mother and father talking from around the corner by the chimney, and I could tell by their voices that neither one of them possessed a good frame of mind. My mother's words were clipped.

"Norman, why in the world would you bring us up here? I can't imagine living in this place. Look at it, for God's sake. There isn't even enough room here for Poppy and the boys."

"Damn it, Frankie. You're never happy. I can't please you, no matter what. I can get this whole place for less than we pay in the valley. Six hundred acres comes with this house. Six hundred acres, Francine. That means I won't have to pay lease for the cows anymore."

"Oh, God, Norman. What about Allen and Timothy? I see two bedrooms in there. What are they supposed to do? And does that creek really run? I don't want Poppy messin' around a creek where she could just fall in and drown."

"I already got a plan for the boys. Don't worry about that. I'm gonna move the little house up here. You're just lookin' for trouble, Francine. Poppy ain't gonna drown in no damned creek."

"You are going to move that house up here? For God's sake, Norman." I couldn't see her, but I knew Mama would be shaking her head like she did when her words ran out.

When we were all back inside the pickup cab, which was hot enough to roast a chicken, my mother had huge, silvery tears swimming in her eyes. They didn't leak out and run down her cheeks. They just stayed right there for a long time.

Two

It must have been hard on Mama to pack our belongings up, leave a place she loved, and take it all to a place she already hated. Maybe because of all the anger and unpleasantness that gripped the event, I have put away the memory of taking our possessions to the new house. To me, it seemed like one day I lived in one place and the next day I lived in another. Just that quick, I had my new bedroom with my own bed, and I felt grown up because I also got to have the big dresser with the mirror that had been my brothers'.

This might sound odd, but in truth, I loved that dresser. When it held their possessions, I would sneak into the room and slide those two small top drawers open to see what lay in the cubbyholes. I never discovered anything important—bits and pieces like pencil stubs and paperclips and erasers. Allen's side stayed neater than Tim's, and he kept his Boy Scout medals in some of the compartments.

I don't believe it was the items I cared about, anyway. It was those divided spaces in the drawers that I liked. I had a keen desire to organize their belongings in the cubbyholes; all of one item in each little square. I liked everything to be in its own special place. Not for neatness sake, but for the things themselves. I thought every single thing should have a place it belonged, fit in that place as perfect as could be.

Mama and I painted my room in the canyon house first. The paint spread a pale, clear blue that one of her friends had picked out down at the Western Auto store. The tin headboard—made to look like wood grain, but didn't at all—had been placed right beside the window with the bubbled glass. I loved sleeping there from the moment I discovered I could see through my open door, across the narrow hallway, and straight into the kitchen.

A bare light bulb hung from a thick, brown cord above the kitchen sink, and I learned right away that, if I woke extra early in the mornings, I could see my father move about the kitchen in silhouette, making his coffee and cooking his breakfast. I could smell the coffee and the greasy, smoky bacon and hear the popping sound as he broke his two eggs into the hot drippings. A deep voice announced the news from my father's radio. The beige Motorola sat atop the old water heater, which added its own occasional belch or gurgle. He timed his breakfast so he would be eating at the table when the Fresno farm report came on.

The living room was tiny, and with all the windows and doors that opened to the outside or other rooms and a huge stone fireplace at one end, wall space was scarce. Our furniture had to be placed willy-nilly to fit in. Mama and I were thrilled over the idea of having a fireplace, but we had no idea how much work it took to use one, or that it was the only heat in the house. We would learn about it all too well when winter came.

As soon as he found time, my father got busy readying the ground in front of the house for a yard. He used a tractor with a disc, pulling it back and forth and around the big black walnut tree. My father saw to his jobs in the same all-out way as his farmer and rancher friends. Land he worked would be plowed looser, holes were dug deeper, fences were higher and tighter and, God knew, they better be straight as a string from brace to brace. In the evenings, he would drag the water hose out and set the tall field sprinkler going—not a lawn sprinkler, mind you—to wet down the hard clods. At last, the hard-packed soil turned over at an even depth, but in spite of the added moisture, the alkali soil would soon dry again and take on an anemic look, not dark and rich like the valley soil.

One early morning, a friend of my father arrived in an old scratched and dented yellow dump truck with a load of cow manure from a valley dairy. I heard the rattle and bang down at the rocky creek crossing, and the whining transmission shifted into low as it came closer. I'd jumped out of bed in a single leap and gone through the door right behind my father. My mother came to stand behind me, cinching the sash of her robe. She looked horrified as the truck backed up to the yard and the driver raised the bed and dumped the load right there in front of the porch. The odor rose in a putrid cloud, and the manure had already begun to generate its own heat. Tiny puffs of steam rose from the pile. My mother clasped her hand over her mouth and went back inside. My father was so delighted he practically danced a little jig right there on our porch.

"Hot damn!" he hollered.

The tractor work started again, back and forth, the metal discs churning the earth until the manure spread evenly and the dirt looked healthy. Postholes were dug by my father and brothers, with the sweat pouring down their faces and soaking their shirts, using a fencing bar to chip away the hardpan out of the depths. The fencing came in huge rolls of wooden slats, bound together by twisted wire. Each section had to be rolled out, held upright, and pulled tight as a fiddle string before being nailed to the posts. My father built gates sturdy enough to hold an angry bull and placed them at strategic places, five of them to be exact. He always said you couldn't have too many gates in a fence.

"Say you want a hammer that's way the hell out there in that tin shed. Now, do you want to walk all the way around the outside of the fence just to get a damn hammer, or do you want to go through a gate right there in the corner and just get it?" He never waited for an answer. The question held the tone of a statement because, of course, there could only be one right answer.

I helped do the raking and loaded the uprooted weeds into the wheelbarrow. The larger manure clods had to be broken up and blended into the soil. Being taller than I, the tools were awkward for me to handle, but I liked helping my father. I always looked to him for approval, and just his mention of me doing a good job kept me bigheaded all day.

When the ground, at last, lay smooth and clean enough to please him, he put grass seed down, scattering it methodically by hand and explaining the importance of doing it just so. His big-knuckled hand reached into the bag and pulled out palms-full of the fine seeds. His long arm swept out from side to side, while his fingers let the seeds fly out into the hot air. We raked again, ever so gently, so the birds wouldn't steal the tiny seed.

The job of watering became my mother's and mine. The heat made it impossible to keep the ground damp. The fine grass would shoot straight up bright green, but to my dismay, by sundown the fine blades lay flat and gray. Only the spots where the ground sank into shallow bowls held enough moisture to sustain the seedlings.

Hard-living man that he was, my father swore like no one else I had ever known. Mama said she'd never heard his daddy say a blasphemous word, not once, so it was beyond her where he acquired his rude habit. Practically every sentence he spoke contained at least one cuss word. I heard him ask my mother why the hell she couldn't keep the damn lawn wet, saw her look down the same way I might when being scolded, and I decided to take over the job. I couldn't tell you now, it could have been five times or ten times a day, I drug the hose out and hand watered the seedlings until my thumb grew stiff and sore from bending over the hose end. My determination began to pay off when the seedlings thickened up and a real lawn took shape.

My mother had discovered a lilac bush barely hanging on to life, sorry looking and in desperate need of pruning and long, deep drinks of water. She managed to protect the scraggly thing from the disc blades by surrounding it with cardboard and keeping an eye out when my father charged around on his tractor like a crazed farmer. When the fencing was all up, the little bush held its ground beside the new path that lay from the front gate to the porch, and it eventually grew tall and healthy.

My mama. Francine, known to all as Frankie. Even though she detested the move and my father for making her be there, she wasted no time in making the dreary house into a nice home for us. Mama was the kind of woman who would never have thought of doing things any other way. She said that once the curtains were hung, a house became a home. Her friends made the trek in small groups and caravans, down the highway and up the canyon to my mother's new house, to help her clean and paint. They talked and laughed and smoked. They scrubbed and scraped and painted every surface. The atmosphere bubbled with fun and silliness, in spite of the work, and my mother was always happiest on the days her friends came to help her out.

"We may be poor as church mice," she'd say, "but elbow grease and a can of paint does wonders."

With her snappy brown eyes and auburn hair, I knew my mother was beautiful, and I thought her elegant when she filled in her eyebrows with a pencil and put on her red lipstick. I liked to watch her swivel up the scarlet stick, swipe her top lip from the little points in the middle to the corners of her mouth and then make the clean sweep of her bottom lip, one way and then the other. Then she would kiss a tissue with a smack, leaving the outline of her lips in red. Her laugh revealed small white teeth—perfect and straight on the top and crowded on the bottom. She was thin as a rake.

Mama took pride in being a good hostess to all who came to our home, always offering up something to eat or drink. "That Frankie," friends would say, "she can make something delicious out of a sack of flour and a pot of beans." She laughed and smiled like a happy kid when she had company around her. When she and her friends stopped to take a rest from fixing up the house, they would take their coffee or iced tea out into the shade and smoke L&Ms and Winstons, putting their pretty heads back and blowing the blue smoke into the heat. I would hang around as close as I could get away with, trying to listen to their conversations, but Mama would always send me away.

"Go on and play, Poppy," she would say. "You don't need to sit here and listen to us old ladies gab."

Of course, sending me off to play made me want to listen all the more. I tried hiding, eavesdropping, but I never heard a thing worth a darn. I don't know what I thought I could be missing.

My mother and her friends worked hard in our house and, to me anyway, it seemed no time at all until the little house was fresh and clean, with sheer nylon curtains from our old place at the windows and rugs on the floor. The house reeked of all the coats of enamel paint for a long time, but the windows and front door were open all afternoon and into the late evening to air it out. Night moths batted themselves against the window and front door screens as soon as the first lamp-light switched on. And, at last, the house would begin to cool.

Mama loved bright colors and used them anywhere she could. To make us laugh, she would say, "I love any color dress, as long as it's red." She swore it was the Indian blood in her that made her love colors.

The kitchen we left behind in the valley house had been a big, high-ceilinged room, painted lemon yellow and looking lit by sunshine. People—my parent's friends and my father's employees—had come and gone all times of the day. Some of the ladies would gather around the table in the mornings several times a week for cups of coffee and Mama's cinnamon cakes. They had charming names like Ivagail, Violet, and Althea, and there were two Mary Alices, who were never mixed up because one was chubby and soft and sweet and the other spoke loud and liked being the center of attention. Some of them talked with southern accents.

They'd come from families who had left the dust bowl seeking work and a new life in California's farmlands. Those ladies didn't hold back if they had something to say, and believe me, they all had something to say. They giggled like girls and howled with laughter over conversations I didn't even understand. The hard lives and hard work that their kin endured made them strong and tough.

Sometimes they got together there in the afternoons to give each other permanent waves and color rinses. They took turns twisting each other's hair around pink curlers. I was allowed to sit at the table and sort the curlers by size and separate the slips of tissue papers that had to be wound around each lock of hair before the curlers went on. The room would be full of laughter and cigarette smoke, and the coffee would be poured by the gallon. After they had all left, the windows were thrown open to the valley wind, letting the curtains billow, cleaning the air of smoke and the smell of permanent solution before supper was started.

The men who drove my father's trucks sometimes came to the house with him for lunch. They would eat fat ham sandwiches—stacked with slabs of cheese and fresh garden tomato and red onion sliced paper thin—with their greasy fingers and dirty fingernails, and my mother wouldn't even say anything about it.

In the canyon house, that same supper table barely fit in the small alcove allotted for it. "Like a size ten foot in a size eight boot," father said. The table was gray Formica with shiny chrome legs, and there were six chairs covered with gray plastic upholstery with bright-red backs. The tall water heater stood in one corner of the alcove, taking up precious space. It crowded in at my father's end of the table, the end chosen by him because from there he could see out of the high window to the hill behind the house. My parents argued about taking a leaf out of the table.

"No, Norman. Then, when the boys are home for supper, there won't be enough room."

"Francine, there's five of us. There's room."

"It's like a bad omen," my mother said of the table's tight space. "It's like we're squeezing my friends right out of my life. Who wants a table in a place where everybody can't gather around?"

I was the baby of the family. My brothers—Timothy, or Tim, and Allen—were six and seven years older than me. I cherished the times they were home from work or sports to eat with us, which had become less frequent by the time we were living in the canyon. They liked to tease me and would until I became frustrated to tears, but I idolized them anyway. My mother adored her boys, too. She was proud of their work ethic and their manners. She acted different when they were around, seeming younger. She showed interest in their lives and asked a lot of questions about what they had planned for the day or the week or their lives. I listened to every word, curious about what their lives were like away from home. They seemed so knowing and clever. But they also seemed like strangers to me sometimes.

They were big boys, going to high school. They played football, went out at night, and worked hard on weekends and during summer vacation from school. They loaded hay during baling season and walked the fields behind the sugar beet wheels, picking up the missed hard, heavy beets and tossing them into the trucks. They were strong and lean and could eat like Hereford bulls. I would watch in awe as their food disappeared. If my brothers were both at home for supper, the table had to be pulled out so I could slip into a chair against the wall.

I picked at my food and ate with total disinterest, which drove my father crazy.

"Eat your damn meat, Poppy. You're too puny, and you're gonna be sick if you don't eat right."

He ate his meat bloody rare, which I couldn't bear to look at, and drank huge amounts of red wine with his supper. Some nights he would sit at the table long after the meal was over and drink and smoke. My mother would clear the table and clean up the kitchen, and I would escape outside, like a paroled prisoner, unless she told me to help with the dishes. I didn't like to be in the kitchen when he was there, watching. He would pick at my mother until she would fly off the handle and yell at him.

"Damn it, Norman. Leave me alone. You're drunk. Why don't you go to bed?"

He would stare bleary-eyed at her with an expression I can only describe as resentment, or maybe blame.

When I was five years old and we still lived in our old house, my mother became sick. I remember the headaches first. Migraines, the doctor said. Some days she took to her bed with the door closed, and I learned quickly to be extremely quiet and to not bother her. Doctor Glasier would come to our house and give her a shot to help her feel better. One day, after attending to her, he came out of the bedroom and saw me sitting over on the couch. I'd been crying hard and feeling scared about him having to come see about my mother. He came to me and gave me a gentle pat on my shoulder and assured me that my mother would be just fine, that she just had a bad headache. After he left, I'd felt so lonely.

On one of her headache days, I followed my brother Tim outside and tagged along behind him with the yard dogs. He climbed up one of the tall eucalyptus trees out by the irrigation ditch and sliced the smallest limbs off with his new pocketknife as he made his way higher. I struggled to climb up below him, thinking I could do whatever he did.

"Get down, Poppy. Go play with a doll or something. Do something like a girl."

"I can climb, same as you."

At that exact instant, as I reached for a limb to pull myself higher, Tim's pocketknife came down and sliced my thumb wide open. I screamed like a banshee and began to wail. Climbing back down, I ran for the house. Without a second's hesitation, I threw my mother's bedroom door open and barreled in, blubbering and bleeding. I stood beside her bed and tried to show her my thumb.

"Mama, Tim cut my thumb, and it's bleeding bad," I'd sobbed.

"Leave me alone, Poppy," she whispered and turned her face into the cool white sheet.

I backed out of the room and pulled the door closed. I stood there in the silence, stunned at being dismissed by my own mother, blood oozing from my thumb and making a little red stream to my elbow. My brother Tim found me standing there when he came into the house. He dutifully led me into the kitchen and stood me on a chair at the sink. He held my hand under cold running water, and when the cut stopped bleeding, he wrapped my thumb in a great lump of gauze and wound white medical tape around it. I never again dared enter my parent's bedroom without asking permission.

Not long after that happened, my mother went away. For sure, someone must have tried to explain the reason why, but even so, I couldn't understand where she had gone or how long she would be away. Arrangements had been made for a family friend to come into our home and help my father care for us kids. Her name was Bertie, a quiet lady we knew and who had always seemed ancient to me. She was a tiny woman, with sharp little bones, and her waist caved into her middle. She wore glasses, and her salt-and-pepper gray hair lay close against her small head and was always under a hairnet. Bertie was from Arkansas, and to me her accent was funny and twangy. Her husband, Roy, had gone away. She explained to me that Roy and my mother both had contracted tuberculosis. I could scarcely pronounce the word, much less know what it meant. All I knew was that my mother was gone and here was Bertie instead.

Bertie treated us with distant kindness, and we treated her with respect because we had all been taught to respect our elders and because my father ruled my brothers with his thick brown belt. I had witnessed the use of that belt one time, and after that, I ran to hide if I even thought it was going to be jerked through the loops around my father's waist and gathered in his hand. The satisfaction on his face while he swung his belt at my brothers stuck in my mind for much too long— the smug look of a man doing the right thing, while his sons cowered from the flailing strap. I cried for my brothers in empathy, an emotion I learned at a young age. Our father never laid a strong hand on me. If he thought I had done something serious enough to deserve punishment, he always sent me to my mother.

"Now get to the damn house and tell Francine what you did."

I would run, crying. Usually, I went to my mother and confessed my wrong, but if I thought the punishment would be severe, which to me meant swats on the bottom with the back of her hairbrush, I would hang back and hope the deed would be forgotten. I cried a lot and over most anything that evoked emotion. I seldom cried for the purpose of getting my own way; I cried because I felt sad and brokenhearted. I would feel the ache and could not stop the tears from coming.

Bertie worked hard to care for us kids and my father and our household. Her children were older than we were and didn't need constant looking after when Roy went into the hospital. But she had her hands full taking care of both families—the cooking, cleaning, and laundry. She never complained to us, and she would say she could take whatever God handed her. She was a Christian woman, and if she was offended by my father's drinking and swearing, she never let on. If there were ever any contrary words between her and my father, I never heard them. Years later, my brothers would relate a story about the time Bertie sent me to kindergarten with holes in the heels of my socks. They said our father had gone into a rage.

"My kids will never go to school looking like poor children," he'd ranted. "If Poppy needs some goddamn socks, go buy her some socks."

Allen and Tim said Bertie never batted an eyelash.

Being so young, the flow of time was not meaningful to me. My mother was gone for more than eight months, and I would recall a sort of emptiness during that time. Bertie fixed my lunch each day, and I sat at the table and ate in the silence. Then I went to afternoon kindergarten.

After all those months of hospitalization, my mother would be allowed to come home if the harshest stipulations could be met. The most difficult requirement for all concerned was that she must live separate from us for an extended amount of time. Tuberculosis was a frightening disease. Quarantine, bed rest, and antibiotic medicine would be the prescribed treatment. So, when I was turning six, the community came together and helped my father and my uncle build my mother a tiny, charming house. Two sides of the white clapboard building were filled with large windows, and it had its own bathroom and closet. Mama's friends sewed curtains and offered homey items like braided rugs and handmade quilts to make her feel comfortable.

The bedroom-sized house stood separate, out beyond our side yard by the pepper trees. Through the daytime, the screen door provided a way for me to see and communicate with my mother. Sometimes she would chatter in her sweet motherly voice, delighting me with her presence. But not always. When loneliness and depression gripped her heart, she would go quiet, often gazing away from us, as if she could see something far away that we could not. The times she became like that, I would think her angry with me for some awful thing I had done, always ready to blame myself for her behavior toward me. She pushed us all away because of depression.

I also didn't understand the fact that she couldn't possibly know what went on in our household. If I'd done something good, or even been in trouble for misbehaving, she wouldn't know anything about it unless somebody went out and told her. But, in my mind, I thought she knew everything because she was my mother and mothers knew. I would sit on the little step in front of her door and cry silently and wonder what bratty thing I had done to make her not want to talk to me.

When Mama recovered enough to be declared cured and no longer contagious, she returned to the main house, and life continued on for our family. She must have been elated to be well and free of confinement. Most of the time, she liked to laugh and look pretty again. Her friends returned for morning coffee klatches. Noise filled our house again.

After my mother moved back into the house with us, my brothers were allowed to move their bedroom out to the tiny house. They, of course, were thrilled with the independence the move allowed them. They had such freedom and probably took advantage of that more than our parents ever knew. Their new dwelling was dubbed "the bunkhouse." I was excited to move from my tiny room into the big room my brothers had vacated, at least for the remainder of time we lived there in the valley house.

But life changed for my family once again. Medical bills had piled up for nearly a year. My father's small trucking business was failing, and money became tight. He and his cattle partner, Mr. Barns, did the paperwork necessary to put all the cows in Barns' name, and then my parents filed for bankruptcy. About that time was when my father found the canyon house. And that is when I first saw the look of blame in his eyes as he gazed at my mother.

The bunkhouse had been built with fine forethought by clever men. Instead of a permanent foundation, the little building had been constructed with axles underneath. With wheels and tires in place, the little house made its slow trek to the canyon, where it fit in perfect order beneath the huge mulberry tree.

Three

The long summer days crept by, riding the heat waves like a bucking bronco—cooling one day, setting record high temperatures the next—making canyon life hard to bear for people and animals alike. Even the birds perched on tree limbs panted with their beaks open for air. We had brought three cats and our little dog from the valley house when we moved. They all suffered, panting in the heat. Our little dog, Goldie—who I had named when I was two and who wasn't gold but white with brown spots—lay around on the linoleum floors, ever moving, looking for a new cool spot. The cats fended for themselves outside and didn't show up until feeding time.

Predawn presented the coolest hour of the day, and then the mercury in the thermometer on the wall of the porch began its rapid climb again. My mother's chores were done early in the morning, hours before the sun crawled up the sky, building up its fire to send straight down into the narrow canyon. By afternoon, she would find herself weak with fatigue brought on by the hot weather. Even in its own swelter, the stucco house still maintained the coolest spot until later in the day when the highest temperatures exchanged places. Then she would escape the house and take a cold drink and a *True Love* magazine out beneath the yard trees and fan herself into a dull doze.

I scarcely noticed the heat and didn't suffer because of it. My days started with breakfast as that was the rule and not because I cared about the food. Except for the thick bacon, fried crisp and brown. I wanted to get breakfast out of the way and do my chores so I could head out through the screen door to investigate my new surroundings.

I prodded and poked and peered beneath and behind everything that looked the least bit interesting. Rocks, rotten logs, rusty tin cans, and holes in the ground were all investigated. During the first few weeks in our new home, I consciously set a boundary for my exploration. A wide and lopsided circumference circling our house became my guiding perimeter.

To the west, or up canyon, sat an old tin barn with its corrals built of silvered boards, aged hard as stone and covered with lichen, a loading chute with ground squirrel mounds pushing at the bottom treads, and cement water troughs that floated with emerald wisps of moss and from which I sipped cool water anytime I wanted to. The tin barn stood dim and empty, except for the scattered piles of dusty straw left over from the oat hay that had once been stacked there and a few pigeons that made their homes in the rafters. There were feathers and tiny bird bones scattered where predators had eaten their meals.

Low windows, cut through the tin siding and framed up with lumber, ran the length of the barn, and there were mangers beneath them for feeding cattle. Here, there also spread a large concrete area sunk into the ground, taking up the entire center of the main corral. When I asked my father about it, he explained that it had been a hog wallow, where pigs could roll around in the muddy water to cool off and keep the damn bugs and flies away. A silence hung heavy inside the barn and made me think of eerie occurrences, and my imagination soared, heightened by the soft cooing of the pigeons. The atmosphere settled right into me as a favorite place.

The opposite end of my out-of-whack circle contained the forty acres that our horses were turned out on. The pasture ran just about a mile long, and the fence lines crowded together in places, making it narrow. Five horses lived there, munching on the dry grass and napping in the shade, flinging their tails at each other's flies. I spent hours a day with the horses. Riding had been forbidden unless my father was at home, but most days I could not resist crawling onto my old mare's smooth, warm back while she stood with the others in the shade. Nicky, old and gentle and kind, hardly seemed to notice me sitting on her back. Sometimes, I would lie forward with my face against her bony wither, and more than once I dozed off in the comfort of her and the warm, earthy smell of horses.

Behind the house and just across a barbed wire fence loomed a hill that began in a gradual upward sweep and then climbed at a steep angle to the crest. A third of the way up stood an old wooden structure, built into the hillside and camouflaged by the low branches and heavy, dark shade of three giant red oak trees. It had long ago been a livable abode for the family who would build the stucco house, our house. There was a concrete floor with massive cracks and broken-up slabs and rotted wooden shelves along one side. Plain to see was the fact that cattle had inhabited the leftover building for a length of time, as there lay spread a deep, rotted layer of manure in the back part of the building.

Around the hillside from the old wooden structure, I found a surprise that made me gasp. Tucked beneath a bulging stone outcropping was an Indian cave. Partially hidden behind scrub oak and chemise, the small cavern dished into the stone. The opening gaped wide and was much taller than I. The floor spread smooth and glass-like in places. The walls and ceiling were stained black with ancient wood smoke. Just where the floor extended out from the entrance, I discovered two perfect, round, deep holes. I shared my discovery with my mother, and she explained how the Indian women ground the acorns and seeds in the mortars with pestles and other types of tools they made from stone. From that day on, when I visited the cave my imagination went wild. I knew for sure I could feel the presence of the Indian families who had lived there. I had watched a lot of westerns on television back in the valley house, so I also knew this as the perfect place to sit quiet and keep an eye out for enemies.

But the best was yet to come. I was not grown-up enough to understand that a sort of kinship could form with a place—a place that would teach me about who I was and then change me into who I would become. There are places and events in our lives that we never forget. Before my tenth birthday came in September, before autumn rains could begin to bring about unforeseen change, I had become happily lost to the land and a simple, seasonal creek. A creek bed in a bone-dry canyon ruled by nothing but Mother Nature.

When I first went out to explore, I stayed within sight of the house or where I could scramble up the bank and see the house from time to time and keep the distance comfortable. I felt timid about venturing too far into unknown territory. I was also a little disappointed at first. I still had in my mind that creeks were supposed to have clear water gushing across mossy boulders and pouring into crystal ponds, making merry noises. What I'd found was hardly any water at all, except for an occasional pool maintained by a seeping underground spring. In fact, there were three such small pools not far from our house.

My disappointment faded as I carefully examined the spring pools and discovered the thriving miniature existence there. I hopped with delight at finding the late blooming, chubby, brown-black tadpoles in all stages of frogdom and dozens of the tiniest frogs hopping madly around in the damp parts of the creek bottom. I would pick up the squirmy bodies, handling them so gently in my cupped palms, and feel the cool, damp tickle of them on my skin. I would lie on my stomach and trail my fingers in the shallow water and watch the tadpoles wiggle away to hide beneath the undercut of the little banks that would hold them in captivity until they grew legs and shed their tails. Water bugs skated across the still surface, leaving the tiniest ripples.

Though the heat wasn't a bother to me, I was aware of the sweet, damp coolness near the little pools. Shaded by cottonwoods and sycamore trees, the sun scarcely found its way into the creek bottom, slightly dappling the water with silver coins of sunlight. The scent of mud and layer upon layer of leaf mulch, rich and strong, filled my nostrils and lungs with a pleasant earthy sense.

I would move from pool to pool, being sure all was well in each one. Every few days I would wander a bit farther up or down the creek, exploring rocks and sand bars. Blue-bellied lizards were abundant where the creek bottom had drained driest. The first snake I saw was a yellow-and-black water snake. I picked it up, two-fingered, by its tail, and three tadpoles fell out of its mouth back into the pool. I commended myself for being so brave and saving the tadpoles' lives. Downstream led me under the barbed wire fence and into the horse pasture. By then, I knew exactly how to watch for rattlesnakes.

"Watch where you walk," my mother called out each time she heard the screen door slam.

"Don't ever put your hand where you can't see," my father instructed me, but just once, "or step over a rock or a log before you look to be sure there isn't a goddamn rattler on the other side. And whatever you do, never pry up a rock without being ready to get the hell out of the way."

The days stretched long, and sometimes I went back outside after supper dishes were done. I sat on the porch or lay out flat on the old picnic table that my mother had painted a bright red and felt the night. At the crest of the high hill that formed the opposite canyon wall stood tall digger pines that on moonlit nights paraded in silhouette. I would study them until it became plain to see that they resembled camels or dragons or any lumpy, bumpy animal I could conjure up. Like the tadpoles and frogs and ponds, the trees felt friendly to me, as if they were getting to know me just as I was learning about them.

I seldom returned to the light of the little house until my mother came to the door and called me in. I avoided the tiny living room where my father sat in his green Naugahyde chair and sipped red wine from a juice glass. The television set in the corner glared its one and only colorless channel, captured from the air waves by an antenna. My father watched the nightly news on the snowy, rolling screen, adding his grumbling commentary.

Four

From the time I was born everyone knew that my father was crazy about his little Poppy.

"That Poppy sure is a daddy's girl," people said.

"Who's that cowgirl you got with ya today, Norm? That your helper?"

My father would brag. "You bet. She's damn good help, and it don't take much to feed her." He called me "Sis" or "Sister" or sometimes "Little Heifer." He liked to make cattle jokes. "Yep, she's kinda puny. Born in a dry year."

By the age of six, I went everywhere with my father. We checked the cows and checked the fences and water troughs on the current leased property. I loved going into the hills on the bumpy, dusty ranch roads. My father would tease me, driving closer and closer to the edge of a steep road, pretending we were going to crash off the side hill. I would squeal and cover my eyes, and he would laugh. He would point out deer across the canyons and ridges and tell me how to find them by using the hands of a clock.

"Look right there at two o'clock, now down just over the top of that oak."

I found the deer and learned how to tell time. I also learned to see my surroundings by keeping an eye out for cows and calves. Once I saw them, my job was to count them. I was learning without either one of us realizing it. But another thing I learned was, if I couldn't spot the deer, I must not be very bright.

"Christ, Sis. They're right there. I don't know how you can miss them."

My father would take me to the livestock sale fifty miles north from our valley house. The Saturday auction had been my favorite place to go. I stood on the pickup seat, near enough for him to fling his arm out and save my life, if need be. I wanted to see the baby goats and pigs, and if I was real lucky, a horse or two would go through the ring. During most of those trips, I slept on the seat on the way home or lay and watched, through the top of the windshield or side window, whatever went by. I counted telephone poles and watched the wires flow by in their hypnotic high and low pattern. When we came to the row of tall eucalyptus trees and their blinking shade, I knew we were close to home.

After we moved to the canyon house, about the only time I went anywhere was the Saturday grocery trips. Mama and I would go into the Foodliner to get the groceries while my father looked after some errands around town. He would go to the Shell station and fill the truck and several gas cans so he would have some for use at home. He also did the banking at the stately Wells Fargo on Broadway.

Through the first part of the summer, the weekends were a merry time for my parents. Friends came up on Saturdays and sometimes didn't leave until the next day. They ate chicken and beans and bread and drank and laughed. And fought. My father placed an old metal water trough in the shade in the corner of the side yard, and as people came, they would bring cases of beer and add ice to the trough. The nights were warm, and everyone stayed outdoors.

I would escape to my room and pull the curtains closed, but I could hear the conversations as the night went on. There was a lot of loud laughter and a lot of dirty words. Without a doubt, someone would get angry about something, and a fight would occur. They weren't physical, and I don't remember anyone coming to blows, but there were loud arguments over issues I couldn't make sense of. Usually, it was the men whose voices grew snarled with sarcasm and dirty words, but sometimes the women would join in the fight, too, and they were worse than the men with their shrill words and crying jags. With my light off and my pillow over my head, I would try to block them out until I slept restlessly. Many times I woke to slamming car doors and revving engines of the people driving away and the screen door slamming again and again with coming and going until the early morning hours.

In those dark hours, my parents would often fight and argue after people had left. I never understood what the arguments were about, but I knew the familiar words and tones.

"Goddammit, Frankie . . ."

"Shut up, Norman . . ."

I would lie quietly and, in spite of myself, strain to listen and feel terrible. It frightened me to hear the spitting-mean tones in their voices. My stomach would ache with worry. That's when I began to look forward to the start of each new week. Mondays were safe from tension. My father returned to his job and I to my lone exploring. I had begun to dread the weekends with all those people coming and the quiet weekday routine changing. I found comfort in my aloneness. The knots would leave my stomach, and my imagination would brighten again.

I started taking Nicky's bridle with me into the horse pasture, and when she would let me, I would put one rein around her neck and lead her to a rock or high place and slip her bridle over her ears. She was old and wise to avoidance, and sometimes I would be frustrated to tears before I finally had the reins on her neck. Once that was accomplished, she would be sweet and agreeable. For a few weeks, I rode her around the big pasture bareback without permission or, as far as I knew, without anyone even knowing.

One day I asked my father if I could ride outside of the pasture.

"May as well. You've been ridin' her all over hell anyway. You'll have to ride bareback. I won't be here to put the saddle on 'er."

"I don't mind. I know how to get on."

"Don't be runnin' 'er around on the hard road. You'll ruin 'er feet."

"I won't," I swore.

"And be sure she gets a drink of water before she goes."

"I will."

And that was all there was to it.

Another adventure took me over. At first, I rode out of the driveway and down the canyon road until it curved away and I couldn't see the house when I looked back. Nicky poked along slowly, ambling from one side of the road to the other, looking for thistle to grab a bite of. When we turned back toward home, her pace would pick up, and I would thrill at the feeling of walking along at a good clip, hearing the rhythm of her hooves on the hard-packed road.

As the rides added up, my confidence grew stronger. I rode a bit farther with each outing until I rode to the nearest neighbor's place. Their house stood up on a hill, looking down at the canyon road like a big eye. I felt the creepy sense of being watched when I came into its view. The horses in their hillside pasture would rush down to meet Nicky, who would toss her head up and nicker a welcome, and I would be wary of riding on past them while they pushed at the fence and pranced beside us. I would turn my horse around at that place in the road and head back toward home, leaving the others watching until we rode out of sight. I turned back for several rides until I worked up the courage to kick Nicky up and hurry on by the snorty horses and around the next curve.

A day came that I rode much farther than I had before. As I rode along, my excitement built while I formed a plan. I wanted to ride to the bend in the creek where the people were building the adobe block house. On our Saturday trips into town, I'd been looking over there for as long as I could as we drove past. Sometimes I would get a glimpse of someone working there, and I eventually figured out that there was a man, a woman, and two kids in the family. I soon became curious about the girl, who looked around my own age. She had caramel-colored hair and was chubby, and she always wore a dress instead of jeans, like me. Her hair was cut shorter than mine and looked thick and heavy behind her bangs. Sometimes she would look busy, bent to some task, but most of the time she sat on a big boulder near the creek, and I often saw a book in her hands. I wondered what her name was.

The day I took my long ride, I hurried Nicky around the curve, anticipating what I would see, and there she was, sitting on her big rock. On the ground next to her, sitting in the creek sand, was the boy who I had decided was her brother. I became self-conscious about riding by them. I had started to turn Nicky around when I heard a voice.

"Hi, girl."

Looking back, I saw that it was the boy who had called to me, and he was getting up off the ground.

"Hi, girl," he said louder.

"Be quiet, Riley," the blonde girl said.

She reached to take his arm, but he moved away from her. That was when I noticed something different about him. His legs seemed to wobble in an uncontrollable way, and one arm was bent tight at his elbow, bringing his hand up near his shoulder. Gangly and thin, with knobby knees and elbows, he reminded me of a newborn foal.

"Hey, girl."

I could see a toothy, crooked grin. I waved to them but stood my place, unsure of what to do. The girl closed her book and crawled down off the big rock, moving awkwardly. She tried to manage the skirt of her dress and hold the book at the same time. It was plain to me right then that she wasn't the tomboy type.

"Riley, be quiet. Come here. If you cross the creek, I'm going to tell."

"Hi," I finally called.

Riley grinned bigger, but the girl looked up and looked away. She held his arm and tugged him back toward the rock. He didn't fight her, but he was clumsy as he moved with her.

"You that girl that lives up the road?" the girl called over to me.

"Yeah. Yes, I am. My name is Poppy. Poppy Wade. This is my horse, Nicky."

"You're lucky. You get to have a horse. Wish I could."

"Why can't you?"

"I don't know." Big shrug. "What do they eat? Where do they sleep?" She was eyeing Nicky suspiciously.

"Oh, they just eat grass and hay and stuff like that. They sleep in their pasture."

I was beginning to feel more relaxed. Nicky was grabbing a nap in the shade.

"What's the matter with your horse?"

"Oh. Nothing's the matter with her. She's taking a nap."

"Oh," was all she said, and there was a long silence. I could see she was looking intently at Nicky's closed eyes.

I looked around for access through the fence and across the creek bed.

"Would you like to pet her?"

"No. We better not. My dad will get mad. He and my mother always think Riley will get hurt or something."

She had a hold on Riley's arm again, and he was bent away from her, trying to get loose of her grip.

"What's your name?"

"Sky."

"Oh." I had never heard of anybody having a name like that. It sounded odd, but I wanted to be polite. "That's a nice name," I said.

"My name is Riley," the boy said. But he spoke in a peculiar way. The word sounded as if he had left the i out and the last part was a long e sound.

"My brother is slow," Sky explained in a grown-up voice. "He can't help it."

I was at a complete loss as to how I should continue the conversation. I couldn't think of the words to fill the silence. For the first time since I had been sitting there on Nicky, I actually looked over at the opposite side of the creek. I could see that, behind the stand of willows, there was a little trailer house. It was short and humpbacked and was a light blue-green color. I saw that it had a huge dent in the end by the hitch, and one corner was separated at the seam. There was a picnic table like ours, but not painted, some wooden chairs, and a kitchen cupboard looking particularly out of place. I could see that there was a green braided rug laid on the ground, right over the dirt, where the doorstep was. The setting looked as if inside had been brought outside. I had never even known the trailer was behind the willows.

"What's that?"

Sky looked, following my gaze. "That's where we live," she said.

I couldn't understand how that could be.

"Your mom and dad, too?"

"We all do. We sleep inside most nights. But we have cots for outside, too."

As she spoke, a man came around from behind the trailer. He looked up as he stepped out from the shade of the trees. He was a lean man, all edges and angles.

"Who you talking to, Sky?" he said.

"That girl from up the road. Poppy," she called back.

"Howdy, Poppy. Out for a ride, are you?"

"Yes, sir."

"That's good. Come on, Sky. Get some lunch, and it's time for Ri to take his rest."

"I better go," I said. "Bye, Sky. Bye, Riley."

Nicky startled when I woke her from her nap with a gentle kick to her side. As I rode away, I could hear Riley saying something with a tone of protest. He looked too old to take a nap.

Five

"They're real nice," I told my mother and father at suppertime. "The girl's name is Sky, and the boy is Riley. He's slow."

"Poppy, that isn't nice to say," my mother scolded.

"Well, that's what Sky said."

"What the hell kind of name is Sky? Those people are damned odd." My father shook his head. "I don't think you oughta hang around down there. They been buildin' on that mud house ever since I been comin' up this road, and hell, they don't have one wall done yet."

"Norm, she doesn't have anyone up here to go and play with. What harm can it do for her to know those kids? It's more than two months 'til school starts, and she spends hours prowling around alone. Let her have a friend, for Pete's sake."

My father never bothered to answer and just kept eating. I said I was done, excused myself, and went outside, letting the screen door slam behind me. I crawled up on the red table and stretched out on my back and looked at the trees making a silhouette across the hill. They didn't look like anything but trees. My imagination would not stir. I thought about Sky and Riley. I guessed Riley was retarded, but maybe not too much. Maybe, in a couple of days, I would ride to the mud house again.

I noticed that, in the hottest hours of the afternoons, the spring ponds seemed to be shrinking. If I went to the creek earlier in the mornings, there was still plenty of water, but as the day went on, it grew shallower. On one particularly hot afternoon, I found that one of the ponds had shrunk down to nothing more than a puddle. Even as I approached it along the sandy creek bottom, I could see an unusual movement in the water. When I saw what was happening, I felt an urgency to do something, and my heart thudded in my chest. All the little tadpoles were flipping around in the shallow water in a crazy frenzy.

I ran downstream to check the next pool and found it still held a fair amount of water. I hurried back to the tadpoles and scooped up as many as my cupped hands could hold and ran to the deeper pool with them, careful not to let any squeeze between my fingers or flop out of my palms to a sure death. I must have made a half-dozen trips, stumbling over the rocks and roots strewn in the creek bed in my rush, until I felt sure I had rescued them all. They all lazed on the bottom for a few minutes and then began to swim around their new dwelling. I went back and examined the drying pool one more time to make sure I had saved all of them. There were still dozens of tiny frogs hopping around the damp sand.

I ran all the way back to the house to tell my mother my concerns.

"I saved them, the tadpoles," I explained to her as I gasped for my breath. "They were dying, and I saved their lives." I was overwhelmingly proud and happy.

"Good for you, Poppy. Do they have little legs yet? You know, even if the pools dry up, they might still turn into frogs, and they will be just fine," she tried to reassure me. But then she grew serious. "You know, Poppy, not every creature survives in nature. It is God's way, and there is nothing we humans can do about that."

I felt the hot tears slip down my face, and a lump big as a gumball formed in my throat. "But, why would God do that? Why would He make so many tadpoles if they can't all grow up to be frogs?" I sobbed in little spasms. The subject of death was foreign and frightening to me.

"Maybe He has to make extra so if some don't survive there will still be some left. God knows what He is doing Poppy. You just have to trust Him. Now, go wash, and I'll make you a honey and butter sandwich."

I stood at the bathroom sink for a long time, letting the cold water run over my grimy hands while I stared hard at my reflection in the mirror. I could see all of my face if I stood on tiptoe. My hair was wild looking, all curly and tangled, and I had clean streaks through the dirt where the tears had run down my cheeks from my dark eyes. I stared at myself and wondered how God decided which tadpoles died and which ones lived—and if He did the same with people. I couldn't understand that part of God's thinking.

The next day, I was afraid to leave the pools to go for a ride on Nicky. I spent all day in the creek bottom, going back and forth between the two ponds that still held water. Even though they seemed to be holding their own, I couldn't bring myself to leave until the evening air cooled my bare skin. I noticed that there were not as many little frogs hopping about in the dampness and wondered if God had killed them. I thought about what my mother had told me and wondered if there had been just too many frogs.

After the ringing of the phone—two longs and one short—woke me the following morning, my mother told me some friends were coming to visit. The lady was my mother's friend Rayleen, and she had two kids around my age. I was so excited, it was hard to eat my breakfast, and I wanted to rush to get my chores done. I hadn't seen my friends since we moved up to the canyon house. Patsy was two years older than I was, and Rex was a year younger. We all liked to play pretend, and being cowboys was our favorite drama. I couldn't contain my excitement, so I planted myself on a porch chair and waited to spot the dust cloud down the canyon road that would announce someone was coming.

When, at last, I could see the dirt that rose and hung in the still air, I ran inside and called to my mother that they were coming up the road. She smiled big, dropped what she was doing in the kitchen, and joined me on the porch. We waved our arms and hands above our heads like two crazy people as they passed by on the canyon road and then turned into the driveway that brought them back to park out front of our house. By the time they pulled up and parked, my mother and I were waiting at the yard gate. As they clambered out of their car, I stepped behind my mother, but she took my arm and pulled me around to her side. Then she quickly let go and pushed the gate open so she and Rayleen could get a hold of each other for a bear hug.

"Oh, my gosh, Rayleen, it is so good to see you," my mother said twice.

"Look at you, Francine. You look like a country girl, through and through, with your Levi's on and everything. And your face is tan as can be."

I looked up at my mother's face, seeing a glint of tears in both eyes, but she blinked them away and never lost her smile. Then Patsy and Rex came into the yard, and we all went up on the porch and through the screen door. The three of us kids stood around, acting shy, not even looking at one another for a few minutes. They looked all around the tiny living room while I watched them out of the corner of my eye. My mother offered Rayleen iced tea, and she told me us kids could have Kool-Aid if we wanted. Patsy said no thanks, but Rex said yeah, he would.

"Yes, please," Rayleen corrected him.

He said, "Yes, please," and I went to pour some for us.

After we all had our cold drinks, we went back outside and sat at the red picnic table in the shade. The day was already getting hot. My mother and Rayleen started gabbing right away. At last, I managed to break the ice for us kids.

"Want to go see our creek?" I asked.

Rex said yes immediately. Patsy hesitated a moment, but she stood and waited for me to lead the way. They followed me through the yard gate, and as we went in single file, I wondered why they seemed like such strangers to me. I took the trail, the one I had worn myself, off the bank and down into the creek bottom.

"Where's the water?" Those were Patsy's first words to me.

"There's pools." She was acting so snooty, and I wanted her to like my creek.

I took them to the pool where I had put the tadpoles. There was emerald-green moss streaming in the water and even more water bugs than before, paddling around on the surface.

"I know," Rex said, "let's put some of these in a jar and watch them turn into frogs. See, these already have little legs." He pointed to some that actually had nice, big, fat legs.

I was disappointed because I wanted to be the one to know the most about tadpoles and frogs, and Rex was stealing my authority. I volunteered to go ask for a jar and ran back up the bank to the house. I found a Mason jar and a lid and took them, along with the ice pick, to my mother. She placed the point of the ice pick here and there on the lid and hit the handle with the heel of her palm. We had done this one time before for a caterpillar that was supposed to become a butterfly. To my distress, the poor thing had died and dried up in its cocoon.

By the time I returned to the pool, the water had been stirred into a cloudy, mucky mess. I was horrified.

"What happened to the water?" I glared hard at Rex, yelling, "You aren't supposed to do that!"

"It don't hurt anything. It'll clear up again."

"If you killed my tadpoles, I'm going to kill you." I spat the words out with sureness, though I had no idea what I was saying.

Patsy turned, starting for the house, yelling, "I'm going to tell!" over her shoulder. "You aren't supposed to say you will kill someone."

I don't know if she told, but she didn't come back to the creek.

I got over being mad while Rex and I sat on some rocks by the pool and waited for the silt to settle out of the water. When we could see them, we carefully scooped up some tadpoles and put them in the jar. We added more water and some strands of green moss and a few pebbles in the bottom and screwed the lid on.

"They eat moss," Rex announced. "I bet they will be frogs in just a couple of days."

I still resented him thinking he knew more about my tadpoles than I, so I thought hard about something informative to say.

"It takes eleven days for them to fully turn into frogs," I said without looking at Rex. "I think these need four more days. Yeah, four more and they will be frogs." I spoke with such authority he couldn't argue with a fact like that.

When we got up to the yard, Patsy was sitting at the table with our mothers, and I thought how she fit in better with them than with Rex and me. Maybe it was because she was tall for her age, but she looked more like a lady that day. I also wondered why my mother hadn't sent her away to play like she did me when her friends came to visit.

"Look at our tadpoles." I set the jar in the middle of the table.

"Oh my. They are almost frogs, aren't they," my mother said.

"Four more days," Rex informed them, "and they will be real frogs."

That made me a little mad. He was acting like a know-it-all and using my information.

We all ate baloney sandwiches out on the red picnic table and drank more cold Kool-Aid and talked nonsense and laughed a lot. After lunch, the three of us sat in my bedroom where I explained to Patsy and Rex how our telephone party line worked.

"We got our phone last week," I announced. "It's a party line."

"What's a party line?" Rex asked.

"We can hear other people talking. You can just pick the telephone up and listen."

Patsy was awed. "You listen to people you don't even know? Can you talk to them?"

"No. It has to be secret." I chuckled at such a silly idea of talking to the people while eavesdropping. "You're not supposed to do it. People get mad and tell you to hang up the phone. You have to be real, real quiet so they don't know you are listening."

"You *do* that?" Rex liked the idea.

"I have a couple of times."

"I'm going to tell." Patsy stomped from my room.

"She won't," her brother said. "She always says that."

I was sad when Rayleen said they had to leave. I cried a little bit as they went to get in their car. My mother hugged Rayleen tight, and they said they would see each other real soon. We stood on the porch as they drove past the house on the canyon road. We waved again, but this time the waves were more like heavy arms being held up in the air. My mother turned and went inside the house, but I stood until the dust settled back onto the road. It took a long time.

When my father came home after work, I was waiting to tell him about our company. I could see, as soon as he stepped out of the pickup, that he had drunk a lot of wine on the way home. He stood at the pickup door for a long moment and shuffled his load around in his arms so he would have a free hand. He carried his lunch box and thermos bottle with one hand, and with his empty hand he reached back inside the cab for the wine jug in the paper bag.

I watched him come through the gate and up the path.

"Guess what," I said as we met at the step, "Patsy and Rex came today. We played in the creek."

"That right?"

"Hi, Norm," my mother said behind me. She took a long look at him and went back into the kitchen.

He didn't answer her right away. He lifted his straw hat off his head and laid it, crown down, on the little table where he always put it. His face was dirty from driving a tractor all day, but his forehead was pale and clean where his hat had been. He carried the rest of the items to the kitchen and put them on the small counter by the sink. He took his juice glass from the cupboard and poured himself a glass of wine. I watched him drink the dark liquid down in just a few big swallows and pour another. He went back to the living room and sat in his chair where he took his work boots off. It was all routine. He did exactly the same every night. He put his feet in his slippers that were always beside his chair and leaned back with a sigh.

He looked worn out.

"So you had some company today, huh?" he said to both of us.

"Good to see them. They stayed most of the day," my mother said from the kitchen.

"And me and Rex played in the creek. We caught tadpoles." I hurried to my room to retrieve the Mason jar full of green slimy moss.

"Look. They have legs." I held the jar up where he could get a good view.

"You can't keep those poor little buggers in that jar, Sis. They'll just die in there. Go put them back where you got them."

I was stunned. "Right now? It's just about dark outside."

"You had no business gettin' 'em in the first place. Go put 'em back."

"Dinner is ready, Norm, and it's almost dark. She can put them back in the morning."

"Dammit, Francine. They'll die before morning."

"They're tadpoles, Norman. They won't die in one night."

It was too late for my mother to win the argument. I was already worried that the tadpoles would die and it would be my fault. I carried the jar gently and with both hands and went out, letting the screen door slam. There was enough light enough to see my way to the creek trail, but as I descended the steep bank into the rough weedy bottom, it seemed as though night fell in that single moment. I stumbled over a rock, reminding me to watch my footing as I picked my way to the little pool.

I bent down and unscrewed the jar lid and, bit by bit, poured the water, tadpoles, moss, and pebbles into the pool. I couldn't see them in the shadows that lay across the tiny pond, but I knew they were swimming away from me. As usual, my father was right. How could they be happy cramped up in the stupid glass jar? I stayed squatted there for a few minutes, taking in how different everything looked, or rather felt, in the near dark. By the time I stood and turned to go back to the house, I was surprised at how dim the light was and how hard it was to see the creek path. Ahead and to my right was the faint glow of the house lights rising above the high bank. Each time I looked that way and then back again, my path grew darker.

I heard a ruffling noise and felt myself jerk with a stab of fear. A buzzing sensation tickled up into the back of my neck. I stood stock still, holding my breath, straining to hear the sound again. Just as I readied to take another step, I heard the same noises again, louder, closer. This time I dropped the jar and ran. I bounded up the bank like a deer and ran until I was in the circle of dim, yellow light from the house and could see the yard gate. I kept looking behind me. The feeling of being chased by something I couldn't see was terrifying.

As I yanked open the screen door and rushed into the living room, I heard my mother call, "Poppy, get in there and wash up. We're eating already."

At the table, hands still damp, I slid into my chair.

"I heard something at the creek," I said as I dished food onto my plate.

"Like what?" my father said.

"It made noise on the ground. Crunching noises."

"Probably a possum or a coon."

"Maybe it was just a deer, Sis," my mother said.

"Could've been anything."

"I think something chased me." Saying so aloud made the idea sound silly.

"She shouldn't have been down there in the dark." My mother spoke to her plate.

"I told her to put them poor damn tadpoles back, Francine. If she hadn't messed around down there, she wouldn't a got caught in the dark."

"I swear, Norman, sometimes you forget she's only nine years old."

"Well, that's how she's gonna learn. It's how I damn well learned."

I didn't go sit on the picnic table that night. I was afraid to go out in the yard in the dark. Not because I conjured up a monster or a giant wild animal. I was afraid of the unknown.

I lay on my bed and thought about the tadpoles and about what I heard in the creek. My mother came in and sat by me on the edge of the bed.

"Tired tonight, Poppy?"

"I guess so."

"You know, there really isn't anything to be afraid of in the creek or anywhere around here. There are the same things in the dark as in the daylight," she patted my leg. "And I'm sorry about the tadpoles. I know you wouldn't want to hurt them."

"We shouldn't have put them in that jar. I think they were happy when I turned them loose in their pool."

"I bet they were. You should get to sleep pretty soon. I think you're pretty tired tonight. You have fun with Rex and Patsy?"

"Yeah, but Patsy acted different."

"Well, she's growing up fast."

Mama stood and said for me to get my pajamas on. We said goodnight. At the door, she turned back.

"Poppy, you know your father loves you an awful lot. I mean, so much, you know?"

I couldn't think of what to say, and she went on out and closed the door.

Sleep wouldn't come for a long time that night. The air that sieved through the window screen felt cool and thin for the first time in a while. I turned my face to it and breathed the night air. I thought about a hundred things, including the tadpoles and my father. By the time he'd left the supper table, his eyes had turned that gray-blue color they faded to sometimes, and he wasn't talking anymore. He had used the bathroom at the end of the short hallway and then shuffled to their room and shut the door. I wondered, even after what my mother said, if he was starting to not love me anymore. That made me feel sad, and I cried until I went to sleep.

Six

I spent most of the next few days playing in the Indian cave. I would catch Nicky and ride her bareback around the pasture then trot fast up the hill to the cave and jump off her at a jog and pretend to hide from the cowboys. I became good at it, and she would stop the instant my body left her smooth back. I would squat down on my haunches at the back of the cave and hold my Roy Rogers pistol aloft—waiting, sneaky-like, to attack the invaders. I was a mixture of cowboy and Indian. That was how I had to play the game when I was alone. Eventually, Nicky started taking off with her bridle on unless I hurried right back after I leapt from her back, so I decided I would teach her to let me ride bridleless. I knew I would be in a lot of trouble if she stepped on a loose rein and broke it.

The lessons happened so easy I didn't even realize what an accomplishment I had made. I dug my little fingers deep into the root of her mane and tugged until she stepped the way I wanted to go. Then I would tug in the opposite direction until she stepped off that way. I would lean way forward and hug her neck when she accomplished what I wanted her to. If she wanted to head off her own way, I would sit up and use my deepest voice. "Whoa, Nicky, whoa." And she would, every time.

The theory worked for a day and a half. She would so willingly go anywhere I wanted her to, until she realized she didn't have to, and there was nothing I could do about it. By the end of the second bridle-less day, she was consistently heading to wherever the other horses happened to be, and "whoa" meant little or nothing.

The smooth stone at the back and floor of the cave remained cool, even on the hottest days. I kept looking through the leaves beneath the huge oak trees for acorns to try to mash by using another rock and the grinding holes in the floor, but all I found were old, dried-up brown hulls. I didn't know I would have to wait for them to grow through late winter and into spring. So I pretended. I spoke aloud to the imaginary cowboys and Indians I played with. I was always the leader, the boss. I got to plan how the story would go and who would live and who would die. The scene could take hours to play out. When I felt too hot, I would go back inside the cave and sit against the cool stone wall.

Two whole days went by without me tending to the creek ponds and tadpoles. When I ambled down the bank late one morning, I was devastated by what I found. All the ponds were waterless. Damp places remained in the sand, but no pool was left. I dropped to my knees where I had turned the captured tadpoles loose and stared at the waterless sight. There was nothing. No tadpole bodies, and no little frogs. My heart was broken. I sat for a while, trying to reason what may have become of them all. Where would all those frogs hop away to? And if the tadpoles just died, then where were their plump, black bodies? I gave up thinking about it and, with tears on my cheeks, walked up the bank and to the little house.

"They're all gone," I told my mother and plopped down on a kitchen chair.

"What's all gone?"

"The frogs and everything," I said.

"Oh, Poppy. You have worried way too much about those tadpoles and frogs in that darn creek. There will be more next summer, and you'll be here when they first start to show up."

That helped me to feel somewhat better. I didn't know there was a cycle. That things could and usually would continue on.

I hung around the house the rest of that day. My mother seemed particularly happy to have me nearby. I followed her around, asking a lot of questions while she watered her new plants and pulled the tiny weeds sprouting up from the new beds. We sat on an old quilt out on the lawn and ate butter and honey sandwiches for lunch. We stretched out side by side in the shade and took a nap together. I would remember that day as the sad-but-nice day.

My mother was afraid of horses. She tried not to be, but I could see fright in her when she was around them. Sometimes she would come to the yard fence and hold Nicky's reins for me while I ran in the house to use the bathroom. She would stand, stiff-armed, and grip the leather in her fist like a vice.

"Hold right here," I would explain.

"Okay, but hurry," she always said.

If I had Nicky near the house, she would bring out a carrot for her, but she always handed it to me instead of offering it to Nicky herself.

"Oh, Sis," she would say, "I don't know how you can handle a big ol' horse like that."

I loved when she, or anybody, showed their admiration for something like that. It made me feel like I could do something special. I would flush with the embarrassment of a compliment.

Anything to do with the horses was left to my father and me. He had acquired an old saddle for me to use, but it was hard for me to lift up onto Nicky's back without pushing the saddle blanket off the other side. It was easier to just bridle her and ride bareback. For a while, the only time my saddle was used was on the days my father was home to put it on for me. The small saddle was a good one, with wide pommels and a high, straight cantle, and held me in place as perfect as could be.

On a Saturday, soon after the tadpole pools dried up, I rode Nicky, saddled, down the canyon road. It had been a week or more since I had been down the road, and I was deciding whether or not to ride to the mud house. As I rounded a curve, Nicky and I were both startled by the whooshing sound of wings as three giant blackbirds with ugly, red, wrinkled heads rose swiftly up in front of us from the edge of the dirt road. Nicky backed a few steps and tried to turn back the way we came. I held her reins and made her stand still. The heavy, sickening stench of rotting flesh made me bring my hand up to cover my mouth and nose. Nicky continued to move her front feet side to side to avoid going forward. I kicked at her sides until she took a few more steps, and then I could see the remains of a dead fawn, scattered in the dust in tawny pieces.

I was shaken at the sight and the smell. I could see a few faded fawn spots on the hide of its back, and its legs were bent and broken, showing delicate, sharp bones. Tears of pity sprang to my eyes, and I felt an ache in my chest. I saw the fawn's face and glassy, wide-open eyes, and I looked away and gave Nicky all the kicks it took to trot her on by the grisly sight. Nicky moved quickly sideways to the far edge of the road and blew a snort through her nose as we hurried by. I wiped the tears from my cheeks with the backs of my hands and wondered where the fawn's mother was and if she was broken-hearted because her baby died.

After I grew calmer and quit crying, I decided, since I was past the horrible sight, I may as well ride down to the mud house and see if I could talk to Sky and Riley again. As I rode past the house that sat up on the hill, I gawked up at it. I was curious to know if someone there rode the horses that had the habit of running down the hill to greet Nicky and me. This time I heard voices from near the house, and then two women walked into view.

The people turned out to be a lady and a girl a lot older than me. They probably heard Nicky's hoof beat on the road because they both turned and looked down upon us at the same time. They waved, and I waved back. I thought how glad I was to be riding in my saddle because I felt like I looked more like a real cowboy and not just a kid. I knew they were watching as I rode out of sight.

When I rounded the curve in the canyon road that bent around the mud house place, I immediately saw that the family was busy doing something at the dry creek bed near their crossing. Sky noticed me first and waved a big wave, causing the others to turn and see me.

"Hey, girl," Riley called and gave a toothy grin. Sky said something to him, and he waved and called, "Hey, Poppy, remember me?"

"Hi, Riley," I called back. He started toward me, but his mother reached for his arm and stopped him.

"What are you doing?" Sky called.

I thought that was a silly question because she could see plain as day what I was doing.

"Riding Nicky."

"Want to stop by?" she asked.

"If it's okay."

"Go over there past the rock and cross the creek where we drive." She started to run in that direction so she could direct me.

I could plainly see the driveway, where a wire gate had been opened back against the fence that ran alongside the road. When we met, she walked beside me, reaching to pat Nicky's neck.

"What are you all doing?" I asked.

I saw a pile of lumber stacked beside a place where the creek channel deepened. The man there was busy with his hands. He was thin to the point of gauntness. Thick, straight, blondish hair fell over his forehead, nearly covering his eyes as he bent to his task. His sleeves were rolled up to his elbows, and his shirt was untucked and hung open, revealing a dingy undershirt. His forearms were long and sinewy.

"We're building a bridge." Sky was excited. "A walking bridge, so when the creek runs we can still get across to our house. My father said, if it rains a lot this winter, there will be a lot of water down the creek, and we need a way to get in and out."

I slid down from Nicky's back and walked with Sky toward her family. Right away, I saw how beautiful Sky's mother was. She was tall and slim, and her dark-brown hair was the longest I had ever seen, besides my grandma's. It was pulled back from her face and tied with a thin, blue ribbon at her neck. The wispy ends hung below her waist. Her eyes were dark, and thick, black eyebrows arched up when she looked at me. She wore a long, drab skirt and a shirt like a man's, sleeves rolled to her elbows, like her husband's. Her hands were rough, and her nails were short to the tips of her fingers. I was shocked to see that, when she smiled, her teeth looked yellow and crooked, one broken half off.

"Hello, Poppy. Sky told me she met a new friend. My name is Maryanne, and it's okay to call me by my first name. We don't hold to much formality around here."

"Hi Mrs. . . . Maryanne. This is my horse, Nicky."

"Nice to meet you, Nicky." She turned to me. "Would you like to tie Nicky over at that tree and play for a while?" She motioned to a small tree away from the creek and near the place where a high dirt and rock cliff jutted up, forming a sort of wall.

"I'm not supposed to tie her up with the reins. She could break them."

I had been in trouble for that before and remembered the consequences. Those reins cost money, Poppy, my father had lectured me. Don't ever tie your horse to anything by the reins, hear me? Kids think every damn thing comes free. Well, it don't. Somebody has to work for them reins. That time the rein had broken close to the bit, so my father had reattached it. We didn't have to get another one, but he was mad, anyway.

"We have a lot of rope around here. Let's find some for you to use."

She and Sky went rummaging around in some wooden crates and came up with a piece of rope just the right length. I led Nicky to the tree and tied her there and gave her a nice pat. Turning back, I was startled to find Riley close behind me. I hadn't heard him come through the rustle of leaves with his odd gait. Now that I was really looking at him, I could see how much he looked like his mother. He had the same dark hair and eyes, and his eyebrows touched each other above his nose. He had long arms and legs like his mother, too. He always seemed to be smiling, and he had a wide gap between his two front teeth. I thought his lips looked too red for a boy.

I said, "Hi, Riley. How are you today?" trying to sound grown up. I don't know why I thought that necessary. Maybe because I knew he was slow, and I didn't know exactly how much he understood.

"I'm good. Want to see our pond?" His words were awkward sounding, and he didn't pronounce his p and t sounds clearly. His mouth and lips became wet as he spoke, and spit sprayed into the air between us. I was anxious to see a pond. Maybe they had tadpoles, like I did.

"Sure. Is Sky coming?"

"I can't be by the pond without Sky or Mama or Father."

I turned to follow him back to where the others were and heard Maryanne say, "Now, Ri, don't be a pest."

His father had not said a word since I arrived, but I could see he was busy measuring some lumber near the creek. He had a coffee can full of nails, a hammer, and a handsaw lying nearby on some boards.

"Can your father really build a bridge?" I asked Sky.

"Sure he can. He builds things all the time."

"Well, I'll be damned," I said.

There was a stunned silence. I knew, an instant too late, I had said the wrong thing. I thought I would sound grown up if I said a cuss word. Maryanne looked startled, but Sky and Riley's father turned in a whirl and said, "What did you say?" in a stern, hard voice.

I could feel my facing burning, as if I was too close to a blazing fire. My skin actually hurt, and all I could do was stammer. "I . . . I . . . I'm sorry."

But Maryanne saved the day when she suddenly burst out with a clear, high laugh.

"She didn't mean to, Carl. It just slipped out. Right, Poppy?"

I was flooded with relief. "Yes, ma'am," I said in a small voice.

Carl looked right at me for a second, and then bent back to his measuring. He spoke while he looked down at what he was doing. "Riley. You stay away from the pond. Hear me? I have told you that a hundred times."

Riley kind of squirmed his body around a little and said, "Okay."

I felt sorry for him, but Sky took my arm and began leading me away as he watched us go.

We walked up-creek for a ways, and soon I could no longer see the canyon road through the thick stand of willows. Now I could see everything the family had behind the growing curtain. The pond was nothing like I had expected. The shape was long and narrow and filled to the top with muddy water. Other than a few water bugs, I could see that there wouldn't be anything living in the thick, brown water. In a large, cleared area nearby were a dozen or so wooden boxes divided into smaller rectangles. Some of the boxes had been poured full of mud. There were a lot of tools scattered about and two wheelbarrows. There was also a high mound of reddish dirt with shovels standing where they had been pushed into the pile.

"What is that?" Sky looked to where I pointed.

"Oh, that's where we make mud blocks for our house. Someday, we're going to have a beautiful, big house made of those." She indicated the boxes full of mud. "It's called adobe. We have to make millions of them." She spoke with authority.

"Millions? That's an awful lot. Then you just stack them up?" I was looking back at the L-shaped wall nearer the creek.

"Yep. We put some more wet mud and then stack them up."

I was amazed at the whole idea. I had never heard of such a thing. I imagined it would take years to build a whole house.

"When will it be done?"

"Father says by the end of next summer, if the rains come and we have plenty of water. That's the clay cliff back there." She pointed to the high, red-orange colored wall at the back of the property. "We use picks and shovels and dig the clay off the bank to mix with straw and dirt and water. Father scoops the mud into the frames, and we have to wait for the sun to dry them all out. Come on. I'll show you my house."

I turned and followed Sky back to the trailer house. She showed me her outside cot with a canvas sleeping bag stretched out on it. What I really wanted to see was the inside of the trailer, but the door was closed. When I asked what it was like, she said it was real nice but that we couldn't go inside.

"Father would get mad," she said.

We wandered back to where Carl and Maryanne and Riley were, and I could see Maryanne was holding a big timber in place while Carl sawed and sawed, back and forth, until he finally cut through the wood. He stood and stretched his back.

"'Bout ready to start nailing these boards here. Sky, I need you to get over here and help your mother hold these long ones up for me." He looked square at me, then turned to his work.

I took that as my signal to leave. "I better go now," I said. "I can't leave Nicky tied for too long. I'll get in trouble."

"Stop by anytime, Poppy," Maryanne said kindly.

"Yeah, Poppy," Ri said.

When I had untied Nicky and climbed back on her, I rode past them through the gate to the canyon road. I waved again, and they all waved back, except Carl. I saw him stand straight and watch as I rode by. Something about him seemed odd to me. His face looked hard and pinched, and his close eyes were set deep. I didn't think I liked Carl much.

Seven

I wasn't supposed to lope Nicky toward home. Another one of my father's rules.

"You'll make her a runaway. Pretty soon, ever damn time you head home, she'll want to take off on ya."

But sometimes I did anyway. Truth was, it was easier to get her into a lope if we were going toward home than if we were riding away. She never went too fast or tried to run off with me, though. She loped big, smooth strides, feeling almost like a merry-go-round horse. As soon as we were out of sight of the mud-house family, I moved Nicky into a lope and had gone only a short way when we just about had a calamity.

While rounding a long curve, me not looking ahead, we came within one full stride of running head-on into another horse and rider. Our horses' instincts saved us from catastrophe as they dodged the collision without any help from us. For me, at least, I just held onto my saddle horn while Nicky figured out what to do. When we were back in control and facing each other, I recognized the other rider. She was the older girl that lived in the house up on the hill.

"You're on the wrong side of the road," she declared with a sarcastic voice and a curled top lip.

I glanced around me, wondering if what she said was true. I felt my face flush at her reprimand and had no words to defend myself. I assumed, because she was older, that she was probably right. I sat, not knowing what to do next.

"You ride on that side going up and this side going down."

She spoke with such certainty, swooping her arm from side to side. I guessed she knew what she was talking about.

"Okay."

"You live up the road in the old Davis place?"

"Who's the Davises?" I didn't know who they were or if I lived in their place.

"The people who used to live in that old house up there across the creek. Old man Davis died, and the widow Davis moved into town. Nobody's lived there for a long time."

"Did he die in our house?" I was stuck on that part.

The girl leaned forward, resting her arm on her saddle horn. Her copper-colored horse spun her bit roller in her mouth, with her tongue making a smooth clicking sound, and stamped a foot at a fly.

"My mom said the old man always wanted to die outside. He told everybody that. 'Just drag me out in the yard when my time comes.' That's what he'd told Marie. People who knew them were worried because Marie wasn't strong enough to help him get outside if he was dying. My mom said he told Marie he could hear the angels coming. He said she better get up and help him out the door, so she tried. Mom said Marie lugged him almost to the front door, and he fell down on the floor, and she couldn't get him no farther. She tried to pull him by his arms, but he was too heavy for her. Mom said he died right there on the floor, and when the sheriff came, poor Marie was sitting by him crying her eyes out because she couldn't get him outside to do his dying. So, yeah, he died in that old house."

I was so interested in the girl's story, I wanted to hear more. I was disappointed when she said she was going to go on and finish her ride. She told me—ordered me, you could say—to stay on the right side of the road and that maybe she would be seeing me later. She said maybe we could go for a ride together. I watched her turn her horse away and head down the road without looking back. I walked Nicky the rest of the way home, thinking about poor Mr. Davis dying in our living room.

After unsaddling Nicky, which was much easier than putting the saddle on her, I turned her out in the pasture and ran to the house. My mother was in the kitchen, cutting up vegetables. I took a glass from the cupboard to get some Kool-Aid, but she took the glass from my hand and told me to go wash. Coming back into the kitchen, I saw she had poured the Kool-Aid for me and had even put an ice cube in the glass. I leaned against the kitchen doorjamb and told her about meeting the new girl.

"What's her name?"

"I don't know."

"You didn't even ask? Does she know your name?"

"I don't think so. I didn't tell her."

My mother smiled and shook her head. "How old is she?"

I was getting frustrated with the questions. I just wanted to tell her my story.

"I don't know, but she's older than me. Anyway, she said Mr. Davis died right here in our living room. Right over there by the door." I pointed to where I envisioned the death of Mr. Davis taking place. "And poor Mrs. Davis sat by him and cried until the sheriff came."

"Well, Poppy, I don't know about that. I think Mr. Davis was ill for a time, and he actually died in the hospital in town."

I sipped my grape Kool-Aid and thought about that. The girl's story about Mr. Davis seemed more interesting.

"Well, she said her mother told her. Her mother knows the whole story."

A time would come later in my life when I would appreciate what a kind diplomat my mother could be. She said, "Well, sweetie, maybe there was just a misunderstanding about where Mr. Davis died. Sometimes stories just get mixed up. What else did you do today?"

I knew the subject was over, but I could still picture Mr. Davis lying on the floor by the door, seeing angels fly around his head and being real unhappy with Mrs. Davis because she couldn't get him out of the door and into the yard to do his dying.

"I visited Sky and Riley again today. They're building a bridge."

"Oh, mercy. Well, now, that must be a big job. Hope it's a better one than that old car trap up to the barn."

"Not a drive-over bridge, just a walk bridge so they can get to their place when the creek runs. Their father's name is Carl. I don't think he's very nice. He's always working. He doesn't talk much at all."

"That makes him not nice?" She had changed from slicing carrots to peeling potatoes into the sink.

"Not that. He wasn't friendly like the rest of the family. I think he looks like a wolf."

"You've never even seen a wolf." She laughed, so I changed the subject.

"I saw where they make their bricks for the house they're building. They make them outta mud. Sky says it's called adobe. By the end of next summer, they will have a great big house to live in."

"Sounds like another big job. What does their father do?"

I thought I had just told her about that.

"What do ya mean?"

"Well, you know, for a job? Like your daddy does farming for his job."

"I don't know. Maybe he doesn't do a job."

"They have to earn money somehow, Poppy. He surely has some kind of job."

I shrugged that subject away. "Their mom's name is Maryanne, and she is real nice. You should see her hair. It is longer than Grandma Taylor's."

Grandma Taylor was my mother's mother. She had gray hair that she wore up in a bun on the back of her head, and it looked exactly the same every day. One night when I was staying with her, I walked into her room and found her sitting at a little dressing table with her cotton

nightgown on, running a brush through her hair. I was astounded to
see the long, thin tresses hanging down in front of each shoulder and
over the humps of her huge, saggy breasts. There were ropey streams
of gray and brown hair nearly reaching her waist. I had run back out,
feeling like I had walked in on something I wasn't supposed to see.

"Anyhow, their mom said I could come back anytime." I paused,
picturing the hurt look on Riley's face when Sky and I went off to see
the pond. "I feel sorry for Riley. He seems pretty smart to me. He's slow,
but I don't think he's really dumb. I think his arms and legs don't work
right."

My mother was scooping peelings into the garbage can and rinsing
the sink. She stopped and gazed out of the widow in front of her where
the giant mulberry tree stood.

"You know, there's all kinds of mental problems. Different things
can go wrong. When I was four, my mother had a baby boy.

I had never heard her say "my mother" before. She always said
"your grandma."

"Ohhh, I was so excited to have a baby brother. He was the sweet-
est little thing. Daddy named him Eric, and all us kids made a big fuss
over him. He died when he was three and a half years old. They said he
was retarded and never knew anything, but I know that wasn't true. I
could tell he liked me, and he would kick his little feet and try to make
sounds whenever I went near him. He didn't talk, but he could look
at us with those eyes, and we knew he loved us like we loved him. He
never learned to walk. Daddy or one of my brothers carried him everywhere. I don't think Daddy was ever the same after Eric died." She
turned back to me. "Anyway, sweetie, that Riley just might be much
smarter than anybody gives him credit for. You just be real nice to him
and treat him like you would anybody else."

I went out to the picnic table and sat, thinking about what my
mother had told me. I never knew she had another brother. I knew my
uncles, her three older brothers, but Eric had never been mentioned. I

felt the same way I had that night I walked in on Grandma Taylor and discovered her long hair. I felt like I knew more than I should.

When my mother came out of the house, she had on her Keds instead of her rubber flip-flops and had held her hair back with a headband.

"Let's go for a walk up by the barn, Poppy. Want to? Your father went up on the hill to check the cows. Maybe we will meet him on his way back and hitch a ride."

I was thrilled to have my mother spend that kind of time with me. It happened less and less since we had moved, and I missed her happy-go-lucky mood. We walked up the driveway, crossed the dry creek bed, and then took the little road that dipped across the creek again and led us to where the barn stood. There was an old wooden bridge that crossed the creek near the barn, but I had been told early on not to step foot on it because I would likely fall through the rotten boards or get a nail in my foot. This was the bridge my mother called the car trap. The heavy wooden gate that closed it off from the canyon road always had a chain padlocked around a post and a "keep off" sign posted so no one would attempt to use it.

Twice I had tiptoed out to the middle of the bridge and looked down at the dry, sandy creek bottom. It looked like a long way down. I tried to imagine water rushing by, but it was hard to get the picture in my mind. I had come to know the creek in its dry state so intimately that it was becoming harder and harder to picture it any other way.

We stopped by the concrete water trough, and like always, I put my face in the water and took a few long pulls, swallowing gulps of cool water.

"Poppy, what in the world are you doing? You drink that water? Oh my Lord. You'll be sick with some cow disease or a bacteria from all the slobber."

"I won't. I drink it all the time. Every time I come to the barn, I get drinks from the trough. It's good. Wanna taste?"

"No. I don't want to taste that." She grimaced.

"Want me to chip you off a piece of salt block?"

I knew my mother liked salt a lot. She was always saying so, and my father was always saying, "Dammit, Francine. Don't put too much salt in them beans or you'll ruin 'em."

"Don't tell me . . . you eat cow salt?"

I had never given a thought to salt being harmful. I would just chip a piece off the block with a rock and suck on it for a few minutes. When I put the salt in my mouth first and then sipped from the trough, the water tasted extra sweet. I decided not to tell my mother any more of what I did when I was alone.

We walked as near the creek as we could, using deer and cow trails, skirting brush and trees when we had to. The trunks of the live oaks that grew there were bigger than any I had ever seen, and the sycamores' long, graceful branches reached out over the creek bed. On our right, out in the long meadow, the two-track road that my father drove on to get to where his cows were dipped and rose across several small ravines. We came to a place where the road headed up into the hills and the creek bed bent away to our left in the opposite direction. My mother hesitated here.

"If we follow the creek, we might miss your father coming this way," she indicated, waving her hand along the road.

"Oh, please. Let's go the creek way. I haven't been this far before." The explorer in me had been awakened again.

"Okay, but we will have to walk all the way back home if we miss a ride."

I was delighted to think that could happen. I would much rather walk with my mother than ride in the old stinky pickup with my father.

In a short distance, we came to a place in the creek that was solid rock along the bottom and up the high, steep bank on the far side. There were a few giant boulders that directed the channel, and we could see the shallow caves of erosion along the stone bank. The rock there was worn smooth, but there were long, deep, horizontal crevasses the entire length of the wall. We tried to peer into them and kept warning each other to keep our fingers out of them. No telling what creatures might be living in there.

At last we moved on around one more bend in the creek, and that is when I first saw a place I would come to love forever. An oak tree with a massive trunk grew up from the creek bank, and one huge limb reached across the width of the creek. The shade was so dense beneath the canopy, we felt an incredible temperature drop as we moved into it. I smelled the rich, mossy scent of creek water. The rock slab was like a floor about the size of our little house's living room, and there were three deep stone holes, each as big as two or three washtubs. In fact, one looked as deep as I was tall. Each was full to its rim with water.

"Look, look," I kept saying as we slowly made our way around the holes. "And look at this one. But, there's no tadpoles."

"I think they have all turned into frogs by now. Let's put our feet in the water. Want to?"

I wasn't so sure about that, but I watched my mother pull off her shoes and socks and roll up her pant legs.

"Come on," she said.

We scooted to the edge of the deepest hole and slipped our feet into the water. It felt like silk. The temperature was tepid, so we were hardly able to feel the wetness on our skin. We sat there for what seemed like a long time, both of us quiet. Blue jays screeched in the oaks, probably not happy to have us there.

"I have an idea," I said. "Let's call this place the spring tubs. This will be a special place to come to, and we don't have to tell anyone else about it."

My mother went along. "Maybe we will bring a picnic lunch here one day."

From somewhere far behind our spot, the sound of an engine whining in low gear drifted down to us. I knew it would be my father. I ignored the intrusion, hoping my mother didn't hear. Or care.

"We're going to miss our ride." She looked back over her shoulder toward the place where the road divided. I didn't say anything, and she made no attempt to rise. The engine sound became louder and then faded again as my father drove on to our house. We both lay back on the smooth stone and let our feet float and gently stir the water.

Finally, my mother sat up and said we had better go. She would need to finish up supper by the time we walked home. She showed me how to shake the water off my feet then wipe them with the outside of my socks before putting them back on.

Later that evening, after we had eaten and were clearing the table, my father asked my mother where in the hell we had walked to.

"The spring tubs," she said.

He just shook his head and drank his wine from the little juice glass.

The next morning dawned the same as all the days before, bright and warm. My mother was frying bacon and eggs, and my father was just coming inside from morning chores when I joined them. I knew, seeing all that food, my mother was either preparing to have company or my brothers were home for breakfast.

"Norm, call the boys in. This is ready."

A stack of toast, a platter of bacon, and three fried eggs on each of their plates graced the table. I scooted around to a chair behind the table, and my brothers came in—making a lot of noise, scooting chairs, and talking at the same time. I was in heaven. I loved the times they bantered and teased and laughed. Our sober father joined in, trying to joke along with his sons. He sounded light and happy. And nice. I soaked up the normalcy.

Our family didn't attend church, so if there was work to be done, Sundays went on like any other day. There was a discussion about how much hay needed to be loaded out for a grower in the valley and how much the boys could earn for the job. I could tell the amount made them happy because my brother, Tim, whistled a long, low whistle when my father told them what the wages would be.

Allen always called me skinny and teased me about how little food I ate. "Careful there, skinny, don't founder on that piece of toast."

I chewed the middle out and left the crust.

"Eat that crust. That's where the vitamins are," my father said, but without his usual supper-time crankiness. I ate the crust, hoping to make him proud of me.

"Mom said you met that neighbor gal yesterday, huh? She gonna be ridin' with you now?"

"Maybe. She said maybe we would ride sometime. Her horse is pretty. Not as pretty as Nicky, though." I looked at my mother. "I'm not going to tell her about the spring tubs. That place is just for us."

"She's lived here a long time, Sis. Chances are, she already knows that place."

I felt protective . . . and stubborn. It was my place now and on our property, so I could refuse to share with her if I wanted to. It was just for my mother and me.

Eight

I think the August heat crushed my mother's spirit. That, and two other matters. There was no relief from the misery of the constant high temperatures. The nights sweltered, and the bed sheets were damp with sweat, even at midnight. I tossed and turned and kicked crazily at anything that touched the skin of my legs. Only my father slept for any length of time, and I knew that because he snored so loud the sounds vibrated through the little house. My mother had often complained about his snoring, but because I had slept the deep sleep of youth, I had not noticed it much until those August nights that robbed me of sleep.

I was edgy and tired and emotional. I cried over everything that was contrary to me. I was a notorious crier anyway, our entire family knew that, and the oppressive heat that stole our rest made me even more of one. I drug myself around like a sack of wool throughout the long days. I flopped down on the lawn in the shade and tried to fall asleep, but the bugs pinched and tickled to the point of annoyance that made me get up and try something else to find comfort. I sat with the water hose turned on my legs and feet, but after a few days, my mother said I shouldn't do that because, "God knows how long the well will hold up in this kind of weather."

Living things lost any semblance of thriving. Plants drooped their heads and leaves. The animals followed the shade as the sun moved overhead. They lay in limp mounds of hair, panting through gaped mouths. No matter how many water bowls and pans we kept scattered around for them, or how many times they went to water, they suffered.

My poor mother. She still fixed meals, washed clothes, and managed the household jobs related to daily living. She kept a damp towel handy and held it against her neck and chest for a brief few minutes of relief. By the time my father came home in the evenings, she would be drained of any energy.

He was the only one who wanted to eat supper. My mother and I took little food onto our plates, and often I didn't eat mine. One night, as she pushed the food around on her plate, she made the mistake of saying how she was tiring of cooking in the blazing hot kitchen.

My father's voice exploded inside the small space of the supper-table nook. "Dammit, Francine. I work all damn day while you sit around here on your butt doing nothing but fanning yourself, and then you bitch 'cuz you have to fix supper. A workin' man has to eat." He drained his wine glass in one long swallow and slammed it back onto the table. I felt my body start at the noise.

For the first time I could recall, I heard my mother talk back like she meant it. "Shut up, Norman." She dropped her fork on her plate and stood, scraping her chair back into the room. "You think you're the only one who counts around here. I hate this miserable place. You stuck me up here in this godforsaken canyon, and all you care about is yourself and your damned old cows. I feel like I'm burning in hell." She turned and left the kitchen, and I heard the screen door slam shut.

I sat without breathing and looked at my father. His face was red as fire, and his blue eyes looked to have a light behind them. He stared after my mother for a moment, then, in a calm voice, said, "Sis, pour me some more wine, would you?" dropped his own fork, and pushed his plate away from him.

My legs felt shaky when I stood up to take his glass to the sink board, where I managed to pour it full from the jug. I tiptoed back to the table, terrified I would spill the wine on my way. I set the glass down and turned and ran out of the house.

My mother was sitting at the red picnic table, smoking a cigarette. I could see the tip of it flare in the dark as she took a long drag. I sat next to her on the bench seat, but neither of us said anything for a few minutes. I could tell by her small snuffling noises that she was crying a little bit.

"Did you finish eating?" she said.

"Nah, I wasn't hungry."

She didn't say anything, and we sat silently for a while.

"I'm just so tired," she said into the dark. "Tired of everything."

There was silence again, and I wondered if she meant she was tired of me, too. I had never thought I caused her much trouble, but maybe I had. I felt so terrible, and I decided right then and there that I would try to be a better girl, nicer and more helpful. Maybe that would help her feel better.

"You go on, now. Get a shower tonight and a clean nightie. You'll feel better."

I didn't think that was true, but at the time, I would have done anything she told me without argument. Stepping back inside the living room, I saw my parents' bedroom door was closing and heard the pretty glass knob rattle. I went to the kitchen and slowly cleared the table, scraping off the plates and putting the dishes into the sink. I washed the table top with the dishcloth, scrubbing the circles of wine spill harder than was necessary.

Standing in the shower for a long time, I turned the handle more and more until the water was cold enough to make me shiver and raise huge goosebumps. I stepped out and opened the window as wide as it would open and stood for a time in the night air.

I expected to see my mother in the kitchen after I was dry and had my nightie on, but she wasn't there. I looked through the screen door into the night and saw that she was still at the table, smoking a cigarette. Tears slipped down my face. She looked so sad out there. So alone. I wanted to go put my arms around her neck and tell her how much I loved her, but I didn't. I don't know why, but probably because I thought she would send me back in the house. I went to bed and lay awake, listening for her to come back inside. I fell asleep without hearing her.

For the next several days, I felt as if something had changed around our house. The canyon was always a quiet place. Only an occasional passing vehicle made any foreign noise. Otherwise, it was the birds and a whinny from the horse pasture or lowing from the cows up on the hills, but I seldom even noticed those sounds. There was another kind of quietness after the night my mother became so angry and sat out in the yard crying, alone. There were no voices most of the time. In fact, during the days, the radio didn't play, and the television's one channel was not turned on. It was as if no humans lived there. After the normal sounds brought on by my father's arrival from work in the evening, hardly any words were spoken. It took two days for me to realize that my parents were not speaking to each other.

My mother still cooked, we still sat at the table, still cleaned up the dishes, but it was like living in a house with mutes. It was only to me that a few words were spoken. "Sis, get the forks," "pass the bread," "rinse the soap off this glass," "goodnight."

As days passed, shear boredom overshadowed the misery of the heat. I returned to the cave and the creek. Hot was hot, no matter whether I was there or in our yard. I rode Nicky around the pasture again and would, within minutes, be wet with her sweat down the backs of my legs. My pants would dry, stiff and dirty, and I knew I smelled like horse sweat. No one told me to get in the shower, so I didn't. My hair became wiry and sprang out here and there of its own accord.

One morning, I asked my mother if she would walk with me to the spring tubs. I stood by her as she sat drinking her morning coffee and asked gently, my voice timid.

"Not today, sweetie. I'm not feeling good. I may have to go lie back down for a bit."

And that is what she did, shutting the bedroom door and leaving me there in the silent living room.

I went to the kitchen and made a honey and butter sandwich, wrapped it as best I could in waxed paper, placed it in a brown sack, and went out the door, careful not to let the screen door slam. That was the first of many trips I would hike to the spring tubs alone.

I was uneasy that first time. I had to keep reassuring myself that I was walking the exact same trail as I had with my mother, and that I left from the pasture road at exactly the same place. I worried, too, that there would be no water and that the tubs had dried up like the tadpole pools had. But, like the first time I was there, I smelled the water before I could see it. The holes were still filled to the brim with crystal clear water.

First, I took my shoes and socks off and sat next to the shallowest hole and put my feet in the water, just like my mother and I had before. After a while, I moved over to the deep hole and dangled my feet there, feeling that same velvety softness as the first time. I swished my feet, wondering how it would feel to slide all the way down into the water. I imagined how it would be smooth and cool on my skin.

I stood and unbuttoned my waistband, slid the zipper of my jeans down, and stepped out of them. Yanking my t-shirt off over my head, I dropped it on the stone slab. In just my underpants, I sat on the edge of the spring tub and let myself slip down into the water. At first, I stood on the bottom and let the water come up above my waist, but then I slowly squatted down and down, taking in a deep gulp of air just before the water washed over my face and head. It felt magical as the apprehension left my scrawny body.

The longer I stayed in the deep hole, the more relaxed and comfortable I became with the velvety smoothness of the water as it covered my bare skin. I lay my head back on the rim and, with knees bent, had room to let myself float on the surface. My white ribcage poked up above the water. I stayed for a long time. When I finally left the tub, I struggled to get my wet body back into my clothes and put my socks and shoes on. I felt good, happy. I unfolded the wax paper from my sandwich and savored the sweet honey and wished I didn't have to go back to the canyon house.

I could see my mother in the yard as I walked up the driveway. She had the hose running in a trickle around her plants. I asked if her headache was better, and she said yes, some.

"I walked to the spring tubs." I said it like a confession, watching her face. I waited for her to be angry, to say how I was not to ever do that alone. But she said nothing about that.

"That's nice, sweetie. So, there's still water in them?"

"I got in one." Another confession.

"All the way, Poppy? Your clothes are dry."

"I took them off."

"Good heavens. You took your clothes off outside?"

I had not seen so much expression from her in days.

"Well, no one could see me. I mean, there's no one there."

"Oh, Poppy," she sighed, "you are like no other child."

And there was the other thing about my mother's sad spirit. Or maybe it was the same thing and I didn't know it. My mother was lonely.

"Nobody comes much, anymore," she said one day.

Much? I'd thought. *More like not at all.*

At first, everybody came. All my mother's friends had visited as often as they could. There had been company every weekend. Eating, drinking, laughing. A lot of laughing. How long had it been since I heard any joyfulness, any at all? No wonder our house seemed so strange. So little talking, less laughing.

My mother had a high, tinkling laugh that would tickle everyone's funny bone and spread like a warm breeze. She could tell a joke with a dry wit like nobody's business. Even if I didn't understand it, and I hardly ever did, I laughed along with the good humor. She got a kick out of doing silly things to make other people laugh. One time, she dyed our dog's little white tail green for St. Patrick's Day. She helped my big, strong brothers dress up like girls for Halloween. She was crafty and colorful.

And there was something else, besides the heat and the loneliness. My mother depended on someone else, namely my father, for her very life. She had never even learned to drive a car.

"I'm just too nervous, Norm. I can't remember to do all these things at one time. The brake, the clutch, the gears. And I can't steer around the corner with one hand while I stick this one out the window to signal. It's just too much."

I'd sat, keeping silent, in the backseat of the old station wagon. She had pulled over and parked on a side street in the valley town we had lived in at that time.

"Dammit, Francine. Anybody can learn to drive a damn car. Put the clutch in and try again."

We jerked out into the street until the engine died and she started to cry. My father scrambled out and slammed the heavy door hard. He stomped around the car and yanked her door open.

"Get over," was all he said.

As far as I know, that was my mother's one and only driving lesson. The other time I remember her behind the wheel was the day she tried to drive to the post office. When she turned onto the main street of town, the car died, and someone almost ran into us. A picture forms in my mind of us pulling right out in front of that other car. Maybe that isn't exactly how the whole thing went, but I can also see in my mind's eye the panic on her face, and I know that was real. She cried all the way home.

Of course, the fact that she couldn't drive probably didn't matter much by the time we lived in the canyon house. We had the one old pickup, and my father drove it every day. While all her old friends were driving to grocery stores and hair appointments and to visit other friends, she was just plain stuck in a bleak and lonely life, living in a way that was foreign to her sensibilities.

Her depression was sly. One day she would be silent, moody, and the look on her face would appear changed, as if she was concentrating on something behind me. And there were those brief, startling moments of anger that bordered on rage. Those times scared me. I would withdraw from her and the space around her, keeping a safe distance from her terrible temper.

I tried to read her mood, tried to anticipate how I should behave to please her, because I felt so positive that I must have something to do with her frame of mind. It was hard work for a little girl, all that dancing around her, so it didn't take too long to figure out that I would do better to stay away from her if things looked unsure. I learned to tell by a glance when my caring, cheerful mother had returned and was available again.

Nine

The next time I caught Nicky and headed down the canyon road, I went at a hair-blowing gait all the way to the mud house. I didn't have to think about whether or not I would be welcomed that time. I didn't take time to wonder if I should or shouldn't stop by. I paid little attention to the neighbor's horses that, as usual, scrambled down to the fence and were extra frisky because Nicky seemed in a hurry.

All I could think about was talking to Sky about a subject that had filled me with such anxiety I had barely been able to breathe. I don't know what it was I expected from her that would make me feel better, but she was the one person on earth I could think of to run to.

The morning had been the same as ever but thankfully, as my mother had said, not as hot as usual. I was dusting the living room furniture for her, using much too much lemon oil, when she came in and sat on the sofa near me. Her mouth smiled its gentle smile, but her eyes looked darkly serious. I thought I was in trouble for something and ran my recent activities through my mind lickety-split.

"Poppy, I am trying to figure out how we're going to get someplace to get you some clothes and new shoes for school. I think I'll call Rayleen and see when she's taking Patsy and Rex, and maybe we can go along with them. I hate to have to ask her, but I don't know how else we'll get it done unless your father will take us on a Saturday."

I must have looked as if I were deaf. There was a rushing noise in my head, drowning out my hearing. School. I had not given one single thought to going back to school. The idea of it belted me in the gut. There had been no one around to remind me. No other kids to bring the subject up.

"But, I don't wanna go to school," I whined.

"Poppy. You have to go to school, for heaven's sake. Don't be silly now. They would put Dad and me in jail if we didn't send you to school." She laughed a little.

"How will I get there?" I asked.

"You'll ride the school bus. Won't that be fun? It comes as far as that wide place in the road to be able to turn around. You're the first kid to get on and the last kid to get off."

She said that like I should think it was a special honor. I stood there, dust cloth in my hand, locked in my private bubble of panic, and tried to listen as she explained how it would be.

"You'll walk down in the morning, and when you get off in the afternoon, you walk back home." Like, see how simple? "Once you get used to the routine, you'll be just fine. You know how there's always a number on the front of the school buses? That's all you have to look for after school so you get the right bus. Just don't forget your number or you might end up in Tucumcari." Big grin. It wasn't one bit funny to me.

"Goldie and I can walk with you until you are ready to go and come all by yourself," she said. I know she meant it as a kindness, but that short walk to the bus turnaround was the least of my worries. That part I could do blindfolded.

But how in the world had I forgotten all about going to school? Maybe, because I was so frightened of the thought, I had put it out of my mind. It would be a new school I had never even seen before, and I wouldn't know any of the kids, and that all made for a good reason for a third grader to be afraid. I would have to give up my time with Nicky and the creek and the cave. And days would be different again.

Just when I had become used to the canyon house being home, things would change.

I finished my chores up and rushed out the door to catch Nicky. I kept thinking of Sky. She would have to go to school, too. At least I knew her.

I reached the curve where I could see the mud house and was relieved to see that Sky and Riley were down by the creek. The new bridge looked amazing. The plank walkway was wide, and there was a railing along one side. I could hardly wait to stand on it.

"Hi, Sky," I called.

"Bridge," Riley called, pointing to it.

"Come on, Poppy, tie Nicky to the tree, and we'll stand on the bridge."

When the three of us were standing at the end of the bridge in front of the step-up, Sky told me the only way Riley was allowed to walk on it was to hold onto our hands and walk between us. We each took hold of a bony, long-fingered hand in our own and began to walk together. Holding onto Riley was not an easy task. His arms stiffened at his elbows, and he kept pulling away in little jerky tugs.

"Stop it, Ri. Don't pull," Sky scolded.

"I not pull," he said, and the hand I held gave a strong yank and came right out of my grip. He stumbled to his knees, banging them hard on the edge of the step. He let out a shriek. I was horrified.

"Sky! You kids get away from that bridge right now, do you hear me? I don't want to see you there again."

There was Carl, a few yards away, standing with a shovel in his hand and looking as hard as a tree knot. I kept trying to get another hold on Riley to help him step back off the wooden planks.

"You there, Poppy, let him be so he can walk on his own."

My eyes flew to Sky.

"You told me to hold onto him," I said, and I could feel heat on my face.

"Yeah, but not now. He has to find his own balance to get going right."

"Well, how should I know that?"

I left the bridge in a leap to get out of their way. I was embarrassed that Carl had yelled at me, and I could feel a prickly blush cross my face. He watched for a long moment before he turned away.

"Now we won't get to go on the bridge anymore unless there's a lot of rain and we have to." Sky seemed to be slightly insinuating that it was my fault. She pouted.

"I did what you said." I crossed my arms with finality. "Besides, I came to ask you about something. It's about school. My mother said I have to go. Are you going?"

"All kids have to go to school." She looked at me like I was dense.

"Me? I go to school?" Riley asked his sister.

I could tell he was excited by his wet, spitty grin.

"No, Ri. You know you don't go to school."

That erased his glee immediately.

Sky had confirmed what my mother had said, so I could see there was not going to be a way out. I was overcome with doom. And fear, for I was so afraid of leaving home to go to school.

"I'll be in fourth grade. What grade will you be in?"

"I'll be in fifth." She seemed as excited about school as Ri. She said "fifth" like a grand announcement. That was disappointing news. Being in the same grade would have been a slight comfort.

"Will you ride the school bus?"

She'd patted her hands together in a mini celebration. "I love riding the school bus. It's fun. Have you ever rode on one? You're high up and can see all over the place. You'll like it. Come on, let's go sit on the rock."

We clambered up, leaving Ri to sit in the sand below us.

"I don't like school," I confessed. "I just want to stay at my house and do things there."

Sky looked over her shoulder toward their trailer house and back at me. "I love school. I get sick of this place. There's nothing to do but work. That's all my mother and father do. Work. All my father thinks about is the adobe house." She paused and looked down at her hands. "They fight."

"Who fights?"

"Father and Mom. He's mean to Mom and Ri sometimes." She looked around again and lowered her voice to a whisper. "He hit my mom one time. Her lip bled and bled. She got blood on her best shirt. She had a big sore here." She touched her lip and looked over her shoulder one more time. "I hate him sometimes."

I knew she did because I could see it in the stiffness of her expression.

"Don't whisper secrets, Sky. That is not nice." Riley was looking up at us where we sat on the rock.

I had no idea what to say. I could picture Sky's pretty mom with her lip bleeding and a scabby sore. I said, "Wow."

We sat for a while, not saying anything. I heard someone coming behind us and whirled with edgy nerves. I was relieved to see Maryanne walking toward us and not Carl, who I had decided was a bully. She smiled big.

"Hi, Poppy. How are you today?"

"Just fine."

"Come on, Ri. Time to go take your rest. You girls want a snack or something?"

"No, thank you." I didn't want to go anywhere Carl might be. I found myself looking intently at Maryanne's mouth. Riley went willingly, holding his mother's hand.

"Your mom is pretty. Mine is, too," I said, looking after Maryanne and Riley. Then, I guess just to make Sky feel better, I said, "My father is mean, too."

"He is?" Her eyes looked big in her round face. "Does he hit your mom?"

I wanted to say yes, just so she wouldn't think her father was the only one who did something so terrible, but it was too big a lie, and I couldn't say it.

"No. He doesn't hit her. He's just mad all the time, and he yells and says cruel words." Somehow, my explanation sounded petty. My words didn't say a thing about how he made my mother feel. Or me.

Sky seemed disappointed. "Well, that's nothin'."

I wanted to tell her that the way he acted was not "nothing." Tell her how worthless he made me feel sometimes, and how he treated my mother like she had no sense. But I guessed, compared to her father hitting her mother, my problem would seem minor. So I said, "He used to hit my brothers with his belt sometimes."

She heaved a sigh and shifted to a more comfortable position on the hardness of the rock and changed the subject as if it had become boring.

"Wait until you see the creek run. We saw it last winter. The water came right down through here, and it was real muddy." She pointed out a high place on the far bank. "It was up to that tree root over there."

I didn't want to say she was a liar, but that was hard to imagine. How could the water get that high just from rain? The gnarly root was three or four feet from the dry, sandy creek bottom.

She was looking at me. "You don't believe me? You just wait and see. That's why my father had to build that bridge. Father said it could be powerful enough to wash a grown cow away if we got even an average amount of rain."

A grown cow? No way could that happen. I decided my new friend was a fibber. I liked her anyway, and it would be good to have her to ride the school bus with.

I rode home slowly that day, looking down into the creek bed from the road when I could see the bottom. I tried hard to picture the high, muddy water running there, but I couldn't see it in my imagination.

After that day, I returned to visit Sky often. We learned about each other and our families while we sat on the boulder. Sometimes I took an extra honey sandwich with me, and we would eat them there and throw the crusts to the blue jays. I liked Ri, but I had more fun with Sky when he had to go take his rest.

Sky told me that her mother had inherited their land from her grandpa when he died, and that was why they were building a house there. I had a vague notion of what inherit meant. She said her father used to work at a tractor company in town but had quit his job, bought the little trailer, and come to live in the canyon. There I had it, the answer to my mother's question.

"Were you sad when your grandpa died?" I remembered how sad I was to think the tadpoles died. And the fawn.

She shrugged her shoulders. "I didn't know him too good. Father never like him. He said he was stingy. He says my mom is stingy, and she got the habit from her father. I don't know how you can get something like that from somebody else."

I agreed. "I don't think you can. Maybe he just says that to be mean. She doesn't really act stingy."

I had more questions about Riley. "What happened to Ri?" I finally ventured onto the subject.

"Nothing. He came out like that."

"Out of what?"

Sky looked at me. "You know. Out of my mom."

I honestly did not understand at first. Then it struck me.

"Oh, yeah. You mean like when our cows have their baby calves. They come out of their moms. Is that the same?"

I got the look again. "Sort of, I guess. But my mom was in a hospital. She says she thought Ri was beautiful the minute she saw him. She said he was teeny tiny." She made her voice go high while she said *teeny tiny*. "And she said he hardly cried at all when the doctor spanked his butt."

"Wow." I was stunned. "Why'd they spank him so soon?"

"That's just what they do to babies."

I wondered if I had been spanked before I even had a chance to do something wrong.

"I don't think I believe in that," I said with sincerity.

"My father didn't want him. My aunt said that. I heard her. She said, 'Carl has a screw loose. He told the doctor right out that he didn't want a baby that was retarded. Poor Maryanne would have a conniption fit if she knew he'd said that.'" Sky had changed her voice, attempting to sound like her aunt, but she just sounded goofy.

"Who'd she say that to? Your aunt."

"Some friend of hers. My Uncle Bill was there, too. He jumped up and said, 'Somebody shoulda done away with that man. He's downright evil,' or something like that." She'd lowered her voice to sound like Uncle Bill. "I wasn't supposed to be listening."

"Your father acts like he likes Ri. He's always fussing over him about something. Like he's always afraid he's going to get hurt or something." I was being a little sarcastic. I had never recovered from the sting of Carl embarrassing me the time Ri fell on the bridge.

"He does," Sky nodded. "He acts like that, but he says such hateful things. That's what my mom says, that he says hateful things. He tells Ri that he's retarded and stupid." She spit the words out like a bitter seed. "Just like that, to his face. He'll say, 'Riley, get away from there,' or 'Quit doing that. Don't be so retarded.' Then he'll laugh, like he's funny. I hate him when he does that."

Tears filled Sky's eyes, and their blonde-lashed rims turned red. "That's what they were fighting about when he hit Mom. About him always saying that Ri's retarded. She told him to shut up and a bunch of other stuff, and he just turned around and hit her with his fist. She fell down in the dirt right over there." She motioned toward the tree where Nicky stood.

"Every time my mom tried to get up, he kept pushing her down on her hands and knees again. Me and Ri were crying like crazy. And poor Ri. He was saying 'Mama, Mama.'" Sky's cheeks were washed with tears, and her lips stretched and gaped as she struggled to control her emotion. "She kept saying, 'I'm okay, Ri. Don't cry. Mom's okay.' I knew she wasn't because the blood ran from her mouth. I thought her teeth came out." A big gulping sob came from Sky, and she stopped talking.

I felt terrible and sick in my stomach. I started crying as hard as she was.

When she could speak again she said, "Promise me you won't ever tell anybody what I told you. Promise." Sky's eyes looked square into mine. I didn't know any better, so I promised and patted her back, wanting her to feel better.

Ten

It was after two in the morning when I stood inside the screen door, waiting for someone to come. My heart was thudding, but I hadn't cried yet. I stood there, listening for a car to come up the canyon road. With all of the lights turned on, the inside of our house seemed so garishly bright compared to the pitch black of the night. I wasn't cold in my nightie, not at all, but I was trembling.

I'd stayed up late, or, I guess I should say, I had lain awake late. My mother and father's friends, Clarkie and Ellen, had been at our house since late afternoon. My mother had fixed dinner—chicken, biscuits, and white gravy—and they'd sat around the supper table for a long time, talking and having drinks. The deck of cards came out, and they played penny-ante poker for a couple of hours. I hung around and watched and listened until my mother told me I had to go to bed.

I could hear them in the kitchen for a while, laughing and carrying on, and eventually they scraped the chairs back and went to the living room. I finally dozed off after that. I didn't feel like I had been asleep long at all when I came wide awake to the peculiar silence. I sat straight up in bed and could feel my senses struggling to understand what was so bewildering. The kitchen light shone in a yellow slit below my door. But I felt a foreboding that made me afraid to leave my bed to open the door, so I sat, listening to the quiet for a few minutes.

At last, I found the nerve. I stepped into the hall and slowly moved into the kitchen and looked around. There were heaping ashtrays, bottles, and glasses still on the supper table. I turned to the living room and saw that the front door stood wide open, but the screen was closed. My parents' bedroom door was ajar, but I knew before I looked that they weren't in there. Their door was never open when they were in there.

"Mom?" I called, in no particular direction. The house was so tiny, I knew they were nowhere inside, but I called anyway. "Mama?" louder. Nothing. The fact that there was no answer, no sound at all, made me shiver. Fear squeezed me around my middle until I felt paralyzed. What happened to everyone? I was all alone in the middle of the night. Why would they go off and leave me?

I sat on the cool Naugahyde sofa, not knowing what I was supposed to do. Every frightening thing I had experienced in my young life came to mind: a scary movie about people disappearing from a house on a stormy night, ghost stories that my brother Tim told me one night when he was babysitting me, and the noises I had heard in the creek the night my father made me go set the tadpoles free after dark. My stomach ached something terrible. After some time, I stood with weak knees and went to the phone, lifting the heavy black receiver and pushing the button twice, calling for an operator. The second I heard her voice say "Operator," I began to cry.

"May I help you? Hello?"

"I woke up and there's nobody here. I'm all by myself."

"Where are you, sweetie? Are you home?"

"Yes."

"Tell me your name."

"Poppy Wade. I'm nine."

"Where do you live, honey?"

I wanted to explain, but my description grew longer and longer. Whatever I said must have made some sense to the operator because she said, "Okay, sweetie. Now, don't you worry, okay? You just sit tight right there, and I'll send somebody to see about you. You're going to be fine. I promise."

I believed every word she said, but I was still shaking and wanted whoever was coming to hurry. Time crept by, and I felt the waiting would never end. Relief rushed over me when I heard a car coming. I watched the headlights pass by over on the canyon road, and soon the car was pulling up right in front of the yard gate. From the shine of the porch light, I saw that it was a police car—a sheriff's car. I saw the policeman get out of the car and open the front gate.

"Hi there," he called to me. "Are you Poppy?"

I nodded.

"Are you okay? I heard you might be here all by yourself."

I nodded again.

"Do you know where your folks went, Poppy?"

"No. I just woke up and they were gone. I got scared."

"Sure, I understand that. Well, I'm Deputy Jay, and you're all right now." He looked back into the dark of the outer yard. "Do you know whose car that is parked out there? That black one?"

And that is when it dawned on me. My brother Allen's ugly black Chevy. He was home. He was out in the bunkhouse.

"My brother's," I answered in a whisper.

"Do you know where he is?"

I nodded. Deputy Jay waited. I pointed.

"Where?" he said, looking to where I pointed. "In there?"

I nodded. "I guess so."

We both saw the lights of another car coming. As it came closer, I saw it was my father's pickup. I felt fearful again and self-conscious about the trouble I had caused.

"That your folks?" the deputy asked, watching the pickup bounce up the driveway.

"Yeah."

We watched them come to a stop. My mother scrambled out first and ran around the front of the pickup.

"What happened? Poppy, are you all right? What happened?"

My father looked from me to the deputy and said, "What in the hell . . . ?"

"It's fine. Poppy here just became a little worried when she woke up and you all were gone. She didn't realize her brother was here and that she wasn't all alone."

My brother Allen came stumbling out of the bunkhouse in his jeans and no shirt or shoes, rubbing his face and eyes. "What's going on?"

"Ain't nothin'," my father said. "Go on back to bed." But Allen stood on the lawn with his hands in his pockets, yawning.

"I'll be going, then." Deputy Jay reached to shake hands with my father, who hesitated but finally shook. "I can see you all been drinking some tonight. I don't want you driving up and down this narrow road when you all are drinking."

My mother wanted to explain. "We just went a few miles to give a friend a ride home. Her husband got mad at her, and they had a big fight, and he went off and left her here."

"Francine. For Christ's sake," my father said. He hated how she went on like that.

"Well, Norman, it's the truth. Wasn't like we were driving all over the country."

I went in and sat on the sofa again and waited to see how everything was going to go. I started to cry again. I had made such a dumb mistake. I knew I never should have called that operator. I should have known my parents wouldn't go away and leave me alone in the middle of the night.

The deputy drove away, and my parents and my brother came into the house. My father tossed his hat down where he always did and sat in his chair to remove his boots so he could put his slippers on. My brother went in the kitchen, looking in the icebox for something to eat, and I followed. My mother began explaining to him, and I guess to me, what had happened. While she talked, she cleaned the supper table off in a big rush, like the Queen of England was on her way.

"Clarkie and Ellen started arguing, and one thing led to another, and Ellen told him she was going to leave him and go home to Nevada. He said, 'Go ahead and go,' and that really got her going, so they were yelling and carrying on. Ellen started crying and telling Norm and me about how she knew Clarkie had a girlfriend. 'Some fat old blonde,' she said. Clarkie just blew up and said that was the stupidest thing he ever heard. He tried to get her to go home, but she wouldn't go with him, so heck, he just drove off and left her here. Must have taken an hour for Norm and me to talk her into going home."

She dried her hands on a towel and looked at me. "Poppy, we'd never leave you home by yourself. Your brother was out there sleeping the whole time." Allen didn't say anything, just chewed whatever he'd found in the icebox.

"Dumb bastard," my father interjected from the kitchen doorway. "He oughta get ridda her. She ain't nothin' but trouble." He turned away and went to their bedroom, scuffing his way in his slippers.

"I'm going back to bed. Night, kiddo," Allen said to me and went out the door.

I slept in late that morning. I had woken to my father's routine morning noises in the early hours. I thought about what had happened during the night and wondered if I was in trouble for calling the operator. I let myself fall asleep again. When I finally got up, I found my mother dressed and puttering around in the kitchen. She looked tired. The kitchen was all back in order, and I could smell the bleach from the sink drain.

"Well, hi there, sunshine," she said when she turned and saw me. "Thought you were going to sleep all day." She was smiling, but there was no light in her eyes. I knew, if the light was gone out of Mama's eyes, something was bothering her. I was afraid she was going to slip away in her mind again.

I went in the living room and sat on the sofa with Goldie. He cuddled with me while I tried to get awake.

"Poppy, did you really think that Dad and I left you home all by yourself?"

"Yeah."

Her brown eyes narrowed, and she kept looking at me. "We could have been in a lot of trouble, your father and I. Do you realize that? You know what else? If that deputy wanted to, he could have taken you away."

"Taken me where?" I didn't understand.

"If he thought we weren't taking good care of you, leaving you alone at night, he could take you away from us and put you in a home or an orphanage. Some place that takes little kids that are abused. He could put Dad and me in jail, too."

"I'm sorry, Mama. I didn't know what to do. I was just scared. I didn't know you went to take Ellen home."

Me, in a home or an orphanage? Whatever that meant, it sure couldn't be good. My parents in jail? I didn't know all that could happen.

Later in the afternoon, I rode down to see Sky. I felt sluggish and slow, and Nicky's pace matched my mood. It took the length of the ride for me to decide if I would tell Sky what had happened in the night. If I told her, she would have to promise not to tell anyone. Not even her mother and father. I worried that she would think I was stupid for calling the police. By the time I came to the mud house, I had decided not to say anything about what I'd done.

We'd been sitting on the boulder for only a few minutes when I said, "Something happened at my house last night." I don't know why I said it. It just popped out, and so I had to tell the rest. She was a good listener. All she said after I was finished with the whole story was, "We don't even *have* a telephone."

Eleven

School started on a Tuesday, the day after Labor Day. I tried to get out of going by announcing I had a bad stomach ache, but my mother said I was just nervous and I would feel better after I was there. I didn't believe that for a minute. Far from it. I was in a new dress, pink as I recall, with a scratchy new slip underneath that I kept tugging up at my waist in an unladylike manner. I wore new, sturdy brown shoes that felt stiff as planks. My stomach was twisting around like a gob of earthworms.

We walked to the bus turn around—Mom, Goldie, and me. We were too early, so we just stood there in silence and waited to hear the bus coming. My mother hadn't said much, maybe because she had said everything she could think of to try to make me want to go to school. We could hear the bus's engine, so she picked Goldie up and said she knew I would have a good day and that she would meet me when I got off the bus in the afternoon. The afternoon seemed a long time away to me.

I climbed up the steps, and the man behind the big steering wheel smiled and said, "Good morning. And who may you be?"

"Poppy."

"Well, Poppy. You are a lucky one. First on the bus gets to pick whatever seat she wants," he said with good humor and a smile full of yellow teeth. The bus door closed, separating me from my mother and my dog. The hulking, round-faced bus driver began to sing a belting song in a language I had never heard.

I didn't know which seat was a good seat, so I just sat down in the first one behind the driver. He backed the bus up and spun the big wheel and headed us down the road on a song. I saw my mother, still holding Goldie, turn to walk back to our house. I had the deepest longing to be walking with her. Going back home.

We stopped for the older girl who lived on the hill. She hopped up the steps with enthusiasm and said, "Good morning, Mr. George" in a voice that matched his cheer.

"Good morning, Loretta. Ready for another year?"

"Yep. Just two more," she said.

"Hi." She spoke to me and went on by. I couldn't see where she sat because I was too shy to turn around to look.

Next stop was for Sky. She clambered up the steps and sat next to me.

"You okay?" She inspected my barretted hair. "Your hair looks different."

Because I tended to look down when I felt uncomfortable, I noticed right away that Sky had on the same rundown, cracked shoes she wore and played in all summer.

"You didn't get new shoes."

"Father said I didn't need more shoes yet. These still fit."

"Wish I didn't have to wear new ones." I didn't say that to make Sky feel better about her shoes; it was the truth.

That was the extent of our conversation for the rest of the bus ride. I felt the swaying and the lurching through the gears with every part of me. I wondered if any kids ever threw up on the school bus. I knew I would die if that ever happened to me.

When we got into town, the bus stopped at the high school first to let the older kids off. Then we drove on a few blocks to the grammar school. With the help of a man teacher who stood at the bus stop, I found my classroom. The pungent odor of sweeping compound prickled in my nose. I chose a desk at the back of the room and sat watching the other kids come in. Some looked as anxious as I felt. There were a few boys that were boisterous and moved from desk to desk until the teacher stood and said "Okay, class" and clapped her hands together. And that began the worst school year of my life.

Her name was Mrs. Gardner. She was married to Mr. Gardner and had a baby boy. She had been a teacher for seven years, and she liked the word wonderful. Surely we would have a *wonderful* fourth grade year and learn a lot of *wonderful* things. She had a kind smile and a short haircut and green eyes.

"We'll go around the room so each of you can tell us your name and something about yourself. That will help us all get to know one another. Come on. Don't be shy." She pointed at a boy in the front row.

I would not remember one single thing any of the kids said. I felt choked on nerves and wondered if I would be able to speak when my turn came around. I started counting down the kids until it would be my turn. Six, five, four . . .

"Next. Next," Mrs. Gardner prompted.

"My name is Poppy Wade." I heard someone whisper "Poppy?" and it distracted me, so I started over. "My name is Poppy Wade, and I like to ride my horse." My voice had a tremor on the last word.

"Oh my, how nice, Poppy. And what is your horse's name?" She didn't believe me. I could tell by her tone.

"Nicky. Her name is Nicky."

"Well, that's nice. Next."

I sat down and felt my knees trembling. Oh how I was going to hate fourth grade. We were given our books that day: arithmetic, history, science, and a reading workbook. Mrs. Gardner called our names and rearranged our places so that I ended up in the front desk of the row near the tall windows. The worst, and the best.

After the last bell rang, I found my bus number easy enough and wanted to hurry to get aboard and get back home. Another girl sat next to me, which irritated me because Sky had to sit somewhere else. Mr. George went back by the high school to let the older kids on and at last left town. The route home took almost an hour. Sky moved next to me as soon as the girl beside me got off the bus.

"Who's your teacher?"

"Mrs. Gardner."

"I had her last year. She's pretty nice."

"I don't like her," I said, remembering her doubt about me having a horse.

"Already? Poppy, I swear, you can't keep on hating school so much. It isn't that awful."

"Is for me."

Looking back, I think, sitting right there on the school bus, I had a real understanding of how life was going to be for me. School would always be hard. I would forever be different, the odd girl out. Of course, being but nine years old, I didn't think it all through in those terms, but I knew. I knew as well as anything that I was in for a struggle. I was a loner, and the other kids would never like me much because of it. Well, except maybe for Sky.

The bus banged and rattled around the curve to the turnaround spot, and I craned my neck to see my mother and Goldie waiting in the road. I could not believe they weren't there, and disappointment flooded through me. I clambered down the bus steps, saying goodbye to Mr. George over my shoulder, and ran up the road toward home. I had to slow to a walk because my new shoes were rubbing blisters on my heels, and I could feel the wet stickiness soak through my socks. I was swallowing back tears because my mother wasn't there with Goldie to meet me.

"Hey, you," she called from up the road.

I felt so thrilled to hear her voice, I started to run again, in spite of the raw pain of the blisters. Goldie spotted me and came lickety-split to meet me. I picked him up and hugged him tight until he squealed.

"Oh my goodness. Look at you," my mother said as she neared. "Your slip is hanging down. And look at your hair. Poppy, what am I going to do with you? You're a mess." She fingered my hair back from my forehead. "So how was school?"

"Fine," I lied.

"Well, good. Do you like your teacher?"

"Yeah. She's nice." I lied again. My mother looked so pleased, I decided right then and there that this was how things would be. I would just act like everything was good, and that would make her happy.

"Can I ride Nicky?" Maybe I felt like I had something to prove. *So there, Mrs. Gardner.*

When my father came home from work that evening, I waited until he sat to put his slippers on to tell him about school.

"I went to school today," I said.

"Hey, that's right. I forgot about that. How did it go?"

"Okay."

"Well, good."

And that was that. By the weekend, I had given in to the routine. Mother and Goldie didn't walk me down or come to meet me at the bus after the first day.

Twelve

September's weather came, fickle as a floating feather. The days would cool, and the nights became pleasant enough to pull the covers up before dawn. But autumn would turn on us, and the mercury would simmer again. Back to triple digits that torched us like dragon's breath. The classrooms were far beyond uncomfortable. My new clothes stuck to my skin, and there was the odor of too many sweaty kids in one room.

Mid-month, there came the buzz of the first rain arriving. My main wish was that rain would never come on Saturdays, but, of course, it did.

It was early when my mother and I scooted onto the pickup seat beside my father for a drive up in the hills to check cows.

"Come on, if you want to go. We'll go up where we can see t'ward the coast." On the way, he talked about lightning storms and how he used to see them coming in the desert when he was a boy and how, one time, he was so scared he lay down in an irrigation ditch, but his father made him get his self up and get back to work. My father had a way of letting us know that nobody ever gave a damn about his well-being, and it was probably a miracle he was even still around.

My mother joined in, "Oh, I hated those desert storms," she said. "They would come so fast. The sky would be blue and sunny one minute and black and crackling with lightning the next. Those big thunderstorms scared me to death. You could feel the ground shake when the thunder rolled. Man, us kids would hightail it for home if we were outside."

"Hell, I never got to go home over a thunderstorm. My daddy would have us out there, digging drainage ditches off the fields so the crops wouldn't wash away."

"Didn't he worry about the lightning?" I didn't know much about thunder and lightning since I had grown up where we didn't have that kind of weather.

"Naw. We just kept on workin'. Couldn't quit for every damn thing that came along. Never woulda got done."

The road that crawled around the side of the highest hill on the place dropped off at a steep angle on one side, and it terrified my mother. She would hold onto the armrest for dear life and scoot closer to me where I sat in the middle. As we drove higher, a new world opened up. I loved to reach the top, the flat place we parked, where it seemed as if we could see forever. Looking west, we could see mountaintops, one after another. East lay the valley. I could practically see the town we used to live in.

On that Saturday, the northwest sky grew black and gray, and the clouds climbed in towering puffs. I had never seen such a dark, moody sky in my life. My father pointed out places where the rain fell in gray sheets, hanging from cloud to ground.

"Won't be long 'til we'll hear the thunder and see the strikes outta those. Hope they don't start any fires. Burn this whole country down 'less it rains enough. Dry as a bone up in this country."

We sat on the hill for a while and watched the storm build. The sight was beautiful and frightening at the same time. I could smell and feel the difference in the air. The moisture traveled out ahead of the storm, and the scent of it blew fresh and tingly in my nostrils. I was jumpy and excited about experiencing a real storm in our canyon. My father turned the pickup around and bumped down the hill road in low gear. On the way, I asked if I could ride to Sky's house when we got home.

"No, not today. You can't be out on that horse if there is a storm coming." He frowned. "Those folks might end up with a pile of mud when this one passes."

I studied my father's face to see if he meant what he said or if he just said it to be mean, like he did sometimes. He looked as if he really meant it.

"Sky's father has canvases he can put over part of the block wall. Sky said he had to do that before."

"Well, what the hell's he going to do later on? Put a canvas over his whole damn house?"

"Sky says that, when the building is all finished, the roof will protect the adobe blocks, and they will get harder and harder. It's just right now that he should cover them from the rain. She knows a lot about building adobe houses. She said the Indians and Mexicans build them all the time, and they last for years and years. She knows how to mix up the mud and sand and add straw and everything. She said, when she grows up, she will build her own adobe house." I liked how it felt to brag about my friend.

Never wanting to give up his opinion, my father said, "Well, I reckon we'll see, won't we?"

The storm raced us home, and by the time we bumped through the bottom pastures near the barn, enormous drops were hitting the windshield in noisy splats. At the house, Mother and I hurried to the front porch. I sat on one of the chairs and breathed as deep as I could to take in the smell of the rain on the dry dirt and weeds. The dove weed, growing pale green and close to the ground, gave off a scent so spicy it burned in my nose and made my eyes water a bit.

It wasn't but a few minutes until I heard the first roll of thunder. It sounded far away, but I felt the rumble in my chest, deep and long. My mother came back out with a cup of coffee and sat by me on the porch. The next rumble was louder and sounded as if it rolled down the canyon, right above us. My mother laughed in fun because I ducked my head.

"This is going to be a dandy. Doesn't the air smell wonderful, Poppy? I could eat it with a spoon."

My father came to join us. "It's movin' fast. Be here and gone before you know it. It'll be hot and muggy for a day or so. Can I get some of that coffee, Francine?"

We sat for a long time. The storm played out a drama, bringing its all: thunder, lightning, and sheets of rain. I felt giddy. I could hear the cracks of lightning, and no matter how many times the thunder banged against the canyon walls, I just about jumped out of my skin at the booming noise. The storm seemed to go on for hours.

"My goodness. This is one of the biggest storms I have ever been in," my mother said.

"Is that bad?" I asked her.

"No, I guess not. Long as the water doesn't flood anything. At least we don't have to worry about lightning fires."

Something exciting occurred to me. "Will the creek run?"

My father said, "Nope. Takes more than one storm to make the creek run. Need about three or four of these. There's going to be some water down there, but that's just puddles. They'll dry up again before another storm this big hits. This is too early in the year for rain. Don't start regular until at least November. Sometimes even later than that. Then, if ya have a drought year, it may not rain hardly at all. Be about my damn luck. Got these cows up here." He pointed with his thumb over his shoulder.

Sunday morning dawned, showing half our sky covered in cotton clouds and half a pale, clear blue. I headed for the creek, and sure enough, there was water lying all along the bottom. The pools where the tadpoles had lived were full. I spent a long time examining them, just to be sure there were none living there again. Every place was wet and muddy, and tiny streams trickled here and there, looking for low spots to gather. I played for hours, poking around with sticks and directing the miniature streams into lines in the mud.

That afternoon, with the storm in the past, I was allowed to ride Nicky to Sky's place, with orders to stay a short time. Riding down the canyon road seemed a new experience that day. Every single leaf and weed, and even the fence posts and wire, were clean and shiny.

I was enjoying everything about the day until I reached Loretta's driveway.

"Hi, Poppy. Wait up and I'll ride with you." Loretta came riding her horse down their driveway.

I stopped Nicky and waited with mixed feelings. How could I tell her I just wanted to visit Sky for a while and then go back home? Besides, I wasn't sure how I felt about Loretta. Sometimes she could be nice, but most of the time she didn't pay any attention to me. I was more curious about her than anything. She was too much older than me for us to be real friends.

"Where you riding to?" she asked.

"Just to Sky's."

"You sure go there a lot. I see you there all the time. Don't you think that family is weird?" We rode our horses side by side down the road. "That boy, what's his name? Isn't he feeble-minded or something? And their father. Gads. That guy is a fruitcake."

"The boy's name is Riley. He's slow, but he's nice. And their mom is nice." I couldn't think of what to say about Carl. I couldn't act like I liked him or stick up for him, but I didn't feel right saying bad things about him to Loretta. She wasn't going to drop the subject, though.

"What's the father's name? Carl? He's mean, you know. He beats his wife and kids. I mean, everybody knows about him. Sky ever tell you about that?"

"No." I lied easy enough to surprise myself. But Sky had confided in me, and I had to keep the secret.

"Well, he does," Loretta said with conviction. "Knocked out one of his wife's teeth one time, and he's always blacking her eyes. My mama says he's plain cracked. She says he goes along nice as can be, then turns on people like a junkyard dog. I am forbidden to ever even stop on the road near that place. I bet you would be, too, if your daddy and mama knew all the talk about Carl."

She must have talked it out of her system because she changed her tone as we rode along together. In fact, we rode the rest of the way to Sky's driveway, talking about the storm.

"Just wait until we get a bunch of storms up here and the water runs everywhere." She gestured toward the hill near the road. "The creek rises so high some kids can't even go to school. I'm lucky because we don't have to cross the creek, so I always get to go to school, no matter what."

Lucky? It had never occurred to me that there could come a time when I wouldn't have to go to school because I couldn't cross the creek.

"You can always walk across that old barn bridge you guys have up there." She sounded happy for me. "The Davises used to park their car out on the road and walk in and out across the bridge and that trail beside the creek."

I was relieved to see where we were. "Well, I have to turn off right here," I said at the crossing to the mud house. "See you tomorrow, I guess."

Loretta rode on without another word.

Nicky sloshed across the muddy water standing in the crossing, and I pulled her up and looked around. Not a soul could be seen outside, which seemed unusual. There was always someone out doing something—usually Carl, working on the house or the bricks. I did not know for sure what to do next. I felt shy about riding up too close to the trailer. I urged Nicky a few steps at a time in that direction, hoping somebody would come out. I saw that Carl had, indeed, laid his big, stained, raggedy tarps out over the mud house walls. The outside cots and some of the furniture had been pushed together and covered.

Just as I started to turn Nicky away, I heard voices. At first, I couldn't understand what the people inside the trailer were saying, but there came the unmistakable sound of crying, and I heard both Carl and Maryanne. The crying turned into a chilling, high wail, and the yelling began.

"Shut him up, Maryanne. He's driving me crazy. Shut up, Riley!" Carl hollered above the commotion.

"If you don't yell at him, he will calm down, Carl. You know that. Why can't you leave him alone?"

The pitch of the weeping lowered to a moan. Riley would gulp a breath and moan again. I knew I should turn away, but I didn't. I couldn't make myself leave. I sat stock-still on Nicky, staring at the trailer house and straining to hear more.

"You always baby him, Maryanne. No wonder he's spoiled rotten. If he had to be born retarded, I wish he would have been born mute, too, so I wouldn't have to listen to all those crazy noises he makes. He thinks, if he hollers and cries, he can do whatever he wants to do. He'll never learn anything."

"Shut up, Carl. You know he can't help how he is. He isn't bad, he just can't help it. When will you ever accept that this is just the way he is? Can't you at least try, for God's sake?"

"I've been trying ever since he was born. What good has it done either him or me? Every time I try to teach him something, he runs to his mommy because he knows she won't make him do anything he doesn't want to do. Admit it, Maryanne. He's your kid, not mine. That is how it has always been." His tone sounded cruel with sarcasm. "You are a crybaby. A mommy's boy. You will never be a man, Riley."

The door to the trailer opened so fast, I had no time to turn away. I'd been caught there, listening to a family's hostility. I felt myself turn hot and flushed with embarrassment at being discovered. But it wasn't Carl who came out of the trailer. It was Sky. Her face appeared pasty gray, and her eyes were enormous. She turned on the top step and pulled at a thin arm I knew to be Riley's. I could still hear him moaning, and he came close to falling forward as he stepped through the door.

"Come on, Ri. Come with me. It will be okay. Just come on."

She saw me then—looked right at me—but never said a thing. She kept tugging at Riley and guiding him down the step.

"Look at that, Maryanne. You have even brainwashed my daughter. She treats him the same as you do." A dull thump came from inside the trailer, and I heard Maryanne cry out.

"Don't hit her," Sky yelled back through the door. "She didn't do anything. Don't you dare push her again."

"Shut up, Sky. This is none of your concern. Take your rotten brother outside and close the door. I said, close the door, Sky."

But she didn't. She led Riley to an old wooden chair and sat him down, then turned and headed back to the trailer steps.

"Stay out," Carl yelled.

"No. You let Mama go." She continued right on through the door.

The next thing I saw was Sky coming through the door backward. I saw her legs wobbling and her brown shoes searching for her next backward step. She missed the stair completely and landed flat on her back on the ground. A sound of pain came out of her opened mouth with a gush of air. She lay still, and her eyes closed.

I flew from Nicky's back and landed hard on the ground, twisting my ankle. I felt the pain shoot through my foot, but I didn't stop to think about it. I limped at a run to Sky and fell to the ground beside her. Riley's moaning escalated again and filled my head so that I could hardly think.

"Sky . . . Sky!" I shook her by her arm until I was jerking her whole body. Her eyes flipped open and blinked rapidly as she took a gasping breath. For a moment, she looked confused, but I could tell the second she realized what had happened because she struggled to rise.

"Sky, wait."

I tried to push her back down, but her determination to rise made her too strong for me to hold. She stood upright, trembling, and went to Riley. She took him by both arms and spoke to him in a stern, rough whisper.

"Riley, listen to me. Listen to me. You must stop crying now. Try for me. I know you can if you try. Remember, Riley, breathe deep. Remember? Deep breaths, Ri. You can." And he did. I watched his body relax a little at a time. "Now, sit right here and take breaths, Ri. Okay?"

I couldn't believe my eyes when she turned and headed back for the trailer door again. I felt attached to the ground where I stood, but I tried to reach out for her. The entire scene felt like the dreams I had where I couldn't move when I needed to get away from something.

This time it was Maryanne who came through the trailer door and down the steps. She met Sky at the bottom one and grabbed her in her arms. They walked, with their two bodies hugged together, toward Riley, and they both collapsed. Maryanne's hair looked wild and tangled and fell across her face. The back of her left arm was scraped raw, and blood ran to her elbow and dripped to the ground.

She kept saying, "It's okay now. It's okay. He only pushed me. I'm okay. Look at me. I'm okay." She cupped Sky's chin in her palm, tilting her small face upward to meet her eyes. Riley had stopped crying and just sat in the chair, staring at nothing.

I'd begun shaking so hard, I lowered myself to the damp, cold ground and tried to take it all in. I saw Carl come to the door, look out, and go right back inside. I couldn't tell if he even saw me there. I became aware that I had let Nicky go when I jumped down to help Sky, but I turned to see her not far away, grazing in a patch of grassy weeds.

Maryanne and Sky struggled and rose and helped Riley stand, and the three of them made their way toward the creek and the big boulder. I pushed myself up off the ground, and as they passed by me, Maryanne reached for my hand and led me along with her children. We made our way there and sat in a huddle. None of us spoke for a long time.

Maryanne tried to tame her hair, combing through it with her fingers and pushing the long strands behind her ears. Tenderly, she did the same for Sky. A few minutes passed, and when she spoke, her voice was in control and sounded soft and kind.

"We're going to be okay. Something happens to your father that he cannot help. He doesn't mean to hurt you or scare you. This will all pass."

"It will just happen again." Sky's words sounded raw and bitter. "He will do it again, and you know it, Mama. Next time he gets mad at us, at you or Ri."

"Maybe not, sweetie. I will talk to him later, after he cools down." She turned to me. "Poppy, I am sorry you had to be in the middle of this, but you must promise me that you will not tell anyone—not even your own family—that this happened, okay? You have to forget what you saw. Promise, because if the wrong people ever find out, something worse could come of it. We will be okay. Hear me?"

"I promise. I won't ever tell."

I couldn't imagine what could happen that would be worse unless, like my mother had said when I called the police the night I thought I was left alone, somebody would come and take Sky and Riley away.

I stood and slid down off the boulder, landing with weak knees and favoring my sore ankle, and told them I had to get back home. Riley, for the first time ever, came to me and gave me the best hug he knew how to give. His arms felt fragile, and he gripped my shirt with clawish hands.

"My Poppy," he said.

I hugged him back, hard. I wondered if he knew what all those horrible words Carl had said to him really meant. I remembered my mother saying to treat him like I would anyone else. I hated Carl right then. It was an emotion that was too grown-up for me. It made my insides feel hot and mean. I wanted to hurt Carl back, kick him with the hard toe of my boot, or hit him with something. Get revenge for Riley. But I held Ri's thin arms, made my mouth smile, and told him I had to go home, but I would see him real soon.

I went to Nicky and found, to my frustration, that she had managed to break one of the reins that had slipped from her neck while she was grazing. The break wasn't fixable, except to tie the ends together to ride her home. I knew I would be in trouble again. I wouldn't even be able to explain why I had left her unattended. It was part of the promise.

I knotted the rein and got on and rode through the creek crossing. I turned to wave and saw that my friends, huddled on the boulder, looked achingly sad and tired. I rounded the curve of the canyon road and was startled to see Loretta sitting on her horse in the shade of an oak. I rode toward her without saying anything, just watching her. She smiled a crooked smile and said, "Told you so. He beat 'em, didn't he? I told you Carl was creepy. I heard what happened." I swear she had a glint in her eye.

"You were listening?" The idea that she had sat there, like a sneak, listening to all that horror and could act like it didn't bother her, well, that felt wrong to me.

"Oh, yeah. Heard it all. Now do you believe me?" She looked so smug, gloating because she was right.

I nudged Nicky on by toward home but stopped after a few paces. "Carl didn't do it. Riley fell and got hurt, and everybody got all upset. They thought he was hurt real bad, but it turned out he was mostly just scared. I guess that's how he acts if something scares him or he thinks he's hurt. That's all that happened." The lie came out smooth as silk.

Loretta looked doubtful at my explanation, but not as confident as she had a moment before. Her tone wasn't as smug when she spoke. "Well, it sounded pretty serious to me. The kid was wailing like a baby."

"I have to get on home. I'm late."

I kicked Nicky into a lope and left Loretta behind me. I didn't want to talk to her anymore.

Thirteen

It wasn't hard to keep my promise. Simple really, because I didn't want to talk about what had happened. I wanted to forget all of it. The burning hatred I had felt for Carl cooled, at least down to a smolder instead of blazing flames. I fell into a sulk that lasted for hours. When my mother asked me if I was feeling sick, I leaped at an opportunity.

"I feel pretty terrible," I said, clutching my stomach and lowering my lids to half-mast.

"Maybe you need some medicine. Come on in the kitchen."

She placed her cool hand on my forehead, like she always did when I wasn't feeling good. I hoped like heck that I had a temperature.

"Cool as a cucumber," she announced.

She took the big bottle of pink medicine from the cabinet and gave me a dose from a soupspoon. My plan went down without a hitch. I began to scheme for the next morning.

It turned out to be quite easy to convince my mother that I wasn't well enough to go to school because, in fact, I felt terrible. My stomach felt sick and achy, and I was twitchy and nervous. My pale reflection looked back at me from the big mirror on my dresser.

"Go on back to bed and rest, Poppy. You can eat something when your stomach settles."

I slipped back into my bed and pulled the covers way up around my face. When I closed my eyes, the events from the previous afternoon played through my mind like a movie reel. I saw, or felt, every single second just as it had taken place from the moment I heard Riley's crying until his awkward hug before I left. I saw how Sky's pale face looked as she lay on the wet ground. Saw her eyes with their thick blonde lashes slide closed. I realized, as I lay there reliving the scene, that the reason I had panicked and flew to her from Nicky's back was because I thought she was dying. That sound of her breath leaving her body with a whoosh and the closing of her eyes and then that silent stillness, all of that made me think of death. Just like I imagined Mr. Davis dying in our living room.

As I thought about Riley, my heart ached. I wished that I knew what he was thinking when his father treated him so awful. Did he understand? Did he know that the words Carl spoke to him were cruel and hateful? Maybe not. Maybe he became upset because his mother and sister did. I imagined a scenario where I was sitting on the boulder by the creek, teaching Riley how to read a book. He was grinning his wet, red-lipped grin. He was intent on listening to me and repeating the words I said to him. I would tell him the meaning of the words, as if he would understand and remember. I dozed off, happily teaching Ri to read.

In the afternoon, my mother made me tomato soup with milk instead of water and sat with me at the table while I spooned it down.

"Are you okay, Poppy?" she asked me right out of the blue.

"Except my stomach," I said. I wasn't ready to give up my illness.

"I mean, how you are feeling about things? Is school okay?"

"I hate school," I said.

I saw her lips tighten. She reached for her cigarette pack and proceeded to light up. I watched her give the little paper match a neck-breaking shake, and the flame disappeared.

"Why, sweetie? What is so bad about school?"

As much as I hated school, I hated talking about it even more. It never led to anything good.

"I just do. I want to be here, at home. I could read here and do arithmetic from my workbook."

I didn't want to tell her how some of the kids were not nice to me. They teased me about what I wore and my tomboy ways. I tended to wear the same few clothes over and over, but Mama didn't seem to notice or didn't care. I wore what felt best, without giving fashion much thought. Marlene Hager was the meanest girl in my class. She called me "hillbilly girl." Some of the kids still insisted I lied about having Nicky. One boy held his nose when we were close.

"You know you can't do that. All children have to go to school. It's a law, Poppy."

I remembered her saying that before.

"Well, it's a stupid law. I could grow up and live here and be just fine." I was sassy with stubbornness. "I don't have to go to school to do that."

"Poppy." She took a deep breath, and the look in her eyes told me how serious she was being. "I know this is hard to understand right now, but we do not know what our lives are going to be like as time passes. The world is changing all the time. You will grow up and be an adult, like your father and me, and maybe you will get married and have kids and live somewhere else, somewhere far away from here. We don't know, Poppy. That's how life goes."

That was all I could take. I was getting angry, and my stomach started to hurt again. I said I wanted to go back to bed and left the table. I expected her to call me back, to be mad at me and tell me to sit back down. But she didn't. I went to my room and closed the door. I sat on my bed, and I tried to picture myself grown up. I couldn't get the concept into my mind, that I could ever live someplace else besides the canyon house. I sure couldn't picture having kids. I was just a kid myself. If I didn't live here, who would take care of the tadpoles when the creek was drying up, and who would love Goldie and ride Nicky? Who would be Riley's friend?

I woke late in the evening to my parent's voices. I couldn't make out all the words, but enough to know they were talking about me. I rose up from my bed and went to the door, where I sat on the cool linoleum floor and put my ear close.

"I'm worried about her, Norman."

"What do ya want to do? Let her stay home?" He said it in a way that made me know he didn't mean I could.

"Don't be smart aleck about it. I don't know what to do. She hates going to school, and I don't know if she's even really learning anything. I mean, she can read and write, I don't mean she can't, but she isn't learning anything about life. I don't think she has a single friend besides the girl down the road."

"I don't know what the hell you're talking about, Francine. Did you learn about life in school when you were Poppy's age? She learns more about life out here than all those town kids put together. If you don't leave her alone, she's gonna grow up about half goofy. Just let 'er be."

"Well, you're a damn big help, Norman. Wash up. Supper's ready."

My mother tapped on my door and asked if I wanted to come to eat supper. I said no and asked if I could go out and sit at the picnic table. It was good to be outside. The air was cool and felt clean on my face. I knew I would have to go back to school the next day. My stomach didn't hurt anymore, and I wouldn't get away with staying home another day, especially since my dislike for school had become a main topic of conversation. I tried not to think about the next day, but I also didn't want to think about the events of the day before. I wished there was a way I could turn a switch, maybe a tiny one hidden in my hair, and not have to think at all.

When Loretta climbed the bus steps the next morning, she flat out ignored me and went down the aisle. I wondered if she told anyone about what she had heard from the road by the mud house. I had an urge to rip her pink bow right out of her hair.

I watched Sky climb the bus steps and tried to tell by her expression how she was feeling. She plopped down next to me and said "Hi," as usual. At first, it seemed as though she had completely forgotten what had happened just two days before.

"You didn't go to school yesterday," she stated, as if she was informing me. "Were you sick or playing hooky?"

"I was sick. I had a stomach ache."

"Hmm. I thought maybe you were too upset about what happened Sunday. You didn't tell, did you? Remember what my mama said? About not telling?"

"I would never tell, but I know someone who might."

Sky gave me a long look.

"Loretta heard what happened. She heard everything." I was whispering, as if Loretta could hear me talking over the rattle and banging of the bus. "She was waiting for me when I left your place. She was around the corner. She said she knew your father beats you guys up and that he was mean. She'll tell. Probably already told her mother." Sky started to look over her shoulder toward the back of the bus. "Don't look," I warned. "Don't look at her. She'll know we're talking about her."

"So? I don't care. What did you tell her?"

"I told her that Ri fell and hurt himself and everyone got scared. I don't know if she believed me." I felt shamelessly proud of my lie.

"I'll have to tell Mama." She was quiet all the way to school.

It rained during the school week, sprinkling off and on and keeping the smell of wet dirt in the air. It was nice to have cooler weather, and I spent the after-school hours outside. I hiked up the hill to the cave and tried to get into my imaginary world of cowboys and Indians, but my heart wasn't in the game like it had been before. I roamed the pasture, found the horses, and hung around them while they grazed. Nicky was always up for a good ear scratch, so I appeased her until my fingers were tired. The horses' hair coats were thickening up, getting ready for winter. I liked knowing they would have the old, dilapidated house on the hillside to stand out of the rain and cold.

One evening, I asked permission to walk to the spring tubs. My mother said I could if I didn't linger there. I would have to come right back. The deal was better than nothing, so I took off in high spirits, walking briskly. As I moved at a fast-paced walk along the trail, I noticed that there were tiny green seedlings sprouting amongst the roots of the thick, dry clumps of grasses and weeds. The trail was not deep with dust like it had been the last time I'd walked it, and deer tracks were easy to read. The damp, decaying leaves under the oaks and sycamore trees smelled earthy, exactly like they had near the creek pools when we first came to the canyon house. I felt restless and giddy without knowing why. I know now that it was an innate anticipation. Change was taking place. Summer was over for good, and canyon life was moving on to the next chapter.

I found the spring tubs near to being full to the brim with murky water. The thunderstorm had carried enough water across the great rock slab to dirty the pools. I sat for a while, remembering how wonderful it had felt to slide, bare skinned, out of the heat into the soft, cool, crystal water. We had lived in the canyon house for just about four months, and the tubs were still a secret kept between my mother and me. I hadn't even told Sky.

I didn't want to get up and go home. I walked slowly going back, having lost my enthusiasm.

Fourteen

I woke on a Saturday morning with a brilliant idea. At least I thought so.

"I'm going to teach Riley to read," I announced to my mother.

"How, pray tell, do you intend to do that?"

"I am going to make a book for him. I'll write a Dick and Jane story and maybe draw pictures and show him how reading works." I was so excited, I was hopping on one foot and then the other while I explained.

My mother smiled one of her big, genuine smiles. "That's a great idea, Poppy, but don't you think you should ask his mother first?"

I hadn't given his mother a single thought since I'd formed my idea. "What if she says no?" I hedged.

"She is his mother, Poppy. She has the say about what Riley does and doesn't do."

"I'm going to make the book anyway, so I'll have one just in case."

So I did. I made the best book any kid could learn from. My story was about Dick and Jane helping a little boy learn to read. I used color crayons to draw pictures of kids sitting on a big rock. I gave them hair like Ri's and Sky's and my own. The story had mostly three-letter words that I had been careful to print in block letters. It told about the kids seeing a cat by the car, how they fed it and petted it, and its name was Puss. The book had five pages when I was finished, and I showed the masterpiece to my mother with great pride.

All she said was, "Just don't be mad if his mother says no."

I had only been back to the mud house one time since the day of the awful incident. That day Carl had given me a brief glance, turned away, and gone on with what he was doing when I rode Nicky across the creek bed, and Maryanne had acted as if nothing had ever happened. The back of her arm was the color of a ripe plum, and a long, oozing scab disappeared up under her shirtsleeve. I wanted to say something considerate, like I was sorry she had been hurt, but nothing I thought of sounded fitting. I had waited for Sky to invite me to come back to visit. She'd told me that it would be all right and that her mother said I should come. She'd said that Riley spoke my name often, and she was sure he missed me. So I had gone there, feeling nervous and hoping I wouldn't have to talk to Carl. I had been able to avoid him, and it was just like any other visit before.

On the afternoon I arrived with Riley's book, the weather was cool. Carl and Maryanne were digging clay out of the red cliff, and Sky and Riley were inside the trailer. Maryanne waved and smiled and said to tie up and go on inside. At last, I was going to see the inside of the trailer.

Sky opened the door for me, and I stepped inside, feeling hesitant. My eyes swept the small room, and I was amazed at what I saw. It was as neat as a pin. There was no clutter, and nothing looked out of place. In fact, there was nothing much in it. The tiny kitchen and living area was low ceilinged and had brown wood paneling on the walls. There was a small table with built-in seats and a stove with two burners next to a sink. The place looked like a large dollhouse. A hallway, even smaller than ours in the canyon house, had narrow beds built along both sides. I could see they were made up with colorful quilts. The room at the far end was dark, but I could see the foot of a bed there.

"Here, sit here," Sky said, motioning to one side of the table.

"Poppy." Riley grinned. "Poppy."

"I brought something for Ri," I said to Sky, "but my mother said I had to ask your mother first."

"What is it?" Her eyes widened.

I felt bashful. I reached out with the book to show her, but I didn't want her to take it from my hand. She tugged. I held tight.

"Well, let me see. Is this a book?"

"Yeah. I made it. To teach Ri to read."

Her wide look turned to a squint of a question. She looked down at the first page and the words I'd printed, and tears filled her eyes.

"That is the nicest thing anybody has ever done for Ri," she said. "But Poppy, I don't think Ri can learn how to read. I mean everybody, the doctors and everybody, said he would never be able to read or write."

I wasn't sure what to say. I didn't want to give up my great idea.

"Maybe I can show him, and we'll just pretend. He doesn't have to really read. I'll read to him. I have to ask your mother first, though."

"She doesn't care. She knows he can't learn it. He'll just think it's a game. Huh, Ri?" She looked across the table at him. He grinned from Sky to me and said something I couldn't understand.

"What?" I looked to Sky for an explanation.

"He said, 'read book,' or something like that."

"Come on, Riley. Let's go sit on the rock and read this book."

Was it ever hard to keep his attention. Riley was a fidgeter, moving constantly, but I was used to that. The hard part was getting him to look at the book. I put my finger below each word as I read him my story.

"Look at my finger, Ri. Now look at the word. See the word? It says car."

He would look at me instead and grin a sloppy grin. I repeated the same thing over and over until I was bored crazy.

"Maybe we can have another lesson next time I come." I looked at Sky, and she shrugged her shoulders to say, *I told you.*

"Do you want to read again, Riley?" I asked as I climbed down from the rock and reached to help him.

"Car," he said and took the book out of my hand. I watched in amazement as he pointed to the word, said "car" again, and promptly dropped the flimsy paper book in the muddy creek bottom.

I yelped with happiness. "Did you hear him? He said 'car' and pointed. Did you see that, Sky?"

I spun a circle and hugged Riley's shoulder. He laughed his goofy,
wet laugh.

Sky had retrieved my book and was wiping a smear of mud from
the back page on her skirt. I saw that she was still doubtful. Her smile
was kind, but she avoided looking at me. I felt that she thought it had
been an accident, him making the association. And why wouldn't she
think that? Everyone was sure that Riley could not learn like normal
people.

It took three more lessons for Riley to learn to recognize and say
the words on the first page of his reading book without hearing me say
them first. At that rate, I figured, he would be able to read the entire
book by February.

I couldn't wait to tell Mama.

"That's great, sweetie. He's probably memorizing it. He's just repeating what you have said so many times. But that's good, anyway."

Her words made me angry enough to shout at her.

"Why do you have to say it like that? You don't know. Maybe he
did learn to read my book. You're the one who said to treat him like
anybody else. Remember? Why can't you ever just say I did something
good? You and Norman both. Why can't you just say I did a good
thing?" I stopped, and we stared into each other's eyes. I had called my
father by his name.

"Get to your room. Now. Don't you be disrespectful to your father,
do you hear me?"

I went. I closed the door and stood. Just stood there for a long time.
I didn't cry a single tear, which for me, under the circumstances, was
a miracle. I started to think about Riley. Maybe he and I weren't so
different from one another. It seemed that no one expected us to do
well. What was the point of trying if it didn't matter to anybody? But I
remembered his goofy grin when he read his first page and understood
that the fact that he had done something new and good made him feel

happy, whether anyone else cared or not. That was how I needed to feel about myself. I had a right to feel happy about helping Riley. Maybe I did teach him to read. I was determined not to care if Mama and my father thought it was great or not. As long as Riley wanted to learn, I would help him.

Later, after I'd heard my father come into the house, I knew they were talking about me again. I heard the frustration in my mother's tone. A short time after, my father opened my door and stood looking at me.

"What's the matter with you, acting like that? Damn it, Poppy, you best straighten yourself out, do you hear me?"

"Yes."

"Two weeks. I don't want you down there around them people for two weeks. If I had my way, you wouldn't go back down there at all. I knew they were gonna be trouble, those damn people. That boy's got a screw loose, and his old man, too."

I felt the hot anger crawling up the center of my body because of the mean words he spoke about Riley. I had to swallow hard and fast to keep my fury from spewing out in defense of him and myself.

"It's time to eat supper," my father said and turned away without closing the door.

Two weeks seemed long, but I knew that I would see Sky on the bus, anyway. Turned out it didn't matter because the rain came and stayed for a long time.

Fifteen

The rain began on a Tuesday or maybe a Wednesday night. I woke to the splatting of the first huge drops on the roof, and I swear, I had a premonition. We were in for a long haul. There was a feeling of permanence in the sound. I listened for a while and began to find the patter on the roof soothing. I could almost find a rhythm to it. I slept, and when I woke again, the daylight was murky.

I couldn't wait at the bus turn around in the rain, so my father would be giving me a ride to school. I knew better than to make him have to wait on me, and I hurried to be ready on time. Pulling out of the driveway, the pickup's tires slipped around in the mud, grabbing for traction. Water was everywhere in puddles and rivulets. The creek bottom was filled across with water, and I would have sworn it was running downstream, but my father said, no, not yet.

"If it keeps this up all day, it'll come down the canyon tonight. Look for me out front when you come out of school. If there ain't much work in the shop, I'll pick you up. Be sure you get on the bus if I'm not out there."

I asked if we could give Sky a ride to school.

"Not today." That's all he said.

"Tomorrow?"

"No reason she can't get on the bus. Hell, it stops right there. They built that fancy bridge to walk across."

I knew not to push the idea. He had never even met Sky, but his mind was made up that if her father was peculiar then she was, too. I wondered if it had occurred to him that people thought us peculiar, as well.

The clouds hung low all day. The classroom air felt damp and close and smelled of wet wool coats and stale air from the heating ducts. The rain slacked up a bit from time to time, but when I looked toward the canyon from the valley floor, the sky appeared dark as nightfall.

"Well, I'll be damned," my father said that afternoon on the way home. We were headed up the canyon road where the creek came into sight. "Musta rained like the dickens up there."

He motioned up the road with his cigarette. The water flowed, slow-moving, light brown and flecked with foam, and spreading out wide where the land rolled low. I gawked through the side window for any glimpse I could get, feeling a thrill of apprehension. The stream wasn't what I had expected, but it was awesome. I'd still had my childlike vision of a clear brook tumbling over logs and rocks.

By the time we rounded the curve near the mud house, the water was moving more swiftly. There was no one to be seen outside, even though the rain had slowed to sprinkles. I knew that Sky was on the bus somewhere behind us. I wondered what Riley thought about all the rain and the creek.

"The radio says it won't rain tonight. I sure as hell hope not. I'm drivin' on in to the house. If this keeps up, we may not get outta here in the morning."

He made the turn into our long driveway, where the tires slid in the mud and the pickup slipped toward the bank of the creek. I pushed myself back against the seat, as if that would stop us from going on over the edge. My father laughed.

"Scare ya? Thought we were going in the creek there, didn't ya?"

I laughed because he did and with relief because we didn't go nose first into the creek. Before I had time to think about what was next, we were in the middle of the crossing, and the water was fanning up over the fenders, sending dirty water spraying across the windshield. When we came to a stop by the yard gate, I opened the door and was astonished to hear the loudness of rushing water.

"Did you see it? It's loud!" I called to my mother, who stood waiting to meet us on the porch. I ran to share the excitement with her.

"I walked out far enough to see what it looked like. I could hear the racket from clear inside the house." She was hugging herself against the damp air.

Behind me, my father stamped the wet and mud from his boots on the cement step. "This ain't nothin' yet. Wait 'til it really gets to runnin'. They're sayin' the next big one's supposed to come in on Friday or Saturday."

I rode the bus the rest of that week. I walked a narrow trail along the bank of the creek to the barn bridge, then back down the canyon road to the bus turn around, being careful at finding my way across the bridge. The old wood felt solid under my feet, but my father had warned me to watch out for loose or rotten boards. There were places where the planks had split away, leaving gaps. If I looked straight down through them, the movement of the water below me made me feel dizzy. The canyon was beginning to look like a different place from the one I had come to know during the summer. The air was cool, cold at times, so that I started wearing my new school coat. The land and the air smelled different—clean and green. The tiny, pale seedlings I had first noticed on my walk to the spring tubs grew thicker and taller. Our land of brown and gold was quickly turning emerald.

The sun rose weak and watery and stayed that way all the way through Saturday morning. I wanted to ride Nicky to see Sky and Riley and had all but forgotten I wasn't supposed to go there for two weeks. I asked to go during breakfast, and my mother said she didn't see why not since it wasn't raining yet.

"Damn it, Francine. You wanted me to tell her she couldn't go there, so I did, and now you say it's okay."

"I think she's learned her lesson, Norm. It won't hurt for her to ride down there for a while. I know what it's like to be stuck in this place. No sense in her going crazy here like her mother is."

I had learned that, when there was trouble, it was always my mother who would back down first. My father, on the other hand, seemed to keep score somewhere in the back of his mind, mentally carving a notch for each argument or disagreement. This one didn't seem worth wasting his time on.

Nicky was shaggy and muddy with her winter coat grown out, so I brushed her for a long time and rode her bareback. I was nervous about riding across the creek, but she forded the crossing like she had done it a hundred times before, and we headed down the road. I trotted the whole way that day. Sky had told me how much fun it was to crawl up on the creek boulder from the backside and sit where the water could be seen swirling below us. I pictured doing that as I hurried down the road, so I was happy to see her sitting there in the weak sunlight as I rode up. We both waved like crazy and called to each other before I had even ridden through their crossing. I tied Nicky and ran to scramble up the rock. It was, indeed, the perfect place to watch the creek.

"Where's Ri?" I asked, turning to look toward the trailer.

"He can't come out here. He can't get close to the creek at all. Mama is afraid he will fall in and drown."

"He can't come outside at all?"

"Well, he has to stay up there by the trailer. My father put a canvas up for a cover. At least we can be out when it's raining now. I wanted to sleep out on my cot last night, but Mama wouldn't let me. She said it was too cold."

I was disappointed, having thought I could check up on Riley's reading. The book was his now, to keep with him. I could have sworn that Sky read my mind.

"Ri read to Mama this morning. It made her cry a little bit. You've done a real nice thing for him, you know. Nobody ever would have known he could learn like that." She laughed. "Now he reads the first two pages over and over until he drives me crazy."

Something new, a feeling I couldn't name, happened inside my chest when Sky said that to me. I was proud like I had never been in my life. I had done something all on my own, and it had been a good thing. A right thing. Not even Mama's or my father's doubtful attitude could take that awareness from me. I dared to hope that maybe one day Ri would read real books. I knew that books would give him the one way he would ever have to know about other people and places.

We sat and watched the creek flow until I knew I had better go back home. The clouds were getting darker, and our spot of sunshine was gone. We said we would see each other Monday on the bus. I didn't mention that I might have to ride to town with my father.

The next storm brought the wind or, I should say, the wind brought the rain. Down in the valley, it blew in gales from the south for two days without letting up, and another deluge poured down on us. A pattern settled in, and for more than a week it would rain hard nearly every day. By the third go-around, the canyon was a mess. I remember that, on that last trip down the road in my father's pickup, what I saw frightened me. Places in the dirt road were buried in thick, slimy mud that made our old pickup slide sideways. The road's edge had eroded, eaten away until the already narrow tract was even narrower. The creek was raging like a brown, foamy monster. Its course had changed completely in many places. Entire hillsides had slid into the creek and forced the flow to go another direction. Banks had been eaten away, and

I witnessed one caving and saw the muddy thickening of the already heaving water as it was swept away. The river it flowed into, down in the valley, was growing higher and wider day by day, and there was a lot of talk of flooding. Homes, livestock, and crops were in danger for miles.

Even my father's tone was anxious at times. Rain and flooding was about all he spoke of. He wasn't able to work because there was nothing for him to do. Farm fields were flooded, and he knew they wouldn't dry out for weeks, even if the rain let up soon. Shop work had come to a standstill. There was only so much work that could be done on the farming equipment that sat idle. He drove me to school and back without complaining because the daily chore gave him a reason to leave the house and get a look at the canyon.

I would look for Sky's bridge first thing around the curve of the road. My father had declared more than once that it would be gone if the creek rose high enough. I wanted to speak up and defend the building of the bridge, but I couldn't bring myself to say anything even halfway decent about Carl, so I had to listen to the cynical remarks.

At school, Sky told me that the last batch of bricks they had made a month before were all ruined. The forms had been flooded out, and the adobe lay soaking. Even when they dried out someday, they wouldn't be good and strong. She told me being in the tiny trailer was getting harder for them all the time. Her mother was silent, and her father complained about one thing or another. The canvas awning her father had put up wasn't much help since the weather had become so windy and cold.

I tried to imagine them all just sitting in that trailer with nothing to do. They were so much worse off than we were in our house. At least I could move from room to room. My brothers came home every few days and grabbed clean clothes and headed back into town to stay with friends. I relished the time they were home and missed them when they left again. So did Mama.

My mother was a wreck. She withdrew into herself again, depressed and moody. One night I heard her say to my father, "I guess I'm going to die in this damn canyon."

"You're not dyin', Francine. It's just rain, for God's sake. It'll stop, and when it does, that creek will go back down so damn fast. That's the way it is in these canyons. It's those poor damn people in the valley that needs to be worryin.'"

"How would you know how I feel, Norman? How do you know I can't be feeling like I'm dying here in this house? It isn't about the rain. I am so lonely here. You go off to town every day and do what you want to, leaving me stuck in this damn place. All I do is clean up mud and cook. I hope the damn creek floods and takes me to the river with it."

By the time they had fallen silent, I was bawling my eyes out in my room. I hated the times she talked about dying. It scared me. They both turned to look at me when I walked into the living room.

"Don't say you're going to die, Mama," I sobbed.

My father gave her a "see what you've done" look. I saw her meet his look with no expression in her eyes. Her spark was gone again.

She patted the couch cushion next to her. "Come here." I sat on the edge, stiff with tension. She didn't hug me like I wished she would, but she put her hand on my shoulder and said, "Quit your crying, sweetie. I'm not really dying. Sometimes us grown-ups just get tired, that's all."

I sat and waited for more. More words, more touch, something. But Mama was finished talking. She stood up, went into their room, and closed the door. I looked to my father, but he didn't look back. I waited, but he continued to stare at the snowy TV screen without a word. I wiped my face on my pajama sleeve, got a drink of water from the kitchen, and went back to my room.

I didn't have to go to school for the rest of that week. The structure of the barn bridge was getting worrisome, and the creek was too high to see the support underneath. My father decided we shouldn't walk across it anymore until he could see to reinforce it.

The days were long and dreary. I could hear the water rushing at night. A hole had opened up in the bank behind our house, and water from underground gushed out. I sat by the back window of my room in the daytime and watched the water flow between the bank and the foundation of the house. A stream formed there, and my father kept going around the house to look at it. He took his shovel and spent an afternoon digging trenches here and there to divert the water to a low place where it could flow across the driveway and on toward the creek. His effort helped for a while.

Sixteen

We survived that storm. The winter sun rose into clear skies for three days in a row. It was freezing cold in the early mornings, with frost on the ground and thin sheets of ice on the puddles. I checked out the creek with a warning from my parents to not go too close.

"It's still going too fast to mess around down there. You fall in and it could wash ya down long enough to drown ya. I mean it," my father had said.

Mama still wasn't saying much to either one of us. She didn't act as if she had the energy to worry about me.

"If you don't get close, there won't be anything to worry about," she said.

To me, that sounded like she was saying, if I washed away and drowned, I had nobody to blame but myself.

I was fascinated by everything I saw near the creek. I still had not become accustomed to the noise of the rushing stream. I discovered that, if I was close enough, I could hear the hard sounds of rocks being rolled and bashed together in the depths of the muddy water. There were gurgling, glugging sounds where the rapids crossed each other and fell off into holes where rocks had been dislodged. One of the tadpole ponds was washed out and as deep as the spring tub I had soaked in.

I hiked up and downstream as far as I dared and then started over, doing it again. There were logs caught up in undergrowth that hadn't been there before, and more than once I thought about crossing the creek on one of them, but the talk about drowning stayed stuck in my mind. I didn't want to be sucked away in the cold, dirty water, so I had to give up the idea. I tossed sticks in the water and raced them downstream, watching them bob and sink, appearing again far ahead of me. I crossed the fence into the horse pasture and found places where the ground had caved away from under the banks, leaving shelves of soil held together by tree and grass roots. Those dangerous areas were easy to spot on the far side of the stream, but I couldn't tell what was under my feet on the side I was on.

I had just decided that I had better move away from the edge when I felt the ground shift underneath me. I scrambled backward so fast, I lost my footing and fell hard on my back and pushed my breath out of my lungs. I struggled to rise in a hurry and watched as, just inches in front of me, the ground disappeared. All that remained was gnarled tree roots poking out over the water, like a tangle of brown, muddy snakes. I was amazed at how fast it had happened. My heart was beating like crazy, and I saw, in a strange vision, my body floating in the thick, rapid water just like one of the sticks I had thrown. I remembered my mother's words about not getting too close. After that, I was extra careful about where I walked, picking the low areas to get closer to the water and staying off the high banks.

That Friday, the water level had lowered enough for my father to see the end braces under the barn bridge. The mud sucked at his rubber boots while he reached as far as he could and nailed up a few support boards, but that was the best he could do for the time being. He told me to walk the bridge on the left side and to walk right next to the nail line where there would be more support. I guess he thought I would be happy to be able to cross and go back to school, but the truth was, except for getting to see Sky, I was disappointed. I only had two more days of freedom.

By the next day, I had formed a grand idea. Instead of riding Nicky down to the mud house, I pictured the fun and adventure of walking there. The plan grew with my imagination. I would take a snack and sit on a rock or a log and eat by the creek. I could examine all the gullies and washes.

"Please, please," I begged my mother. "I promise I will be real careful, and I will stay up on the road the whole way."

"Why can't you ride Nicky, like you always do? What if it starts to rain again? It will take you too long to get home."

"No, it won't. I can run most of the way."

It was true. I could have jogged most of the way home. I was strong and light as a feather and could run like a deer. When she gave in and said yes, I hurried to make a sandwich, shoved it in my coat pocket, and headed out on the trail to the barn bridge. I don't know why it seemed so exciting to me, just because I was on foot instead of on my horse, but it did. As I walked on past the bus turn around, I felt light and happy about my new freedom. I sang songs and skipped and spun around in silly circles, like some girl maniac. I felt loose and unburdened on the walk to the mud house that day. I didn't stop anywhere along the way, like I had imagined I would. The sandwich in my pocket stayed put in its waxed paper. I hurled sticks and rocks into the water wherever I could reach it. The road left the creek side where Loretta's house sat up on the hill, and I felt like ducking low so, if she was outside, she wouldn't see me down on the road. I didn't like talking to her anymore. I looked at the ground and hurried by as fast as I could.

When I came to Sky's bridge, I stopped and looked all around the property, hoping to see someone outside. My happiness was fading fast. I saw that their old truck was there outside the crossing, so I knew they were at home, but I would have to go knock on the trailer door, and I felt intimidated by that. I stood at the end of the walk bridge, trying to decide what to do. I had walked all that way, and I didn't want to go back home without letting Sky know that I was there, even for a little while. That was when I heard Riley.

"Hello, Poppy. Hey, Poppy, hi. I can read now." He was calling to me from up the slope by the trailer.

"Hi, Ri. Where is everybody? Where's Sky?"

Riley started down the slope toward me, stepping as carefully as he knew how, but his balance was always off, and he kept slipping in the mud. I started toward him to head him off.

"Stay there, Ri, and I'll come up. Hey, I know, go tell Sky I'm here. Okay?"

He said okay and gave me his silly grin and turned toward the trailer. He fell then, and hit the ground hard. I saw the look on his face and thought he was going to start crying, but he grimaced and closed his eyes for only a second and struggled to get back up again. I hurried to help him, and when he was up, I saw that the knees of his pants and his elbows were covered with mud. After he was upright, he saw his pant legs, and I was taken aback by his look of horror. He turned and looked straight at me with his deep-set, dark-brown eyes.

"Father will be mad." His face broke up and tears welled in his eyes.

"It's just mud, Ri. It will wash off."

"No!" he yelled. "Father will get mad!" With that, he sat flat down in the oozy mud.

I hollered before he met the ground, "Riley, no! Don't!" But it was too late, and I doubt he would have heeded my words, anyway. I was relieved to see Sky step from the trailer door and come to us.

"What's wrong? What happened to him?" she asked me, and I heard a tone of accusation.

"He fell, slipped down in the mud. Then he started crying, saying he was going to get in trouble, and that's when he just sat down." I was talking fast, wanting to explain.

Riley looked at his sister through his tears and repeated that his father was going to be mad at him. She squatted down so she could be closer to him. She held her hands on the sides of his face and spoke real soft.

"Ri, listen to me. You will be okay. I will tell Father you had an accident so he won't be so mad. Okay? Stop crying. That will make him madder." She wiped his tears with her thumbs. "Come on, get up. We have to get you cleaned up."

Ri struggled up, and I followed behind as Sky led him under the canvas awning and sat him on a bench.

"I'll be right back," she said.

I stood there, not knowing what I should do. I watched her go up the steps and quietly close the door behind her. I could hear her say something, and I heard Carl answer back. Then Sky again, and then Carl, "Get him in here right now. Now, Sky. He wasn't supposed to go out at all, now he has to be cleaned up and his clothes washed again. Does he think we have nothing else to think about but him? Riley this and Riley that. Riley always needs something. A good whippin' is what Riley needs." He sounded like he was running out of breath.

"He doesn't need a whipping. He just had an accident."

"Don't make excuses for him. Hear me? You and his mother. Always making excuses. If he would do what he's told to begin with, these things wouldn't happen, would they? Well, would they? Answer me, Sky."

I heard her voice but not the words. She came through the door with a wet cloth and a towel. She had clean jeans over one arm. I saw Carl standing in the doorway, looking down at us.

"What are you doing here, Poppy? You run around like a little orphan. Don't you have anything to do at home?" Carl's face was red, and his eyes intense with anger. I was dumbfounded. I stood there and looked back at him. He looked back at Sky. "Clean him up, and bring him in." He turned and closed the door.

Sky was already washing Riley's hands and arms. He had begun to tremble, and I saw that his nose needed to be wiped. I surprised myself when I bent for the towel and used the edge of it to wipe Ri's snotty nose and the drool hanging from his chin. He stood when Sky asked him and dropped his wet, muddy pants, stepped out of them, and into the clean ones. Sky fussed over him for a moment, pulling his shirt down and smoothing his dark hair back off his forehead. He had calmed down a bit and, except for a slight tremble, had quit shaking. He reached his bony arms around my waist, like he had one other time, and hugged himself to me.

"Poppy. Poppy, I can read a book."

I gave him a hard hug back. Sky was picking up the wet jeans and towel and watching the hug.

"He loves you, you know. I honestly think he does."

I didn't say anything, but I felt like Riley was my brother. I had felt that since I taught him to read. I knew something else, too. Riley was terrified of his father. I wondered how often Carl punished him, hit him and belittled him. I thought probably a lot. Maybe every day.

"Is your mom here?" I asked Sky. I hadn't heard her voice from inside the trailer.

"She's sick. She's been in bed for two days. Her fever is high, and she hasn't eaten much at all. I think that's why Father is so upset today. Let me see if I can get Ri to take his rest, and I'll come meet you by the rock."

I was glad to get away from the trailer and Carl. I crawled up on the boulder and sat, losing myself in the movement and sound of the rushing of water. I drew my knees up and held them tight and stared into the current until I felt hypnotized by its motion. What a strange life these people led, I thought. I knew my own life was different from anyone else I had ever known. Different from kids at school or even the few friends I had. But I had a home and a room and, even if my parents didn't always treat me too good, they weren't cruel like Carl. I thought about Maryanne being sick, and that led me to thinking about death. Seemed like I thought about death a lot. First there were the tadpoles, then the deer on the side of the road, and then there was the story of Mr. Davis dying in our living room. And the worst of all, my mother talking about dying. I wondered if Sky thought about death.

I had sat for such a long time, I had almost given up on Sky coming down to the boulder. When she did, she came so quiet she startled me when she sat down close beside me.

"He finally went to sleep. Poor Ri." She stared down into the water, like I had been doing.

"Do you think about death?" I blurted out.

"Sometimes." She didn't even look up.

"You do?" Her answer made me sit right up. "How? I mean, how do you think about it?"

"I don't know. I mean, people just die, don't they? And animals? Animals die all the time." Her eyes found mine. "Father killed our dog."

"Why?" I was stunned. "On purpose?"

"Yeah." She was looking across the creek again. "I didn't see it happen. Later, I found a stick out by the willows with blood and Chipper's hair stuck on it."

"You mean he beat him with a stick? Until he died?" I was incredulous, but I had a clear vision of Carl swinging a big clubby stick down on a little dog over and over, and I was sick at my stomach at the thought.

"I think so. He and Mama fought about it after. He said the dog tried to bite him, but I know he didn't. Chip would never do that. He was a good dog." Sky sucked in a big breath. "I really, really loved him."

Huge tears slid down Sky's face at her memory. "When I grow up, I will have as many dogs as I want, and he will never be near them."

We went quiet, looking at the water again.

"I don't want Mama to die," she whispered the words. "She is so sick, and Father says we can't afford to take her to a doctor. I don't know what to do."

I didn't know what to say. I thought that Sky always knew what to do. She seemed so sure of herself. She was good at taking charge, and she cared for Ri like a mother would care for her special child.

We sat there on that boulder in our shared misery. The sunshine came and went as clouds began to build again. I knew I should start my walk back home. I felt the sandwich in my pocket and pulled it out.

I unwrapped it and pulled the soft, warm bread in half and handed a part of it to Sky. She took it, and we ate, licking the butter and honey from our grimy fingers.

All of a sudden, Sky turned toward the tree behind us where I always tied Nicky.

"Hey," she said. "How did you get here? Where's Nicky?" She stood to look around.

I started to laugh at her belated realization that Nicky was not there. "I walked."

"No. You walked all the way from your house? Why?"

"I just wanted to. It was fun. You should walk to my house sometime."

We shifted around on the boulder to face the tree where it seemed Nicky should be standing, taking her nap like she always did while she waited for me.

Had I left when I knew I should be on my way, everything about my life would be different to this day. But that's how it goes, right? Mama said each decision we make guides the course of things, even though we're not aware of it.

Seventeen

My day had started out full of fun and anticipation. I had skipped and spun circles on my way to the mud house, so anxious to see my friends and surprise Sky. That was just before the darkest cloud came and stayed for a long, long time.

I had wadded the waxed paper and shoved it back in my pocket and was wiping my sticky fingers on my pant legs when I heard Carl yell.

"Riley, get away from there! Riley!"

I turned to see Ri loping down the slope toward the creek where the willows grew. The curve of the rise prevented me from seeing him, but as I watched Carl run, I realized that Riley must be near the creek's edge.

Sky's brows lowered and came together. She had left Ri taking his nap. I think we both knew at the same instant that Riley was in some kind of trouble—or danger. We jumped from the boulder and started to run upstream toward the trees.

I see it now in slow motion. Riley leaving the ground in one determined step into the edge of the water and then one more, falling forward into the gushing stream. Beside me, Sky was screaming his name in a wild, high-pitched voice. She stumbled and fell to her hands and pushed herself up, trying to gain her feet under her. I grabbed her arm and pulled, and we ran again.

The three of us met at the creek edge, all running and calling Ri's name. I saw him face down at first, and his blue shirt full of air puffed out of the water like a parachute. His thin legs came up, bent at his knees, showing the soles of his shoes. He moved in the current that way for about a second. Then he slowly tipped to one side and turned face up. His eyes were closed, but his mouth was working, as if he was talking.

My mind must have disconnected from my body. I remember the energy that shot through me, catapulting me into the water. I was not prepared for the force that grabbed me up and shoved me around at will. I struggled to position myself so that I could see Riley, who I thought should be right next to me. I caught a watery glimpse of his dark hair, and I saw that he had already been whirled around so that he was going downstream headfirst.

I grabbed for his hair over and over again, but I could not control my reach against the pressure of the water, so I kept missing. My unbuttoned coat was being ripped off my arms, and the weight of it pulled at my elbows. I straightened one arm and let the sleeve slip away and continued to grab at Riley's hair. I felt myself being scraped and bumped against the rocks. If I was shoved into one with force, my body would be sent off in a ricochet. I heard nothing but the muffled rushing of the water.

When I felt Riley's thick hair between my fingers, I jammed them through as much of it as I could and clenched my fist tight, holding on with all my strength. My other arm was still caught up in my coat sleeve, and I began to feel afraid that I wouldn't get loose from it. I tried to use my feet to brace against the rocks or the bank to slow us down. Because my body would not stay upright, I could not find leverage on the creek's bottom. The water was too swift, and the holes, too deep.

My coat sleeve was at last pulled from my arm, freeing up my hand, so I started wildly grabbing at anything I could see through the muddy water washing against my burning eyes. I was dragged against exposed tree roots when we were washed close to the bank. I felt one, like the sharp end of a stick, slide up my stomach beneath my shirt, and I was yanked into a tangle of weeds. For a split second, I had hope that I had found something I could grasp, but the shallow-rooted grass pulled out of the soft mud. While struggling to hold my face above water, I saw a blurred shape that was coming fast and realized that it should be the walk bridge. I held my free arm out of the water as straight up as I could and waited for the bridge.

I went under, allowing the water to close over my face, and felt a horrible burning sensation in my nose. I began to cough, which caused me to suck in water as I gasped between the throat spasms. After that, I felt myself weaken. I kept squeezing the fist that was gripping Riley's hair, but my hand was tired and it ached. I wanted to scream out my frustration. Time was bewildering. Seconds flashed by with extreme speed, but at the same time, I was aware of everything happening and even wondered, in what seemed like logical order, why no one was coming to help us.

Riley and I started to pass beneath the bridge, where I thought I saw a person above us. I could not have said at the time if it was Carl or Sky. It was a human form, a watery vision. I felt the back of my hand hit hard against a support underneath the bridge. I missed grasping it with my fingers, but I grabbed at another and managed to hook my wrist around the post and hold on. Two arms reached down, and strong hands grasped onto my forearm. For the first time, I heard a faraway voice.

"Hold on to my arm, Poppy. Hold on so I can reach Riley." He kept saying the same thing over. "Hold on to my arm."

I heard him say, "Okay, I've got him. I have him now, Poppy. Let go of his hair, and hold on to my hand."

I do not know where my strength came from, but somehow I did what Carl said to do. I forced my hand to open and let go of Riley's hair and grabbed Carl's hand and forearm. Suspended there, with the water pulling at my body, I twisted my head sideways to look for Ri. I saw, with joyous relief, that Carl's other hand was cupped firmly under Ri's chin, holding his head above water. Riley's body rolled to the side just enough that I was able to see his colorless face. His dark eyes stared directly into mine. I saw his wet lashes close and open with one slow blink and his hand lift toward me. I saw Carl's hand open and his long fingers slide up Riley's face from his chin. His open hand pressed down gently on Riley's forehead, and with its long fingers spread wide, linger there in the water. And just like that, Riley was gone.

I kicked with strength that must have come from God because I had none. I heard my own weeping voice calling, "No, no, no . . ." I twisted and turned, trying to get away from Carl's grip on my hand, but his fingers were like iron, and I could not get loose from them. He pulled me sideways toward the shore of the creek, and I knew he was going to drag me from the water onto the bank. All I wanted to do was get away and try to reach Riley again. I didn't know that reaching him was already impossible.

Carl pulled me up the steep embankment, and I struggled to get my feet beneath me. I could picture myself running along the water, swift as a deer, and grabbing Ri up again. But I couldn't stand. I couldn't even lift my head. I coughed and coughed until I vomited. I felt warmth spread up my stomach and knew I had wet my pants. There was such a rushing in my ears, I could not hear anything else.

I thought a long stretch of time went by with nothing happening. I just lay there in the mud, thinking about how cold I was. I drifted in and out of consciousness several times, and each time I would come to, I had a vague feeling of being all alone. At last, I heard a familiar voice that seemed to come from far away calling my name.

"Poppy? Poppy? Can you hear me?"

I tried nodding my head and thought that I had. I felt someone shake my shoulder and heard her voice again.

"Poppy. Answer me. Say something. Can you hear me?"

I kept thinking, *I know you. Who are you? Ah, I know. It's Loretta. What is Loretta doing here?*

As I became more aware of my surroundings, I heard footfall and voices and, above all of my bewilderment, hysterical sobbing and wailing. I heard Sky howling. I struggled to sit part way up and managed to raise my head and try to look to the sound. I saw the image of her far downstream, sitting on the bank, her face tilted to the clouds. She keened like an animal.

I lay back again and focused on the face near me and was surprised to see that it really was Loretta's.

"Listen to me," she said, "My parents have gone to get help. I know you're cold, but you have to be still until help comes. Mama will bring a blanket for you, okay?"

"Is Riley gone? He's dead, isn't he?" I remembered then. I saw the fingers of Carl's iron-strong hand open up and let Ri go. Just let him go. I saw Ri slip away as smooth as could be. "He let him go. Carl let Ri go down the creek."

"Shhh," Loretta hushed me. "Don't think about that right now." Her face was ashen, and I could tell that she was trying not to cry. Looking up at her, I could see she kept swallowing in gulps that made her throat move.

I faded away again, and the next time I opened my eyes, it was quiet except for the creek noise rushing inside my head. A lady was bending over me with a pink-and-white striped blanket, trying to raise me up so she could tuck it around me. I clutched at the warmth. I looked for Sky, but she wasn't there anymore. The lady must have known because she said Sky was up at the trailer with her father.

"I'm Janelle. I'm Loretta's mama. We called your mama and daddy, honey. They'll be here soon."

"Where's Riley?" My teeth were clattering so that I could barely get the words out.

"They're getting him, sweetie. Don't think about that right now, okay?"

I didn't have to ask anymore. I knew by what Janelle said that someone was down the creek looking for Riley. I knew Riley was gone. I wondered where Maryanne was and if she knew yet. I think it was at that time when I began to shut down, consciously that is. I remember knowing that my father and mother were there by me, but that's all I knew until I awoke in a bright-white hospital room.

I lay on a narrow gurney in an examining room. I think what woke me was the warmth of the heated blanket being tucked around me. A nurse—I knew she was one because of her cap—told me Doctor Morse was going to come in to see me. When he came, I had to give up my hold on the blanket so he could pull it away. With him on one side of me and the nurse on the other, they gently rolled me back and forth. I listened to them speak in whispers, as if not to disturb me.

"She is really banged up," the doctor said. "Some of these are pretty severe. We'll have to scrub them. Let's give her a little something for pain to take the edge off, and I want x-rays of her lungs. She'll have to be on antibiotics. I don't like that the water was so dirty. We will have to be careful of infection." I felt like I was hearing them speak about someone else. "Let's keep her here overnight and see how she is in the morning."

The nurse came back with my parents behind her and told them what the doctor had said while they all stood looking down at me. My mother held my hand and smoothed my hair from my face. My father stood with his hat in his hand.

I awoke in frightened confusion the next morning. Several minutes went by before I remembered where I was and why. I was so stiff and sore I couldn't even roll to one side to look around. When I tried to turn my head, the deepest ache stopped me. I moved my hands around my body as far as I could reach and felt gauzy bandages everywhere. Some were wrapped around my arms and one hand, and some were taped to my skin. My hips and shoulders hurt, and the skin on my stomach and chest burned like fire.

When I remembered that poor Ri was gone, the devastation swept over me from top to bottom. I felt the sadness settle down in my very center like a stone, like it was there to stay. Between that morning and the first time I knew that I was at home in my bed, there was little awareness of my surroundings. Getting from the pickup to my room was painful, and later I remembered some of that as if it were a dream. I sank into an emptiness where time would mean nothing.

I was supposed to be propped upright with pillows part of the time and eventually sitting on the edge of my bed for a few minutes every hour or two. To keep my lungs clear, Doctor Morse had said. I had to be awakened every time there was to be a change because all I could do was sleep. My mother fussed over me, bringing soup and juice and crackers that I had no interest in, and from time to time my father stood in the bedroom doorway looking awkward.

Mama insisted my door be wide open all of the time, in case I called for her. The house had seemed eerily quiet whenever I had been awakened, but as I opened my eyes on the third morning, I could hear someone talking softly from the living room. I listened for a long time and decided the voice was that of one of my mother's friends, or maybe two. For the first time, I pushed myself up in my bed and leaned back against a mound of pillows.

"Poppy, look who came to see you." My mama's voice chirped like a happy bird.

I looked past her and saw that it was one of the Alices—the round, soft, nice one. She could not hide her expression quickly enough. She looked horrified for a single second but tried to cover with a smile.

"Hello, honey. How are you doing?" She moved around my mother and came to take my unbandaged hand in her soft one. "Are you feeling a little bit better? I brought you some baked goods to eat when you feel up to it."

"She sure did, sweetie. She made three kinds of cookies. You feel like trying one?" Mama looked so hopeful. I started to say "Okay" to be polite and realized my voice was barely there and nodded instead.

I hadn't said maybe five words in days. My throat had been grated raw from coughing up the creek water and from all the screaming for Riley. Mama went to get the cookies and Alice stayed.

"Do you remember what happened, Poppy?" sweet Alice asked.

"I think so," I whispered with a rasp.

She nodded, like that explained something to her. "Well, try not to think too much. Keep resting and get yourself feeling better. Okay, sweetie?"

After that morning, people came and went like they had the first months we lived in the canyon. My mother looked and acted more like her old self. I saw her moving around the kitchen, fixing food for company to eat and for me. She helped me get up, clean up and wash my hair, and she talked the entire time. I saw my face in the mirror, and I stared for a long time. One cheekbone was bruised to a deep blue, and I had a lump the size of a jawbreaker on my forehead. I had scraped my chin, so it was beginning to look scabby. Mama ignored me looking at myself and kept talking.

"The creek is way down now. It has not rained since the day . . . well, the day of the accident."

The accident. I had played it over in my mind a dozen times by then. True, I had come to hate Carl, but I could not grasp the idea that he had let his own boy drown. Maybe I saw it all wrong. Maybe I didn't see his long fingers slide from Riley's chin in the dirty water.

But I did.

Eighteen

Deputy Jay came to our house to ask me questions. My mother brought in a kitchen chair and placed it beside my bed, patting the seat as if being sure it would be comfortable enough for someone of such importance. She backed up into my father, who stood in the doorway, and I saw him elbow her over. She had propped me up as straight as I could sit and told me to listen and answer politely. I was glad it was Deputy Jay who came. He was as nice to me as he had been on the night I thought I had been left home alone and called the operator. He took a seat and arranged his clipboard on his crossed knee and clicked his pen.

"Hey, Poppy. How ya doin'? You look like you're healing up pretty good." His eyes smiled.

"I'm good. Better." I smiled a weak smile back at him.

"I have to ask you some questions about the other afternoon, Poppy. I don't want to upset you, but we do have to know exactly what happened at the creek there. All of us down at the station are real sorry about what happened to Riley." He looked over his shoulder at my parents. My mama nodded. He turned back to me and took a breath that made his chest swell inside his sheriff's shirt. "Can you tell me how the day started out down there?"

I looked to my parents and back at Deputy Jay. This would be the first time I would speak about what happened. Even my mama and my father had not heard my version of the events. My insides tightened. Mama must have known because she brought me a glass of Kool-Aid.

Once I started talking, even with my throat being sore, the story flowed smoothly and easily because I pictured every single minute as I spoke. I told about walking down the road and wanting to surprise my friends. I went over the whole part about Riley falling in the mud and crying about Carl getting mad at him and all the hubbub that took place after that. Deputy Jay wanted to know every single thing. What we all said, including Carl, where we were standing, and exactly what I saw. I could picture all of it perfectly, but I hesitated to tell it.

"Poppy, think hard now. Did Riley jump into the creek like he meant . . . well, like he meant to hurt himself? Was he just playing, maybe?" He looked away to give me the time to answer.

"I just saw him take a big, long step and go into the water."

"Did he look happy or scared?"

"I couldn't see his face too good. He was turned away. Maybe Sky saw."

I had not even asked about Sky. I just couldn't. When I thought of her, I would see her sitting on that bank and hear her wailing for Riley. What if she had gone crazy or just died right there from a broken heart? I'd heard people say that could happen. I was too afraid to ask.

"Yeah." He was speaking in such a kind, soft way. "Well, what were you thinking when you jumped into the water? You just wanted to get him out?"

"Yes. I guess so. I didn't think anything. I just jumped in."

I told as much as I could about what happened. I showed him with my fingers and fist how I had finally gripped Riley's hair. I told it all until I came to the part where Carl had grasped my hand. I stopped there.

The deputy looked at me intently for a long moment. "Then what, Poppy? What came next?"

I couldn't look at Deputy Jay, so I watched my hands turn and twist in my lap. I explained how Carl was holding Ri's chin in his hand and how he was keeping his head from going under the water. I said how I felt good, relieved, knowing Carl was saving Ri.

"Okay, Poppy. I know this is hard, but I have to ask. Do you really think that Riley was alive then? Right at the time Carl was holding on to him?"

"Yes. I know he was," I nodded.

"You know he was? How do you know that?"

"Because I saw his face, and he looked right at me, and he blinked."

"He blinked?" Deputy Jay uncrossed his legs and leaned slightly forward.

"Yes. Real slow and big. I saw his eyelashes close and open again when he was looking at me. His hand sort of reached out to me." I knew what was coming next, so I didn't wait. "That's when I saw Carl's fingers slide from Ri's face. He let go of him. He just let go of him." I was beginning to cry.

My father said, "I think that should do it for now. She's had enough for today." He left the doorway.

It was true that I felt completely exhausted. Deputy Jay stood and thanked me for being brave. "I may have to come back again," he said. "There could be more questions."

"Is Riley's father going to be in trouble?" My gravelly voice was almost gone again.

"I think he may be, yes. We are investigating what happened to Riley. We have to know everything before we can decide what to do next."

I slid down in my bed and lay back after they went off into the living room. They talked quietly, but I could hear some of what they said. I heard Loretta's name spoken, which really perked up my interest, so I started straining to hear more. I sat on the edge of the bed and slid my feet onto the floor. I felt like my legs were made of rubber, and I was shaking like mad, so I held onto the bed and wobbled closer to the door. I tried to breathe quieter so I could hear.

"She is a witness, of sorts," Deputy Jay was saying. "They were driving on the road when she saw that something was wrong and yelled for Ward to stop. She was out of the car and almost to the bridge when she saw Riley slip away and go downstream. She said poor little Sky was running and screaming at the top of her lungs. She saw Carl drag Poppy onto the bank and then, she said, he just stopped and stood there, looking downstream. He finally saw that she was right there across the creek, and he looked really surprised. Shocked, is what she said. You can't hear anything over the noise of the creek, so he probably didn't know how long Loretta had even been there. That's when her mother caught up to her, and Ward, he drove on home to call you folks, and he hurried back down." The deputy paused, and I thought he was finished, but he said, "What a damn crazy thing."

Dr. Morse, who had treated me in the hospital, came to see me the next day. He was worried about the wound on my stomach from the tree root that had gouged so deep. He took off almost all my bandages and looked carefully at the scrapes and cuts. He apologized while he swabbed them with something that burned like fire.

"I don't like the looks of this one. It isn't right at the edges. In fact, it doesn't look healthy there." He pointed out some areas to my mama.

I knew right where it was that he was talking about because that is where it was the most painful. He said he would leave some more pills.

I couldn't go to school. I'd felt so bad, I had not given it much thought. The doctor wrote a long note about me and told my mother to be sure to get it to the office, not my teacher.

"Might help quell the gossip," he'd said, "if it goes straight to the school office." He told Mama he thought the fewer people who knew of the situation, the easier it would be later on.

That night, I asked to read the note. It took a long time to decipher the doctor's handwriting that Mama said looked like hen scratch. I made out that it said that I, well, Poppy Wade, had recently experienced some mental and physical trauma and was under his care. It explained that I would be in no condition to attend classroom school for an indefinite period. He suggested that, in due time, I would possibly be able to have some lessons sent home so that I wouldn't get too far behind. He gave them phone numbers where he could be reached.

After reading it through, I lay back and closed my eyes. I had always hoped I wouldn't have to go to school, and now I didn't, but I didn't feel happy about it. Sleep wouldn't come to me easily again that night. Sky was on my mind. And Maryanne. I decided that the next day I would ask about them until someone told me what was going on.

Beginning mid-morning the next day, our house was like a town cafe. A carload of my mother's friends came from the valley, staying to visit through the afternoon. Mama was giddy with happiness at having them there. She flitted around in the kitchen while they gathered at the table. The chatter sounded like old times in the lemon-yellow kitchen of the valley house.

They poked their heads in the door to say hello to me and asked how I was feeling. I said, "Good," and they smiled and said, "That's good," but I saw that their faces changed when they looked at me. The lump had gone down some, but not enough to really notice, and the bruises had yellow-green edges. The scrapes stayed scabby looking because, no matter how many times I was told, I couldn't keep my fingers off of them.

I could hear them talking plain as day, and I learned more from eavesdropping than I had from asking questions, that's for sure. Their voices were full of drama and concern, and the story came to me through their conversation.

Althea said, "That boy's poor mama. What's happened to her? Can you imagine, layin' up there in bed in that doghouse, and somebody comin' to say your boy just drowned in the creek? If that'd been me, I'd probably have died right there in the bed. And her bein' so sick, poor thing."

Mama said, "I guess that's about how it was. I heard that Carl himself told her. I don't think little Sky could talk at all yet."

I could hardly hear Mary Alice's voice. "Where are they now? It didn't look like there's a soul around that place when we drove by."

Mama said, "I heard that they went to stay at Maryanne's sister's place. I guess, from what everybody's saying, she's the closest relative they have around here. I don't know where she lives, but not far, I don't think."

Ivagail asked, "So what was it that was wrong with the mother? Somebody said she had a case of the flu, and somebody else said no, she had some kinda food poisonin'. Maybe that boy had food poisonin' and that's why he ran inta the creek and drowned. Some sickness can make people go crazy and do things like that."

"Poppy told Deputy Jay that Sky said her mama had a real high temperature and hadn't eaten in two days. She told him that she, Sky that is, was scared about how sick her mama was, and that Carl said they didn't have the money to take her to the doctor." I could hear her spitting out the words.

"Well, there ya go. It could've been the fever. Maybe that boy got the fever so bad he had those hallucinations people get from it." That was Ivagail again.

"Who had to fish the boy outta the creek?" one of them asked.

Then I really listened hard because I had no memory of any of this.

"Well, turns out, Ward was the one," Mama said. "He's the neighbor just down the road, the one who called me and Norman. I guess Riley was tangled in some brush at a fence crossing quite a ways down the creek. I talked to his wife, Janelle, on the phone, and she said Ward was in real dreadful shape after he had to pull that boy out of the brush. Took him a long time to untangle him, and the water was running so fast, it was hard for him to stay standing. He said the boy's eyes were still open, and he kept thinking what if he was still alive, but he knew he just couldn't be. She said Ward said the child was snow white, and his lips and tongue were gray. Said poor Riley was all beat up from hitting all the rocks. I guess he looked way worse than Poppy does. Anyway, poor Ward, he can't sleep or anything. Janelle said she'd never seen him cry like he did that day. Not in over twenty years. People don't get over these sorts of happenings, you know?"

"Do you know about that poor girl? What's her name, Sky? Now I heard that child was worse off than anybody. You know, in the head I mean. They said she was like a little mama to that boy," Althea said.

Mama said, "She's with her mama at the aunt's place. It's Carl I wonder about. I can't believe a man could let his own flesh and blood die like that, but I know Poppy wouldn't fib about something so important."

"Oh, heavens no. Poppy ain't like that. Besides, poor thing, she's going through her own hell. She looks just beat to pieces. Her emotions, I mean, not, you know, how she looks or anything." Althea apparently thought she'd said something wrong about how I looked.

I couldn't stand to hear any more. I turned onto my least painful side and pulled the blanket over my head. I curled into a little knot under there and closed my eyes tight. That made me feel worse because I kept seeing the mental pictures of Riley in the creek. Remembering his eyes made me feel so sad. I don't know why, but I started humming a little made-up song so I wouldn't keep thinking about it all, and then I hummed "Twinkle, Twinkle, Little Star" and went on to "How Much Is That Doggie in the Window," and I guess I finally went to sleep.

I slept more often and more soundly in the daytime than at night. I guess it was the dark that made me lie awake and worry. I relived Riley and me washing down that creek together a hundred times over. Sometimes I would think that, at the end, I saved him from drowning, but other times I would see Carl letting him go, and I could see myself hitting Carl with my fists and kicking him. I hated him so much it made my stomach hurt inside. Sometimes I even wondered how I could kill him for what he'd done.

Nineteen

My father hadn't gone to work because the fields weren't dry enough, so it became his routine to drive down the canyon, just for something to do to get him out of the house in the early mornings. He would come back and have some lunch, then go on up the hill and check on his cows. He loved those cows. He'd borrowed a good bull and was hoping to get some nice heifer calves so he could build up his herd. Being a cattleman was really all he had ever cared about. He had his dream to own enough cows to sell the calves to pay off the bank and have an income doing the thing he loved. But if there was no work, there was no income, and I knew it was hurting him.

"It damn well figures," he said to Mama one night. "We needed the rain for the feed, so we got it, and now I might have to sell my cows to get us by."

"Well, Norm, I guess eating and paying Poppy's doctor bills is more important than those cows."

I knew she had started something.

"Francine, you don't have no goddamn idea what those cows mean to me. You never did. Hell, I've done everything I can to build up a little herd and get some money comin'. Cows are a damn sight better than a few bucks sittin' in a bank. What do you think we would've done if I hadn't had them calves to sell last year? We'd be in the poor house, that's what."

"I'm sick to death of hearing that. We wouldn't even be living out here in this hole if it weren't for you having to keep those cows. I don't know how much longer I can go on being here knowing those damn cows mean more to you than I do."

"You ain't goin' anywhere, Francine, and you know it. Where you gonna go?"

That did it. Mama started crying, and Father went to the kitchen and poured more wine. I didn't get up. I had only been in the living room a few times since I got hurt in the creek. I mostly just wanted to stay in my room. It wasn't long until I heard Mama go to their bedroom and shut the door. The lamplight was still on when I dozed off.

I woke sometime later, which wasn't unusual because I never slept long, and I could hear Mama crying. I lay real still and listened until I figured out that she was outside. I pushed myself up, slow and stiff, and went to the front door. It stood open a crack, letting cold air in. Mama was sitting on the porch on the opposite end from their bedroom window, looking small and hunched in the porch chair. I slipped through the door and stood looking at her back. I didn't want to startle her, so I spoke in a whisper.

"Mama, what are you doing out here? It's cold. Are you crying?" I saw her head come up and her spine straighten.

"You don't need to be out here," she said. "I'm fine. I'm just having a little sad spell is all."

"Why are you sad, Mama?"

"I don't want you to be worrying, Poppy. It doesn't have anything to do with you. You go get back in bed so you don't get chilled out here." I sidled back to go inside, but she spoke again so I stopped.

"I hope you get to have a good life," she said out into the dark. "I hope you grow up and meet a nice man who will treat you like the Queen of Sheba."

"Who's the Queen of Sheba, Mama?"

She gave a soft little laugh. "It doesn't matter," she said. "I just mean I hope you have a happy life, that's all. Go on now."

I felt awful leaving her out there in the cold, but I knew she really wanted me to go and let her be. I lay back on my bed and stretched out all my sore places and listened for Mama to come back inside. When, at last, I heard the door open and close, I started to think about other things. I had been wondering a little bit about the creek. That familiar feeling of curiosity was creeping back into my thinking, and I decided maybe it was time to go out and take a look around. I missed Nicky and was sure she missed me, too.

We'd had a few rains pass over, but nothing like we had before. It would shower some and go on by. The creek rose and fell according to the rain amount, but not drastically, and my father had been driving his pickup across just fine. The reports he brought home from the valley had lost their urgency. The river had receded back into its channel, and there had been only slight damage to crops along the banks.

"Them people don't know how damn lucky they are. One more day of that kind of rain and they would've lost the whole damn she-bang. Now they're sayin' the river silt is going to grow a bumper crop. We'll see."

After four or five days of a little midday warmth, he was finally able to go back to work. He would come home in the evenings and kick the mud off his boots on the bottom porch step. The cold would be flowing right out of him.

"Here, Sis, just put your hand right here on my leg and feel that. I'm cold to the bone." It was true. I could feel the cold through his Levi's, like it was leaking out of his body. He would pull his boots off with the bootjack and put his house shoes on and stand in front of the fireplace drinking a glass of wine while he waited for supper to be ready.

My first morning out was an amazing adventure. I dressed warm like I was told to a half-dozen times, and Mama wrapped up in her coat and walked out with me. The sun was weak, and the breeze coming up the canyon was cold on my face. The bruises had turned into sallow yellow-green splotches, and the lump on my head was gone, leaving only a place that was sore to touch. The scrapes and cuts on my cheeks and chin had healed enough to show new, bright-pink skin. I still looked terrible but, except for the wound on my ribs and chest, it wasn't as painful.

I shoved my hands deep in my coat pockets and walked, slow as molasses, out to where the bank dropped off to the creek. I saw that my well-worn trail had been washed away, leaving a deep slash where the water had run. I stood looking down at a place that was no longer familiar to me. The channel of the creek had widened out and left rifts of debris where the highest water line had been. Tangles of sticks and limbs and rotted sycamore leaves lay in piles. But what I saw that amazed me most was the expanse of sand that lay clean and smooth along the edge of the water, like an actual beach. I wanted to find a way down the bank to get closer, but Mama said no, not yet. I could see one of the tadpole pools. A limb had jammed and created a waterfall into the hole. I could hear the deep glugging sound of the water pouring into the depths of the pool.

We walked on to the crossing in the driveway, where my mother pointed to some huge rocks and told me how my brothers had removed their shoes and socks, rolled up their pant legs, and waded out one morning to push them aside so they and my father could drive across. We took the barn trail, and I saw where an oak limb had fallen and blocked the way. My father had sawed it into lengths that he used to shore up the creek side of the trail. We went on to the barn bridge, and Mama told me about how Father and my brothers had used ropes to pull the brush and limbs away from the bridge so the weight of the debris wouldn't cause the bridge to give up and wash away.

My energy was fading, so we turned to make our way back to the house. I asked about Nicky, and Mama said she was good, just shaggy, and next time out, we would look for her.

I sat out on a porch chair for a while to avoid going back inside. I thought about what we had seen on our walk, and I was surprised that so much had happened, changed, while I had been in bed. In the days I had lain there, thinking only about what had happened to Riley and about how I felt, life had just kept going on. Work still had to be done, and my brothers had gone on with their busy lives. The school bus had come and gone, and kids went to school every day, as usual. The reality of that was hard for me to grasp. I felt as if time should have waited for me. But, once I grasped it, it was like being granted permission to let go of some of the emotion that had taken me over in all its gloom. I had suffered both mentally and physically, day after day, and now something within me was trying to lighten my burden. One day I would understand that it was a simple walk outdoors that gave my spirit back to me. After that, I improved quickly. Too quickly, my mama would say.

"I can't keep her down anymore. She's nearly her old self, only a little different in a way that I can't quite put my finger on," I'd heard her tell Althea one day. I was up and out every day, unless the weather was just too awful. I started walking the creek banks again, examining every change in its new design.

Mama said, "I thought she would be scared to death to go near that creek. After what happened to her and poor little Riley, you'd think she would hate it down there."

Althea agreed, "She's a strong-willed one. I think most kids her age would end up terrified of creeks for the rest of their lives. Don't you? You know, how kids are afraid of dogs forevermore if they get bit when they're babies. Don't you wonder, Frankie, if she thinks about that boy and what happened when she's playin' along the water down there? Heaven sakes. If that was me, I'd be seein' it over and over in my mind all the time."

"Me, too," Mama said. "I still see her little body layin' there on that creek bank, all beat to pieces, and her daddy and me both crying and scared absolutely to death. I was so scared she was going to die. Norman was, too. He didn't say so, but I could tell by his look. He picked her up so gentle-like and took her up to the pickup, and she was limp as a noodle. She doesn't remember that at all."

"I wonder how often she thinks about it all these days," Althea said.

I thought about it every single day. That day's heartbreaking ordeal, or at times snippets of it, would blindside me. The pictures would roll through my thoughts like a movie and leave as quickly as they came. I missed Ri and Sky with an ache in my heart, but I wasn't crying much anymore. I guess, by then, I was all cried out. Because of the aching inside my chest and the dull, lingering pain from the scar running up my stomach, I would sometimes need to sit down on a rock or the ground and take some deep breaths until I felt better. If I sat still for a few minutes, the smothering sensation would ease up so I could breathe naturally. I didn't tell anybody about those episodes for fear of having to stay in the house again.

On the days I felt I could, I would ask my father if he had seen anyone around the mud house when he drove by. He didn't like me asking, so if he was drinking much, I knew to leave it alone. I could see a little fire in his eyes when Sky's family was even mentioned. He hadn't liked them before, and it had turned personal after the tragedy.

"I couldn't ever come back to that place again, if I was them," Mama said.

She had a good heart, and I think that, someplace down inside of her, she couldn't come to completely believe that Carl killed his own child. I didn't mind that sometimes it seemed like she couldn't believe my story about Carl letting Riley go down the creek still alive. I knew how hard it was even for me to realize that someone could do such a thing, and I was the one who actually saw it with my own eyes.

"I don't ever want to see that son-of-a-bitch again anywhere. I'd like to hold him under the creek for a while." My father had no doubt at all that what I saw was real and that Carl "ought to be hanged for what he done."

On a Saturday when my father came in for lunch, I heard him tell my mama that he saw some people down at the mud house.

"They were all gathered up around the bridge, the girl and her mama and some other people. I didn't see old Carl there, but he coulda been. The little gal waved, but nobody else did."

I ran into the kitchen, nearly jumping out of my skin with excitement. "Can I go see Sky? Please, please," I begged. I was shaking and looking from my father to Mama and back and forth.

"Damnit, I knew I shouldn't say nothin'. I knew this would happen." I saw him look to Mama, and I knew he wasn't going to tell me no. He didn't have the meanness in his heart to deny me seeing Sky. "What do you think, Francine? Think she should see that gal?"

"You're only asking me because you can't say no and don't want to be blamed if it turns out to be the wrong thing. If you didn't want her down there, you'd just say so." She gave me a long look while I worked at being still and keeping my mouth closed. "Let's drive her down there. She doesn't need to go alone, and it's too far, anyway."

I ran for my boots and coat.

I sat on the edge of the pickup seat with my hands on the dashboard all the way down the road. I wanted my father to go faster, and I guess my anxiousness made me brave because I came right out and asked him if he could hurry. I thought I might have felt the truck boost up about one or two miles per hour. My parents both gave me instructions, and I tried to pay attention.

"We ain't stayin' long," my father told me, "so if your mother or I say 'let's go,' that means let's go now."

Mama said, "Sky might be feeling awful bad by being back out here, so let her do the talking if she feels like it. Don't push her, okay?"

The closer we got, the harder it became to breathe, and I felt trembly. We drove around the last curve in the road, and I just about broke down into tears because I didn't see anybody at the bridge where my father had seen them. But I noticed the long, blue car parked by the creek crossing, and I knew somebody was still there. We came to a stop, and I almost stepped on Mama's shoes, trying to get out of the pickup in a hurry.

I looked up by the trailer and saw that some people were sitting in the outside chairs. I spotted Maryanne first, and then I saw Sky come out of the trailer door. I forgot all about my parents, and I ran across the bridge, my boots making a racket on the wooden planks. When I was halfway to the trailer, Sky saw me and dropped something she had in her hands and started running to meet me. I squealed, and then we were clutching each other, and we both started crying. We stepped apart and stood there facing each other, wiping our faces with our hands, and we didn't say a word for several moments.

Finally, Sky spoke. "I'm so glad you came. I didn't think you would."

"Why?" I said, wiping my snotty nose on my sleeve.

"I don't know. Because it would be hard, I guess. And because everything is all different now."

I honestly didn't know what to say. She was right, of course. Everything was different. The air felt odd somehow, thicker maybe, and of course the rain had changed the landscape to a rich, mulchy dampness.

"Well, I wish you still lived here. I wish we could see each other, like before."

We held each other's hands.

"Mama says she can't live here no more. We're staying at my aunt and uncle's house." She looked over her shoulder, where everyone sat watching us. Seeing them peering down at us like that made me want to go over beyond the willows where we would be private. "My father took a room in town. The police said he couldn't leave to go anywhere else for now."

"The police said that? Why?" I asked her.

"Don't you know?" Sky looked at me with her brow pinched together. "There's going to be a hearing, is what Mama says. She says we'll all have to go and answer questions again. Did the police ask you questions about what happened?"

"Right after." I didn't want to say after Riley died. "Deputy Jay came and asked me lots of questions."

"They'll ask them again. My mama says a judge will decide if my father has a trial."

"What will happen? To your father, I mean?"

"I don't know. Mama says, if the judge thinks that Father could have saved Riley and didn't do it, he can make Father go to prison."

"Prison?" To me that was some faraway, evil kind of place with cement rooms and tiny windows, and I could not imagine someone I actually knew going there.

Sky nodded. I saw tears well in her eyes. "Did you really say my father could have saved Riley?" She squinted at me, waiting.

"I guess." I looked down at the ground. "I told Deputy Jay that I saw him let Ri go down the creek."

"Tell me honestly. Was Riley alive when he floated away?"

"Yeah," I nodded. "I thought you knew that." I had a hard time understanding that she didn't know the same things I knew.

Sky and I stood there, side by side, and looked downstream to where the creek curved and disappeared out of sight. The water was clear, and though it still moved fast, it was calmer and had a friendly look.

"I hate that creek." Sky's words came out hard and mean. "I hate this whole place. I don't ever want to come back here anymore. If my father goes to prison, Mama's sellin' it. My aunt and uncle want her to. So do I."

Seems wrong now, but what she said hurt my feelings. Wouldn't she want to still live there so we could stay friends? Wouldn't she miss sitting on the boulder with me and just talking? Didn't she know she was my only friend in the whole wide world? I wanted to say something mean to her, but I couldn't think of what to say, so I turned and looked for my parents.

"I have to go," I said. "I'm not supposed to stay here very long."

I waited to see if she would say she didn't want me to leave yet, but she didn't. I saw that Maryanne and my parents were making their way down the slope, and my mama and Sky's were talking back and forth. Father was just walking along beside Mama with his hands down in his Levi pockets and kind of kicking at the ground as he walked. Maryanne had something in her hand, and as they came closer, I saw what it was. It made my heart start to ache again.

"Poppy, honey, you should have this." Tears came to her eyes so fast. "You did such a nice thing for my boy, and I know, if he could be here with us longer, he would have learned to read real books, and it would have been because of what you did for him."

She held the paper book out for me with both hands, as if offering something preciously delicate. I took it in two hands and stared down. It was smudged and had the brown mud streaks on the back page from Riley dropping it in the creek bottom that first day we'd read together. The day he read the word "car." The first page had a tear at the corner, but someone had put a piece of tape there. I held the book flat to my chest so tightly the pressure made my wound there hurt a little bit.

"What do you say to Maryanne, Poppy?" Mama said.

"Thank you." My words came out as barely a whisper.

My father said we needed to get going, but we all just stood there for a minute. Finally, I looked at Sky and said, "I guess I'll see ya."

"Yeah. At the hearing, I guess."

I followed Mama and Father back down the slope and across the bridge to our pickup. We were all three silent and slow. I crawled into the middle of the seat and leaned back. Mama got in and shut the door and reached to hold my hand. Father started the pickup and backed around to head home. He had pulled his hat brim extra low above his eyes.

"All this court crap is sure goin' to be hard on those people," he said.

I still had no idea what a hearing was or what "court crap" he was talking about.

Twenty

I hadn't worn a dress since the last day I'd gone to school, but Mama made me put one on. She had polished my school shoes, tamed my hair with a barrette, and helped me find the sleeve of my button sweater. I felt stiff as a paper doll.

My father had put on his clean Levi's that weren't so faded and a plaid shirt instead of the plain blue one. Mama wore her navy polka-dot dress and had changed things over to her navy-blue purse. She wouldn't go anywhere without Kleenex folded neat and tucked in one of the side pockets, and I noticed she carefully folded an extra thick pad of it this time. In it went, along with her lipstick and compact. She went to a kitchen cupboard and took a pack of cigarettes out of a carton and pulled the little red strip, peeling the cellophane off the top. She opened her purse again and pushed them down into the bottom. She snapped it closed with a final, loud clack and heaved a big breath. I watched Mama push her hair back from her temple with flitting fingers. I couldn't think of the last time I had seen Mama put on her good clothes and wear lipstick. She looked beautiful.

We drove to town in near silence, and my father parked in front of a long, low office building right on the main street. My stomach ached, and I felt like I needed to pee.

"I have to go to the bathroom."

"Well, you'll have to wait, Poppy."

"I can't."

"Yes, you can. We'll ask when we get inside." Mama sounded mad because I had to go.

Father pushed through a glass door and then held it for Mama and me. The room was all wood and windows and smelled like lemon oil. There was a lady sitting behind a desk across the room. She wore glasses down on her nose and had a pencil stuck in her thick, dark hair by her ear. The clatter of her typewriter stopped, and she peered at us above her glasses.

"May I help you?" Her voice was so loud it startled me.

"We're the Wades," my father said. "We're here to talk to James Parker."

"Mr. Parker is with someone right now. Would you like to take a seat?"

"Mama," I whispered.

"Is there a restroom we could use?" Mama asked.

The lady appeared to check Mama out, seeing if she was worthy of using the toilet. She pursed her lips and looked toward a door to her left.

"I suppose," she said. "Over there. Turn the light off when you've finished."

"Mama, why doesn't that lady like us?" The restroom was small and smelled like Juicy Fruit gum.

"I don't know. Sometimes town people don't care much for people who live way out in the country."

"Why?" That just seemed stupid to me.

"I don't know, Poppy. They think we are dirty or something. Your own grandma thought that same thing," she said while she pulled up my slip and twisted my skirt around where it belonged. "She used to tell me some of the kids at school were dirty because they lived in the country."

It still sounded stupid, even if my grandma said it.

As soon as we came out of the restroom, I felt like I had to go again, but I kept it to myself. We sat in chairs by a tall, paned window and waited for a long time. My father stood, holding his hat in his hand.

"Well, shit," he said loudly enough that the desk lady glared at him. "Didn't he say ten o'clock? I'm not gonna wait around all damn day." He sat next to me, crossed his leg over, and hung his hat on his knee.

A door opened in the wood paneled wall, and two men stepped out into the room where we waited. The man wearing a suit said he would be calling the other. Then they shook hands, and one went out of the glass door.

"I'll be ready in one minute, Maggie." The man with the suit went back in his office and closed the door.

"Well, shit," my father said again.

The next time the office door opened, the man came out and walked across the room to meet us as we stood up. I clung to my mother's arm. The man stuck out his hand to my father and said he was sorry we had to wait. My father shook his hand and turned to me and Mama and said who we were. The man motioned to his door and told us to come in.

"Have a seat," he said toward a row of wooden chairs in front of his massive desk. We sat, me in the middle, and waited.

"I'm James Parker. I spoke with you, Mrs. Wade, on the phone a few days ago. Nice to meet you, Mr. Wade. And you are Poppy, am I right?"

He smiled at me, showing big, white teeth. His hair was thin and colorless, and he wore the wisps combed to the side. I could see little white flakes on his scalp and across the shoulders of his suit coat. He sat and rolled himself closer to his desk.

"Yes, sir." The words came out sounding as if I wasn't sure.

"Well, it is nice to meet you, Poppy. I heard that you are a special, brave young lady. I also heard that you have a story to tell me." His right hand went up and scratched his pointy nose.

I thought, *I do?* I must have looked dim-witted because he started over again.

"I don't like having to ask you to tell the story about Riley Hogan drowning in the creek, I want you to know that, but I have to hear it for myself so I will be able to explain it exactly as it happened when we go before a judge. Maybe it would be good to let you begin telling me what happened, and then I can ask some questions. Would that be okay with you folks?" Mr. Parker looked at my parents.

Mama nodded, and my father slid forward in his chair. "Seems to me," he said, "that she's told the whole thing to a deputy of the law, and it's gonna be hard on her to tell it all over again."

"I understand your concern, but if I am going to be speaking for Poppy in front of a judge, I need to hear what happened in her own words. There will be questions from Mr. Hogan's attorney that will sound to you and to Poppy like he doubts some events that Poppy says took place. Mr. Hogan and his attorney will be striving to convince the judge that it is unnecessary to continue to trial. They will be listening for the tiniest little cracks, inconsistencies in Poppy's version of what happened." Up went his hand to scratch his nose again.

"I have spoken with Sky and Mrs. Hogan, so we know some background on Mr. Hogan and the relationship he has with his family. I will also need to hear anything Poppy recalls seeing or hearing that might reflect on that relationship. Some people who have kept their personal relationships private tend to hold back some of the more, um, unpleasant occurrences, shall we say. It is also often difficult for family and loved ones to believe the worst of one another. Loyalty oftentimes trumps harsh truth."

So far, I really had not understood much of what Mr. Parker had said. I was feeling strongly like I needed to use the bathroom again. I crossed my ankles and swung my feet to and fro. Mama laid her hand on my leg, which I knew meant to stop doing what I was doing.

Mr. Parker went to the door and called for Maggie to come in. She came, quiet as a mouse, and sat somewhere behind us. He brought a yellow tablet out from a desk drawer and laid it on the desk in front of him. "Okay, Poppy. Are you ready?"

"I guess so."

"I want you to begin wherever you are comfortable." He smiled his teeth at me again.

So I did. I started with me walking down the road to the mud house. He held his hand up and stopped me right away.

"The mud house? Can you tell me what that means?"

I explained, and I sure wanted to tell him the whole thing about how to make adobe blocks and how Sky knew all about it. But I didn't get too far, only about to the part when you put in some straw.

"You don't need to tell him all that, Poppy," my father said. "Just start with when you got to the bridge there."

Father stopping me like that threw me off so that I already felt self-conscious. Mama patted my shoulder and said, "It's okay, sweetie. Just relax and tell what you remember, just like you did for Deputy Jay."

I started over again, at the bridge, like my father said. The telling went easier after I got a good start and the pictures came to my mind again. In fact, I told it so real that my heart was pounding when I came to the part about being in the creek with Riley, and I almost choked on my own words when I told about Carl letting Riley float away, but I didn't.

Mr. Parker's face, in fact his whole body, was still as a tree trunk when I finally finished. There was no nose scratching. He had been writing something on his yellow tablet, and when I quit speaking, he laid his pen down and wove his fingers together in front of him. He looked past me for a while, so I guessed he was looking at Maggie, who still sat behind us and hadn't made a peep the whole time.

He scooted forward in his chair and gave a little croak to clear his throat. "That is quite a story and such a sad one, Poppy. Maggie, maybe you could get Poppy something to drink?" I heard her go out of the office door. "Let's take a little break, and then I have a few questions, if that's all right with you all."

Maggie brought me an orange soda with a straw, and she smiled a pretty good smile as she handed the bottle to me. Mama poked my arm. "Thank you for the soda," I said. Maybe Maggie didn't think we were really so dirty after all.

We all—Mama, my father, and me—used the restroom and then sat back in the chairs in front of the big desk. I finished my soda, and Maggie took the bottle from me. Mr. Parker took his seat and pulled his yellow tablet closer to him and picked up his pen, giving it a few clicks.

"Now, Poppy, just a few questions, not too many. How many times would you say you had been to the Hogan's property before Riley . . . before that day? Let's say it like this. Would you say ten times? Twenty times? More?"

"More," I said without a doubt.

"Ahh, so you had been there a lot, hadn't you?"

"Yes, sir."

"When you were there, did you usually see Mr. and Mrs. Hogan? Or did you only see Riley and Sky?"

"Most of the time I saw Carl or Maryanne, or sometimes both of them. They were usually doing something outside. They built the walk bridge, and they were always working on that mud house."

"Uh huh. Did they tell you that you should call them by their first names?"

This question made me think I just might be in trouble. I knew I was only supposed to address them as Mr. and Mrs. unless they said I could call them by their first names.

"Uhm, well, Maryanne said so, I think. Carl didn't say. I just called him that if I talked about him, but I didn't call him anything to his face because I didn't really talk to him much."

Mr. Parked smiled a little. "Okay. What were your feelings about Mr. Hogan? Carl?"

"I know we aren't supposed to say we hate anybody, but I guess I hated Carl." I looked at Mama, thinking I was going to hear about saying I hated somebody, even if it was Carl. She didn't say anything to me then, so I supposed she would later, if she remembered.

"What caused you to feel that way? Can you tell me something he did or said that made you hate him?" He was smiling at me a lot, but all that smiling was making me kind of uncomfortable. I didn't see any good reason for it.

"Lots of things. He was mean. He yelled at Maryanne and Riley a lot. He said bad things to Riley, like he was retarded and dumb and he would never be a man, never amount to anything. He hurt Ri's feelings all the time. Sky told me he did that all the time. And he hit Maryanne, and he killed Sky's dog." My words were coming so fast I was breathless.

Mr. Parker held up his hand so I would stop talking and asked me to explain about Carl hitting Maryanne and killing Chipper. I told what Sky had said to me about all that. He frowned and scratched his nose again when I told him about Sky finding a stick with blood and dog hair on it. Next to me, Mama made a funny sound. Probably because she was so upset about the dog, just like me. I went ahead and told him about seeing Sky get knocked out of the trailer door and how I thought she died and how, when I jumped down from Nicky, I turned my ankle, and about the big sore on Maryanne's arm after that day.

I guess Mama couldn't keep quiet anymore. "Poppy, why in God's name didn't you ever tell me any of this?" She looked like she might cry.

"I couldn't. I promised I wouldn't tell anyone."

"You promised Sky?"

"Sky and Maryanne, both."

"Maryanne made you promise not to tell me?" I don't think she understood my reason. At least, that's how she looked at me. I had to look away. I didn't want her to be mad at Maryanne.

"Poppy, do you think that Riley was afraid of Carl? Would you say he seemed to understand that his father was saying mean things to him sometimes?" Mr. Parker went on like he didn't notice that Mama was upset.

"Yes, sir. I didn't know at first. Riley seemed so happy most of the time. He loved Sky and was happy to be with her. When Carl was mean to Maryanne, and then that day when Ri fell down in the mud, he was real scared because he knew his father was going to be mad at him.

And he was, too—mad, I mean. I heard him yelling in the trailer about how Ri thought nobody had nothing better to do than look after him. Ri was crying louder and louder." With all this talk coming out of me, I could feel the hate creeping up inside me again. I was shaking some.

"I'm just about finished here, Poppy. Tell me, could Riley talk? Did he speak much?"

"He could. Only he didn't talk much. He said words, but not whole sentences much. He said my name a lot and Sky's, and he said Mama and some other words. He knew stuff though. I was teaching him to read."

"Riley was learning to read?" Mr. Parker looked amazed. He leaned way forward and kind of lit up. His eyebrows went way up on his forehead. "How in the world did you do that?"

I told him about my idea and how I made Ri a book. I told him how we sat on the boulder by the creek and I showed him over and over about the words and pictures. I started to tell about how Ri picked up the book and pointed and said "car," but my voice just stopped on me, and I was so overtaken by my feelings, I couldn't speak anymore. My heart about burst right out of my throat. A big loud sob came out of me before I could do anything about it.

"Okay. That's all. We're through here. Poppy, I am so sorry I made you feel bad. I didn't mean to do that. I have to say, though, that if we end up in a court with a jury, I will likely have to ask these questions again. I won't if I don't have to, but I can't say I won't."

He told my father and Mama that he would be in touch as soon as he heard from Mr. Hogan's lawyer. Maggie smiled real nice at us when we went out the glass door.

It felt wonderful to be out in the fresh air, and I felt a nice, calm feeling return inside of me. I could hardly wait to get back home.

Twenty-One

Anyone who could say they were happy that such horrible things had happened as those that happened to Riley and the rest of us would be crazy as a loon, but I admit, I sure was never one bit sorry I didn't have to go to school for a while. It couldn't last forever, though, so I finally had to start doing my schoolwork at home. I guess someone, maybe the school principal, decided I should stay out of school until after Christmas vacation. I suppose the school district had to agree to that, and must have, because my father came home one day with a bunch of mimeographed worksheets and my schoolbooks that had lain in my desk for weeks and not opened a crack.

The papers smelled like the sharp, sweet scent of the bright-purple copy ink. Most of them were for arithmetic, my worst subject in school. I'd held my own until I had to memorize the times tables and, even then, did okay until I got to eight times nine. I had figured out that, if I went all the way back to the times six answers, I could start from there and go on until I got to the answer. Division was a mystery to me. Just looking at all those worksheets stacked on our table made me cringe.

Our reading book and the questions at the end of chapters were easy. In fact, back in school before the accident, I had gone ahead and read the book clear to the end when I was supposed to be doing my arithmetic. Mrs. Gardner tried to help me get a better grasp on numbers, but when I was caught reading, she was so exasperated she would just shake her head and send home another note, which I either forgot to give to Mama or hid in my dresser drawer.

I had to start doing the work at home, and was I ever surprised to find out that my father was so good at arithmetic. He ended up being the one to help me the most. We would sit at the kitchen table a couple of times a week before supper, and he would help me figure out the problems. I learned that, if I paid attention and said "uh-huh" a lot, he ended up doing most of the figuring.

"Now, look here at this one, Poppy. If you take fifty-six here, see it, and divide it by seven, what do you get? Think, Poppy, is six times eight fifty-six? No, it ain't. So what's seven times eight, then? What comes next?" He would point here and there at the numbers with the point of my pencil. "Does seven times eight come to fifty-six?"

My fingers were popping up under the table while I counted to myself.

"Uh-huh."

He would hand me the pencil, and I would dutifully write the answer on the line, as if it was all my idea.

"Good. Now this one, here." And on we'd go.

Usually, on Fridays, he would drop my work by the school office so the teacher could correct it over the weekend. On Mondays, we would get them back, along with the week's new assignments. One time Mrs. Gardner wrote a note on a worksheet that she marked a hundred percent: "Good job, Mr. Wade." After that, I worried that he wouldn't help me so much, but he did. I think he liked getting those good grades back from Mrs. Gardner.

Doing schoolwork together was the most attention I'd received from my father for a long time. Probably since we moved into the canyon house. I liked the time with him, and I felt special again if I pleased him with a right answer, even if I was counting on my fingers under the table. I didn't try to figure out why he was being nicer to me again.

I guess I didn't want to think about it too much because I wasn't sure how long it would last. Maybe he felt sorry for me. But then another problem arose. I could tell that Mama wasn't happy because he could help me and she couldn't. She would keep coming around the table where we worked, mentioning things about reading or spelling.

"Poppy, sweetie, when you get done there, I can help you with your spelling words. You have a new list to learn, you know. How about after supper?"

Sometimes I would let her help me, even if I didn't need her to. I knew my spelling words quick as a wink. I could look at a word just one time and know it. Looking them up in the dictionary took time, but I liked using it so I didn't really mind. I could get way-sided reading the definitions of other words for the fun of it.

In some silent sort of way, our home life changed after Riley drowned. Not that it was the same as it had been in the valley house, but at least life felt kinder, for the most part. I know we all thought a lot about Riley's death, and my father still got drunk a few nights a week or on Saturdays. So, not everything had changed. He would rant about lawyers and judges and how he didn't trust any of them. They were crooked, he'd say, though I couldn't see how that could be true. He hoped that Carl would never, ever see the light of day again. Of course Mama would say it was all up to the Lord. Then later she'd say the Lord sure as heck better do His job. I thought Mama would do a good job if she could sit by God at the Pearly Gates and help Him decide what to do about some of the souls that maybe shouldn't get into heaven.

The day that father brought home a fat envelope from Mr. Parker's office, we instantly became all stirred up again. Father opened it carefully across the top with his pocketknife and pulled out the neatly folded papers. He unfolded them and sat in silence while he read until Mama said, "For God's sake, Norman, what does it say?"

"It says Poppy has to appear in court as a witness for the District Attorney's office. Says old Carl entered a plea of not guilty, but Judge Hoover says he has to go to trial. Says we have to bring Poppy to meet with Parker again."

He tossed the papers to Mama and, without looking at me, stood and went out of the house. I heard his pickup start up, and he drove down the driveway. I knew he'd gone to see his cows.

Mama's hands trembled a little while she read. I just sat and waited for her to be finished so I could say what I wanted to say. She finally put the papers down on the table and leaned back in her chair with a big, tired sigh.

"Don't worry, Mama," I said to her, "it'll be okay. I'll just say what happened, and it'll be all over."

The next few days were dark and chilly, both outside and inside. Our calm was gone again. Even my brothers were home more, and they asked a lot of questions about what could happen to Carl. Tim played cards with me until I was sick of it and had to tell him he didn't have to play with me anymore. They teased me and said I would probably be on the *Perry Mason* show on TV. Allen hung out in the house with us until Father came home. Then he would either go into town or out to the bunkhouse.

I had nightmares again. They were the same as the ones I'd had right after Riley died. I would wake crying or shaking and trying to holler out or sometimes so angry at Carl I could hardly stand it. I would dream wild dreams of hitting him and yelling at him that he had killed Ri. My heart would pound so hard my chest wound would hurt again. I felt like I was right back where I had been when I woke to Loretta calling to me on the creek bank. All the horribleness that had taken place that day was as clear as if it had just happened.

When we went to Mr. Parker's office again, Maggie met us with a big smile, like an old friend. She chirped for us to take a seat and Mr. Parker would be right with us, which he was. We sat in the same chairs as we had before.

"Well, I figured it would come to this," he said after we were seated. "At his hearing, Mr. Hogan pleaded not guilty to the charge of homicide. His attorney, Mr. Wright, is a public defender. I know him well. He is completely adept and is going on the idea that Riley died because he wanted to and it was purely an accident that Carl was not able to save him from himself. Poppy, you're our star witness, but we have other folks to tell what they know about Mr. Hogan and his relationship with his family. Unfortunately, for us and for herself, Sky will be a witness for the defense. I can see that she cannot bring herself to believe that her father caused Riley's death." His hand came up to scratch at his nose.

I was stunned. What Mr. Parker was saying was that Sky didn't believe what I'd told her. I remembered our exact conversation the day I saw her at the mud house. I thought sure she had known I was telling the truth. I hardly heard anything Mr. Parker said after that. Mr. Hogan was in jail until the court proceedings, which were to begin the next week. We would have to drive almost fifty miles to the county courthouse in a bigger town up north, but for the time being, all I could think about was Sky.

"It's hard for kin to turn on their own," Mama tried to explain on our way back home. "She can't help it if she can't believe her father would do something like that."

"But she knows how mean he is. She's the one who told me the things he's done to her mother and to Riley." I couldn't get it through my head.

"If Dad or I did something that awful, would you be able to believe it?" she asked me.

I may have hesitated a second too long because she said, "Poppy, for heaven's sake. You mean to tell me you wouldn't think right away that we wouldn't be capable of something like that?"

I could see that she was truly shocked, so I said what I thought sounded right.

"Well, what if you really, really hated me or Allen or Timothy? Then maybe you could."

"Don't be talkin' like that," my father said. "Just be quiet about the whole damn business for a while."

"Well, I'm still mad at Sky for not believing me."

I guess I had to get the last word in.

Twenty-Two

The days went by beneath a dreary shadow. The closer time drew to court day, the more uneasy I felt. I spent as much time outside as I could, but it was mostly cold and cloudy, and it rained often. Mama said it made her worry when it rained any at all for she was afraid the creek would rise up again. For some reason, I didn't think about that happening. I couldn't believe it could ever get so high and mean again in a million years. I messed around down by the water every day. The stream didn't flow clear for long because of the runoff from the hills each time a rain came along, but it was never again that thick, brown demon like it was that day Riley drowned. I sat by a place where a tadpole pool had been and wondered if there would still be a place for them in the summer. I longed for summertime.

Sometimes I just walked. I would go from the Indian cave to the barn and then up to the spring tubs. I didn't play pretend as much as I had in the summer. I didn't seem to have an imagination like I had back then. When I tried to make up a story about an Indian girl or a cowboy, reality would keep getting mixed in and take the fun out of my game.

I wondered how Carl was in jail. I don't mean I cared how he was doing; I just wished I knew if he was mean as ever or if he was regretful about what he had done. It was hard to picture Carl being sorry about something. I didn't think he would ever be the type of person to just say, "Okay, I did that bad thing, and I am so sorry about it." Sure could have made my life easier if he would have.

Being a witness was nothing like I'd expected. Maybe because I started watching *Perry Mason* after my brothers teased me about being on the show. The old court building we went to was the biggest building I had ever been inside of, and for the first time in my life, I rode in an elevator—only up to the second floor, but the motion made me feel giddy on top of my nervousness. The hallways smelled like floor wax and men's cologne. I had also never in my life seen so many men dressed up in suits and ties. Most of them carried briefcases or leather-covered books, and they all walked like they were in a hurry to get somewhere.

Mr. Parker was there, right where he said he would be, and showed my parents and me where we could sit in a little room off the corridor. He sat with one leg up on the edge of a table, showing us his argyle sock, and looked at all of us.

"Poppy, I want you to stay here until someone comes to get you, and that person will show you the way into the courtroom and up to where I will be. I will be right there waiting for you, and I will tell you exactly what to do next, so don't worry about any of that. Okay? Norman and Francine, if you like, one of you can come on in and sit in on the trial so you can keep up with what's going on. I will most likely have a chance to get back here to talk to Poppy again before she is sworn in."

I knew what being sworn in meant, and I was really dreading that part. All of those people would be looking at me. Mr. Parker had told me to try not to worry about that too much. He said I should just look right at him and try not to pay attention to anybody else.

I saw the look that passed between my mother and father, and I thought, *uh-oh, now they are going to argue about who stays with me and who goes into the courtroom to listen to the other people testify.* I didn't think I could stand for one of their hateful disagreements to happen right then. I hadn't cried in a long time, but that probably would have done it.

For maybe two whole minutes, the room became so quiet we could hear each other breathe, and then I was never as shocked in my life as I was when my father said he would stay with me.

"I think you oughta go in," he said to Mama. "I don't know if I can keep my mouth shut when ol' Carl is up there spewin' lies. You know he will be. What else is he gonna say? No," he was shaking his head side to side. "No. You better go listen in, Francine."

Mama looked as surprised as I felt. But I saw her glance away and wondered if maybe she didn't really want to be the one in the courtroom. It would be a lot easier to just sit in that little room with me. I think sometimes people want to do something until it's time to do it, and then maybe it doesn't sound so good after all. Like learning to swim or ride a horse. Things where you have to be brave.

My mother's depression had her down real low for a while. She'd slept an awful lot and was quiet when she was up and around. She just wasn't ever a brave type of person, anyway. When she became sick with tuberculosis and had to go away for such a long time, I think it made her afraid of a lot of things about life. It's no wonder she didn't like for things to change much. Seemed if, when they did, it was always for the worst.

If she drank along with my father, or in spite of him, as she'd say, her depression would get worse. There had been a lot of days through all this mess that I felt as if I lived by myself. I don't mean I had to do everything around the house, all the chores and things like that. It was the way the house felt on some days. Empty. Cold and empty.

Anyway, Mama finally rose from her chair and headed out of the door. She didn't say a word, but I thought it was because she was scared and not because she was mad at me or anything.

Sitting in that small room with my father started out to be one of the most awkward times in my life. We looked here and there—at an ugly picture on one wall of a man standing by a horse, at the floor, the door—anywhere but at each other. There was nothing to keep us busy in there. Nobody had said, and it sure never crossed my mind, to bring a book to read. My father would never have thought of that. He probably hadn't read a book since he was in eighth grade. That was when he left school, after eighth. I'm not saying he couldn't read because he could, but he never showed an interest in books.

Finally, I said, "So, what do you think about that horse in that picture, there?"

He smiled a little and said, "Well, I never have seen one of those English horses, but I don't think they really look like that. That's a big ol' head on that pony, that's for sure. I don't believe that guy was gonna ride that horse, either." He poked an unlit cigarette toward the picture. "Look at that silly, ruffly shirt he's wearin'." The idea of that made me laugh a little bit, too.

After that, we felt easier with each other and talked about this and that. The silent times weren't as uncomfortable. He found his matches in his shirt pocket and lit his smoke. I grew drowsy and put my head down on my crossed arms. I think I must have slept a while because next thing I knew the door opened and Mama and Mr. Parker came into the room.

Mama was white as Casper. She promptly took the chair nearest my father.

"It's good you didn't go in," she told my father. "Carl was so awful."

She saw an ashtray on the end of the table and reached quickly down in her purse for her pack of cigarettes. Her hands trembled while she lit up and took a long drag. That must have been contagious because my father lit up again, and soon the room was a gray haze.

"Mr. Hogan's testimony was extremely graphic," Mr. Parker interrupted. "His entire testimony dwells on the fact that he did actually run down the hill to the creek as soon as he saw that Riley was not at the trailer. He says he went looking for him immediately and, because of the danger there, he knew he better look to the creek first thing. He told how he called to Riley as he ran and how he was horrified to see Ri slip and fall into the water—"

"Ri didn't slip and fall," I stood and exclaimed. "I saw him. He stepped into the creek on purpose."

"Well, see, that's just it, Poppy. We will need to show the jury that Riley planned on going into the water on purpose and that the reason could very well have been because he was feeling so troubled about himself." Mr. Parker paused a second and scratched at the side of his nose, then went on. "Mr. Hogan says that he ran, desperately, along the creek bank to get ahead of you and Riley so he could jump in and grab for you, meaning both of you. He says there was no good place for him to plow into the rushing water, so he thought to get on the bridge and try to snag you as you passed below. That is how he grabbed hands with you, Poppy, and then got a hold on Riley's face and head. But here is the most important part. He says that he was holding on to Riley with all the strength he had in him and that Riley himself reached up and pried Carl's fingers from his grip. He tells it in vivid steps. He said Riley clawed at his hand and then pulled his fingers away with power-ful determination. He said that, because he was holding on to you with his other hand, he panicked because he didn't want to let you go, either. So, the story ends with Riley gaining his way and escaping Carl's hold. Oh, except he says he ran downstream again to try to reach Riley, but it was just too late.

"Loretta testified, too, you know." He shook his head. "She was no help. She said that she hardly noticed what Carl did because she was worried about you. I tried to get her to say something about Carl's ex-pression or if he appeared to be frightened or desperate in any way, but she just couldn't remember."

I was so mad I could not be still. I had to keep myself from wiggling around as I waited to speak.

"Those are lies that Carl told. That is not what happened at all." I started to cry, but it was because I was so frustrated, not sad or any-thing like that.

"I know that, Poppy. Take it easy now, if you can. Don't worry. I know Carl is lying because I remember every word you told me about what happened. So when you go in today, we need to let the jury know, too."

I sat again. Stared at the floor. I wanted to know about Sky, but I couldn't work up the nerve to ask, what with being so upset about Carl's lies. I still had hopes that Sky would change her mind and tell the truth.

Mama must have wanted me to hear about Sky, too, because she brought it up.

"I think you should tell Poppy about Sky's testimony, also. I don't think it sounded near as bad as Poppy expected it to be."

Mr. Parker nodded. "That's true, Poppy. She told us more about the family relationships than she did the actual drowning of her brother. It was difficult to get her to say how unpleasant things were between Carl and Riley. She dug in and insisted they weren't so bad. It was important that I did not come across as a bully to the jury. They don't like to see us attorneys picking on children for even one second. I couldn't be too stern with Sky while getting her to admit Riley's abuse from his father."

"What about when Carl let Riley go? What did she say about that?" I asked.

"She says she didn't see her father do that. She isn't allowed to say what you told her because that would just be hearsay, not something she witnessed herself. The best I could get from her was that she could not see for herself whether Carl let Riley go on purpose. That much she had to admit.

"You will be called up after a lunch break, and we can clear up some of the unknowns. I have to get back."

He left quickly, and we sat, not knowing what to do next.

We found a cafeteria down on the bottom floor and ordered some sandwiches, but I had a hard time swallowing any of mine. I sat and watched people come and go and wished I was home and that the day was over with. Mama told us more about what was said in the courtroom, but I think it made me feel worse. She said Sky spoke so soft that both attorneys had to keep asking her to speak louder.

"So remember that, sweetie," she said to me. "It will make it sound like you really mean what you say if you speak up."

"Well, I will mean what I say, Mama."

"You know what I mean," she said.

I opened my mouth to talk back, and Father leaned forward and laid his big hand flat out in the middle of our table.

"Don't start, you two. Ain't no damn place for a quibble about something like that."

I looked away from both of them and saw Maryanne come through the cafeteria door. I was stunned to see how she looked. She'd been a thin but sturdy woman because of all the hard work she did, but she looked frail to me in her green and white dress that hung from her shoulders like it was on a coat hanger. Her cheekbones were high and sharp, and her eyes were sunken into dark circles. She had slicked her long hair back from her face and attempted to wind it into a bun at the back of her long neck. It was hard to believe I was seeing the Maryanne I knew.

Behind her came her sister, who I had seen at the trailer, and then I nearly threw myself from my chair when I saw Sky, who was overshadowed by a huge man who I assumed was Mr. Wright.

Mama and my father both reached for an arm at the same time and gently sat me back on my chair. I stared at Sky, willing her to look my way. She looked the same as ever to me. Round and soft, wearing a nice dress, and she had a little bit different haircut, like one you'd get at a beauty salon.

"I only want to say hi to her. Please. I won't say anything else, I promise." I pleaded to my parents, but they wouldn't budge.

"You can't, Poppy," Father said. "You won't be allowed to talk to her. Her father's lawyer is right there, and he won't let you. And even if he did, it could ruin the whole damn trial."

"Why?" I didn't understand.

"Well, he could go right back in there and tell the judge that you influenced his witness. Then, if she had to be questioned again, they would use that."

He looked at Mama and nodded once toward the door. I stood when they did, and they hustled me past Sky's table and through the door into the wide hallway. I pulled away and looked back, and Sky looked right at me. Our eyes met, and I saw a spark of the Sky who was my best friend cross her gaze. But she looked down, and that was it.

We rode the elevator again, and I thought for sure I was going to be sick. Back in the cramped waiting room, Mama sat me down and gave me a glass of water from a pitcher and fiddled with my hair with her fingers.

"I wish this was a dream and I could wake up." I didn't say it to either one of them, I just said it because it was how I felt.

That was the end of my talking. I sat back in the hard chair and never said another word. I felt myself change from being so upset to being angry. Really angry, and it was building up something fierce. *What is the matter with all these people?* I kept thinking. *And all these stupid rules?* Carl killed his own son, and that was all there was to it. He hated Riley because he wasn't like other boys, and he was ashamed of being his father. Having Riley for a son was like saying he had something wrong inside himself, and he couldn't stand that. He didn't want Ri around, and he found the perfect chance to get rid of him. I sat in that chair and glared at the whole world until a big, heavy lady in a brown uniform came into the room and said it was time for me to go. I stood and walked with her, my parents trailing behind. I didn't even feel much emotion. I felt lifeless. All I had to do was answer questions, and I didn't really care much about it anymore.

The courtroom was terribly warm, and paddle fans up in the high ceiling were going around in lazy circles, doing no good at all, as far as I was concerned. I looked straight ahead, finding Mr. Parker by the little gate in the low wall that divided the room. He opened it and let me go through. I felt him pat my shoulder, and he bent and asked me if I was all right.

"Yes, sir. I'm fine." And I really was.

Mr. Parker stood by protectively while I was sworn in and helped me onto the chair in the witness box. I looked up at the judge when he spoke.

"I am Judge Hoover, Poppy. I want you to understand that if you need to rest or have a sip of water while you testify, please feel free to ask." He was a big man, and his voice resonated out into the room.

The first questions were simple. Mr. Parker asked me my name and age and where I lived and about how long I had lived there. He went on to ask how I came to know the Hogan family. He made the conversation easy, mentioning that I rode my horse to my new friend's house. We spoke briefly about the mud house and what that meant.

"And that is what you called it, right, Poppy, the mud house?"

"Yes, sir. But they really lived in a little trailer."

There were so many questions. They went on and on. How big was that trailer? Was the area flat? Was the boulder where we sat by the creek? Did I know what a Volkswagen car was? Was the boulder bigger or smaller than that?

Then he said, "Okay, Poppy, now I am going to ask you some questions about the Hogan family, and I want you to take your time and think before you answer."

I was ready. I knew the answers.

Twenty-Three

"Did you like Maryanne and Carl?" Mr. Parker asked me.

"I like Maryanne a lot. She was nice. Right away, she said I could come back anytime I wanted."

"And Carl?"

I couldn't help but glance at Carl, sitting next to Mr. Wright at a long table. He was staring straight at me with little eyes, and he was still as a stone. Mr. Parker stepped into my line of sight.

"Well, at first I didn't know what to think because he mostly ignored me. He was always busy doing something. But I don't think I liked him from the beginning."

"Why would you say that, if he didn't even talk to you?"

"Well, that's why. That wasn't a very polite way to be to a kid."

There was a little ripple of soft chuckles, but I really didn't see what was so funny.

"So on the days after that first one, did Carl ever talk to you? You know, say howdy, or make any kind of conversation?"

"No, sir. Not until I had been there a bunch of times. After he built the walk bridge. Sky and I were going to help Ri onto the new bridge, and he fell down, and Carl yelled at me to leave him be. He scared me and made me a little bit mad because I was only trying to help Ri."

"When you say Ri, you mean his son Riley, don't you?"

I nodded.

"You have to answer," Judge Hoover said, so I did.

Mr. Parker changed the subject and asked me if I ever heard Mr. and Mrs. Hogan argue. He also wanted to know if I heard either of them say harsh words to their kids.

It took a long time to go back over all the times I heard Carl hollering at Maryanne and even longer to tell about the things he said to Riley. It was the fight I had heard go on inside the trailer that took the longest to tell because Mr. Parker asked question after question.

"First, I heard him, Carl, yelling at Maryanne to shut up, and then there was all kinds of commotion. The trailer even moved a little bit, and I heard Riley crying, well, more like howling. I thought I should leave, but I couldn't right then. That's when the door came open, and I saw Sky helping Riley down the steps. She took him to a place to sit him down, and she was kind of hugging him and talking to him. Next thing I knew, she was up and headed back inside the trailer. She was screaming at Carl to leave her mama alone, and she came flying out the door backward and landed right there on the ground."

My heart was speeding up, and I was beginning to be mad all over again. I drank some water from the glass in front of me and looked right at Mr. Parker, like he had told me to do.

"Did that scare you?"

"I thought Sky had died. I jumped down off of Nicky so fast I hurt my ankle, but I didn't care. I ran to Sky just as she took this big breath, and her eyes kind of rolled around. I shook her and shook her and kept on saying her name. I was praying to God that she wasn't really dead. She wasn't."

There was a little ripple of laughter again.

I told how Maryanne came and sort of collected us up, and we went down to the boulder and sat together until we became calmer.

"How did Riley seem to you, Poppy?"

For the first time during the questioning, I was afraid I would cry. "He put his arms around my middle and said my name. He gave me the biggest hug."

"How did you feel about Riley then?"

"I loved Riley. I wished he was my little brother. Maybe I didn't love him as much as Sky did, being his kin, but I really did love him."

Eventually, I had to tell all of the story. Even about the time Sky told me Carl had killed her dog, but Mr. Wright stood up and objected to that because he said it was hearsay. That hearsay rule didn't seem right to me, because a man killing a dog with a stick seemed important, that's for sure.

I drank some more water and looked over at where the jurors were all sitting. Mr. Parker was busy at his table, so he wasn't there to keep me from looking around. I saw that there were only two ladies sitting there, and the rest were all different looking men. A couple of them smiled at me when they saw I was looking at them. One of the ladies had real red-rimmed eyes, like she'd been crying. I felt sorry for her.

Carl and Mr. Wright sat close, with their heads nearly touching, and they were whispering while Mr. Wright wrote on a yellow tablet. I got the creeps if I looked at Carl, and a weak flutter of sickness crawled around in my stomach. I knew the worst part of the whole thing was still to come.

Mr. Parker asked me a few more questions to get us up to the part about Sky's mama being sick. I told about Ri falling down in the mud and being scared that Carl would be mad. I said that Sky told me she was worried about her mama dying because she was so sick, and Mr. Wright objected again, but Judge Hoover said "overruled." I don't think it really mattered much because the jury already heard me say how sick Maryanne was, and no matter what anybody said, they couldn't just act like I didn't say it.

"Now, Poppy, can you tell us what you heard and saw when you and Sky were sitting on the boulder by the creek?"

I told every single thing, like I had so many times before, and when I reached the part where I saw Riley take that big step right into the water and throw himself forward, a murmur of voices traveled around the room.

"Did you think for even a second that Riley had fallen into the water accidentally? Maybe his toe caught on a root or a stone?"

"No, sir. He went into the water on purpose, that was plain as day. I saw him take two long steps before he went headfirst into the creek. Ri didn't trip on anything, sir."

"It must have been hard for you to decide to jump in that water to help Riley." Mr. Parker said it like I was going to agree and say, "Oh yeah. It was real hard." But he knew that wasn't the truth of it.

"No, sir. I didn't think about it much at all. I only remember jumping in and then feeling how strong the water was pushing me around."

I went on, telling how I got a grip on Ri's hair and how I tried to stop us by grabbing bushes and putting my feet down on the creek bottom. I told how I saw the bridge and thought there was someone on it.

"Now, Poppy, you know this is especially important and that, no matter what, you must tell the truth."

Mr. Wright stood and said, "Your Honor, I would hope that Miss Wade has been telling the truth this entire time and does not need reminding to begin telling it now. Or, sir, perhaps Mr. Parker is feeling a need to stress the accuracy of a testimony that has been previously determined."

"So what exactly is your objection, Mr. Wright?" Judge Hoover rested his chin on his folded knuckles and looked down at Mr. Wright. I peeked at Carl. He was still stone-faced.

"It does seem that Parker is leading his witness, Your Honor."

"Sustained. Be careful here, Mr. Parker."

"Tell us please, Poppy, what happened beneath the bridge. Can you start from when you knew someone had hold of your hand?"

I did. I told every second of what happened. I told about seeing Ri look at me and how I saw his beautiful eyelashes when he blinked that long, slow blink. I could hear one of the lady jurors sniffling and blowing her nose, trying not to be loud about it. As my eyes traveled the room, I saw a lot of tissues being dabbed at wet eyes. I swear, it was the peoples' sadness that made me start to cry. I didn't sob, but the tears came fast and washed down my face. Mr. Parker handed me a tissue. I wiped at my face and took a big breath.

"I saw Carl's hand on Ri's face, and his fingers were wrapped under his chin. Carl kept hollering for me to let go of Ri's hair and grab onto his other arm. He was holding my hand real tight, so I did what he said."

"Did you feel like everything was going to be all right then, Poppy?"

"Yes. I felt so relieved. Carl was going to save us and get us out of the water."

"And you knew Riley was still alive and needed to be saved quickly, is that right?'

"Object," Mr. Wright boomed. "He is not only leading, he is asking her to make a judgment call she cannot possibly make. There is no way she could be positive that the boy, Riley, was still alive."

"Yes, he was!" I heard myself yell out. "He was too alive, and I am tired of people saying he wasn't."

Mr. Hoover pounded his gavel, and Mr. Parker was shushing me. I was so mad, I was holding my breath, like a tot having a temper tantrum. When everyone calmed down, Mr. Hoover told Mr. Parker to finish up, and we would start again the next morning.

Mr. Parker said his next questioning was central to the trial, and he needed to go slowly. Mr. Hoover asked me if I was comfortable going on.

"Yes, sir. I'm sorry I spoke out of turn, sir."

He nodded down at me, but I couldn't tell if he was mad at me or not.

"Poppy," Mr. Parker said, "tell me what you thought when you looked over and saw Carl's fingers holding Riley's face above water."

"Well, I thought about how good it was that he could breathe." But then I told how I saw Carl's fingers unwrap from Ri's chin, letting go one by one, and how I saw his hand touch Ri's high, white forehead and give him the gentlest, little, tiny push and at the same time the water grabbed him up, took him away, and how the next thing I knew Riley was gone. I told how I started to scream and struggle to get loose from Carl's grip on my hand so I could go after Ri again, but he would not let me go.

I covered my face with the limp tissue and sobbed.

Twenty-Four

I slept all the way home after that first day in court. Lordy, was I ever tired. I didn't even dream that night. It seemed like I blinked and it was time to get up and drive all the way back to court. Mama helped me as I fumbled around getting dressed, and she made me eat some toast and drink my milk and off we went.

I was scared. I knew this time I had to answer Mr. Wright's questions, and he wasn't going to be nice to me like Mr. Parker was. Mr. Parker tried to make me feel better by saying he would be right there for me to look to for encouragement, and he would try to protect me if Mr. Wright overstepped his bounds. I know he was trying to help, but he didn't really. I was still scared.

After I was back up on the witness stand, I looked over all the people for my father and Mama and found them near enough to give me some comfort. That's when I saw Sky and her family sitting in a tight row directly behind Mr. Wright's table. All of them met my gaze, even Sky, but I couldn't see a great deal of feeling on their faces. Maybe just tiredness.

Mr. Wright started out asking some of the same questions as the day before about who I was and if I was a friend of Sky's.

To that, I spoke right up and said, "I am," because I felt like I still was, or should be, even if she didn't think so.

But he threw me for a loop with his first important question. "Poppy, do your parents ever fight? Shout at one another?"

Mr. Parker jumped right up to object because he said that question didn't have anything to do with anything, but Judge Hoover let Mr. Wright ask it anyway.

"Sometimes they do."

"And when your parents act like that, does it scare you sometimes?"

"Yes, I guess sometimes it does." I could not for anything make myself look at my parents.

"So, Poppy, would you say that it is probably a, well, a natural feeling of fear for a young child to have when parents fight or argue?"

I looked at Mr. Parker, who actually smiled at me. I wondered why the heck he was smiling at a time like that. But, you know, I felt better somehow, like I should just say what I wanted to.

"I think that depends, sir."

"Explain that, please." Mr. Wright tipped his head back and looked at me around his bulbous nose.

"Well, if parents are arguing about something like who lost something or who forgot to do a certain thing, that's completely different from fighting about saying one is dumb or stupid, something mean like that."

Mr. Wright walked around behind his table and looked down at his yellow tablet.

"Okay. Do your parents do that? Argue about being dumb and stupid?"

"Once in a while." I didn't want to say that, so the words came out in a whisper.

"And you get scared, right?"

"Yeah."

"So, do you think that Sky felt scared when her parents argued like that?"

"Yes, I know she did."

"But those arguments don't always mean that something worse happens, do they? Do your parents abuse each other when they argue?"

"No, sir, but they—"

Mr. Wright held up his hand to stop me.

"That's all, Poppy," he said, "We'll move on. How many times would you say you actually saw Mr. and Mrs. Hogan fight?"

"Maybe one time."

"Maybe?" He raised his eyebrows at me.

"One time."

"But weren't they inside the trailer, Poppy?"

"Yes, but—"

"So you didn't really *see* them fighting, did you?"

"No."

Maybe I was just a little girl, but by then I was beginning to understand what was going on. I would not be allowed to explain anything. I couldn't tell my story. I could only say as much as Mr. Wright wanted me to say. I felt helpless. I looked at Mr. Parker, who actually smiled and nodded at me again.

"So, if Sky happened to mention to you that her parents had a fight and it frightened her or made her feel bad in some way, that doesn't mean they hit each other, does it?"

"I thought we couldn't say any hearsay, sir. Isn't that a hearsay?"

Everyone in the courtroom laughed out loud. Even Judge Hoover gave a big laugh.

"Poppy, you don't get to question Mr. Wright, although that was an appropriate question."

It took a while for the people in the courtroom to calm down and be still again. I had time to look at my parents and see that Mama was wiping her eyes with a tissue, probably laughter tears, and my father still wore a thin smile. And Sky. I looked at her for what seemed like a long time, but she just looked down at her hands.

"Now, Poppy, while you and Sky were running toward the place where Riley went into the creek, didn't Sky fall down on the way, trip on a rock maybe?"

"Yes, sir."

"And you helped her up, right?"

"Yes."

"Could it be possible that you were in such a hurry and a little panicky as you got closer to where Riley stood that you remember incorrectly?"

"He wasn't standing, sir. He was running pretty fast. For him, anyway."

"Well, you know, Poppy, when we are in a high emotional state, sometimes we don't see or remember details correctly. Didn't you say yourself that you don't remember deciding to jump into the water?"

I thought, *here we go again. Somebody trying to tell me what I saw and what I didn't.*

"Yes." Up came the hand. "But I know what I saw."

Mr. Wright looked to Judge Hoover, who leaned down and said kindly, "Poppy, you have to answer the questions without adding on."

"Let me see if I have this right, Poppy. After you dove into the creek and started to wash downstream, by the time you reached the bridge, you had a tight grip on Riley's hair, correct?"

"Yes, sir. A ways before that."

"So you were able to stop washing downstream because you got a hold of one of the uprights beneath the bridge. Tell me if this is correct. Mr. Hogan would have been lying on his stomach and chest and reaching down with both hands, right? So he got a hold of your right hand with his left and told you to let go of Riley and grab on to his same arm with your left hand also, right?"

"Yes."

"Okay. When you looked to your left, you saw that Mr. Hogan had his right hand underneath Riley's chin and seemed to have a pretty good hold, right?"

"Yes, sir. His fingers—" The hand came up again.

"It must have felt wonderful to know that the two of you were going to be saved from drowning."

"I guess, but I didn't really think about drowning. Not myself, anyway, just Riley."

"So, Riley looks at you, and then you see his hand come up. Yes?" I nodded to that.

"That meant that Riley, as bad off as he was, was still able to bring his hand up by his own will, doesn't it? And that would be when he began pulling against his father's hold on his face and chin. And when poor Mr. Hogan here," he turned and looked kindly at Carl, "when he couldn't maintain his hold on both Riley *and* you, Miss Wade, it only took a split second and Riley was gone. Isn't that how it happened?"

"That doesn't even make any sense," I blurted out.

"No? Why not, Poppy?"

"Because what father would let his own kid go washing down a creek where he was sure to drown and then save some kid that he didn't even like? I mean, if Riley was your kid, wouldn't you save him and let me go?"

The courtroom rumbled. Judge Hoover was pounding his gavel up there on his bench, but nobody paid attention. The judge finally said it was time to recess, and we would come back after lunch.

Mr. Parker came to help me down from the witness chair and led me, weak-kneed, to Mama and Father.

We went together through a door behind the judge's bench into a small room that looked exactly like the one we had used before. The only thing missing was the goofy picture of the big-headed horse and man with the ruffled shirt. I was tired already and plopped myself onto a chair at the table. My parents scraped chairs back and sat near me. Mr. Parker sat across the table.

"You did a great job out there, Poppy. I could see that the jury was taken in by your testimony." He looked at my father. "Great answer to that last question, don't you think, Norman? What man would not save his own child, given the choice?"

"I sure as hell don't know. But how do you reckon Francine and I feel when we think about that? I mean, if he hadn't made that choice, chances are damn good that Poppy wouldn't be sitting here with us now. Yet, there's that boy, gone."

I swear I saw a look of sadness, or something like it, wash over Father's face, but I couldn't be positive because I didn't really know what sadness looked like on him. Mama was the opposite. Tears sprang into her eyes really quick.

Mr. Parker said we should finish up with my testimony pretty quickly when we went back into court. He warned me that Mr. Wright was most likely going to have some tough questions about Carl pulling me onto the bank and exactly what happened there. This time around, I was dreading going back in there so much I felt sick. I pictured myself jumping up and running away down the hallway, bursting out the doors to the courthouse steps. Maybe I was just so tired of it all. The pressure on me to be the one to decide Carl's guilt was beginning to get to me. In fact, I felt a little bit like crying just sitting there at that table.

I think it was hard for me to separate all the feelings about Ri drowning. I mean, to me, that was the most important thing about the whole mess. Riley died. Died. And now everything seemed to be about everything and everybody else—about me and about Carl and even Sky. What difference did all that talking make? Why should it matter what happened way before Riley died, like fighting and arguing and all that stuff? Why did it matter when I got a hold of his hair—his thick, dark, silky hair—while we washed down the creek? All that mattered was that Carl didn't save his son like he could have, and now Ri was dead. The rest of it all seemed stupid to me. Sitting at that table right then, my insides ached so badly I wanted to scream out. I didn't know what, but something to make all those people remember what this was all about.

"Poppy," Mama was saying, "do you want us to get you a sandwich or something to eat?"

I said I would try to eat a grilled cheese if they could get one and maybe a chocolate milkshake. That made everybody smile, and they all stood and left the room—my parents to get food and Mr. Parker to do some business. I rested my head on my arms I'd crossed on the table, closed my eyes, and let myself float on the quiet. I missed my time being alone by the creek or up in the Indian cave. I so badly wanted to be somewhere where there was no one talking.

We went back into the courtroom and "proceeded," as Judge Hoover said. Mr. Wright strolled back and forth in front of the witness stand a few times, and I couldn't help but notice a dark, greasy stain on his blue tie. I wondered what he ate for lunch. Probably a big, drippy cheeseburger.

"Have a nice lunch break, Poppy?"

"I guess." I was thinking, *don't be nice to me.*

"So, Poppy, when Riley became loosened from his father's grip, what happened next? To you, specifically." He really hadn't looked at me yet.

"I remember that Carl had my hands with both of his, and I think he just drug me to the bank of the creek."

"You *think* you remember it that way." It was a statement, not a question. "So, Carl most likely had to get up on his knees, at least, or maybe he got to his feet and bent down to keep his hold on you. Would that make sense?"

"Yes, I guess it would. He couldn't pull me while he laid on his belly."

"And you could see him above you?"

"No. I don't think so."

"You don't remember?" he asked like I was a moron.

"Not exactly."

"Not exactly?"

I hated when he repeated what I just said. I wasn't going to answer it again.

"Now, you have just told us that you couldn't *remember* two things that happened immediately after Riley floated away. You *think* Carl drug you by both hands from the creek, and you do not even recall *seeing* him above you. That makes me wonder how you can be so sure about what happened just seconds before so clearly. It is hard for us to perceive how, in your panicked state, with filthy, brown water flooding your vision and your instances of memory loss, well, how in the world a young girl like you can be so sure that you saw this father let his own son float away down a raging creek." He whirled around dramatically and pointed to Carl, who didn't look one bit sad or sorry to me.

"I object, Your Honor. Mr. Wright is badgering her. She has answered his questions, and he is using them out of context against her." Mr. Parker's face was turning pink.

Judge Hoover overruled that, if you can believe it, and Mr. Wright looked like he had a mouth full of bees and was looking down his fat nose again.

"So, now, what do you think you remember next, Poppy? After you were on the bank?"

"I remember hearing Sky. I heard her crying, but a loud, scary kind of sound. I looked toward the sound, and I could see her sitting on the creek bank downstream. I tried to get—" Up came Mr. Wright's chubby hand.

"Were you completely aware of everything around you at that time?"

I knew what he was getting at, what he hoped I would say. I wanted to say, "Yes." I wanted to say I saw and knew everything, but that wasn't quite true.

"I knew that Carl stood near where I was lying."

"Did you, at some point, lose consciousness? Sort of pass out?"

"Yes."

"More than once?"

"Yes, a couple of times."

"And what was it that brought you back? Do you remember?"

"Yes. Someone kept calling my name over and over. I figured out that it was Loretta."

"So then, you wouldn't have known if Carl had run after his son as he was floating away, would you? Because you wouldn't have a way to even know how long at a time you were not conscious, right?"

"All I know is that he didn't go after him right away, like he should have. He—"

"That's all, Your Honor. No more questions."

Twenty-Five

Mr. Parker said we had to come back again the next day. My father threw one of his obnoxious fits, but we were too tired to really care, so we just let him go on.

"What the hell? What if I said we can't come another day? What would you do then?"

He sounded so unreasonable, I didn't even want to listen, but we were in that little room, and I had no choice.

"I've already missed two days' work and spent money I don't have on gas for my pickup. What the hell else is there for her to say about anything? All this lawyer crap. Most of it ain't got a single thing to do with that boy drowning."

Which was what I thought.

When he quit ranting, Mr. Parker, who had held his tongue, was pink faced. My father could frustrate a saint.

"Norman, listen to me. This here," he motioned a big sweep with his arm, "this is what going to court is. Decisions have to be made on peoples' statements. On what we and the jury and the judge hear these people say. We can't send a man away to prison because Norman Wade thinks we should. What if you were being blamed for something like this? Wouldn't you want a fair shake in a court of law?"

There was no conversation on our way home. I leaned against Mama and watched the farmland roll by and thought about Nicky and the cave and the creek. The weather was cold, and I could feel the wind gusting against the pickup. Pushing and letting go, pushing and letting go. It seemed like it took a year to get home. Mama fixed a quick supper and made me take a shower before I crawled into bed.

I could hear her and Father talking in low voices about what may happen. The defense could bring back witnesses for more questions, and I wondered who that would be. Maybe Maryanne, since she had already agreed to testify for Carl and had done so in the beginning.

That is exactly what happened. First, Maryanne was called back up by Mr. Wright, and according to Mr. Parker, she would not budge one bit in her testimony. She insisted that, even though Carl could be moody, he was not abusive. Moody! Can you believe that? I can be moody. Carl could be crazy as a mad dog. When Mr. Parker asked her why I might have thought differently and repeated some of the stuff I saw go on, she said that I misunderstood because I didn't know Carl very well. I simply didn't recognize his cantankerousness.

The trial was over by that afternoon. Both sides rested their case. We didn't stay any longer. We went home and waited for Mr. Parker to call us. He said it could be the following Monday before we knew the verdict, anyway.

Mama and my father talked on the way home about what might happen. I could tell Mama was real nervous, and I wondered why. It wasn't until later that night that I figured out why she was so worried.

"It scares me to think that that maniac could be set free," I heard her say. "You never know what men like him might do to someone who would testify against him. My God, Norman, what if he doesn't go to prison?"

I didn't hear my father answer. I don't think he said anything. I felt a shiver of fear that I didn't understand run along my spine.

The next day was full of anticipation, enough to keep my skin goose-bumpy over certain noises or quick movement. There was not a minute that one of us wasn't within hearing distance from the telephone. Once in a while, I would skillfully pick up the receiver without making a sound to see if someone was on the line. I could slide my finger off the button so slow and careful that, if someone was talking, they would never know I was checking. Mama caught me once, but she pretended she didn't see what I was doing.

When the telephone rang late in the afternoon, two longs and one short, I felt like I had been electrocuted. Mama and I stood, staring at the phone.

"Answer the damn thing, for cryin' out loud," Father hollered at us as he strode across the living room in a half-dozen long steps. We both stepped aside and let him pick the receiver up.

"Hello," he barked. "Mr. Parker. Is there a verdict?" I stared at Father's face, his eyes, and the creases near his mouth. I knew. "Crazy damn people. What the hell's the matter with them? Twelve idiots who can't make a right decision. Were they bribed? They were bribed, weren't they? What did they get for a verdict like that? Bastards." He dropped the receiver on the table and pushed me out of his way to get by and slammed out the front door.

I heard Mama say hello in a feeble voice. I could hear the drone of Mr. Parker's voice, and Mama just listened and nodded her head. The color drained from her face until she was a sickly gray.

"Yes, she's right here." She handed the phone to me.

"Poppy? Poppy, you there?" Mr. Parker sounded sad and kind.

"I'm here. Carl isn't guilty, is he." I felt like I weighed a ton and any second I would just go right down through the floor and into nowhere. Just disappear from the room, the world.

"Poppy, you and I know that isn't true. Carl *is* guilty, but we just weren't able to hold up against his family's lies. Don't blame yourself, Poppy. You did a great job, and you told the truth. That is what matters right now. Try to remember that, okay, sweetheart?"

Mr. Parker had never called me a sweet name before. That was probably what made me break down like I did.

"Why? Why would they do that?" I heard myself wailing. "Why wouldn't they believe me?"

Tears poured down my face, and my mouth was so contorted, I couldn't even close it and the drool hung in strings. I felt so weak, I just plopped right down on the floor where poor old Mr. Davis had died.

"Poppy, I want you to hang up now and try to calm down. I will see you here at the office tomorrow afternoon, and we will talk some more, okay?"

I hung up and sat on the floor with my face pressed against my drawn-up knees. I wished I could fold myself up into nothing.

The next afternoon, we drove into town to Mr. Parker's office. Maggie saw us coming and met us at the glass doors. She gave me a quick hug and put her hand on Mama's shoulder as we walked through Mr. Parker's door. We sat in those same old chairs. I must have looked a mess, and I know Mama didn't look good. Our eyes were red rimmed, and my lids were so swollen I was narrow eyed. Of course Father looked the same as he always did. He didn't wear his good clothes to Mr. Parker's office anymore, so he was just in his regular old work clothes and dirty boots. He did, at least, take his sweat-stained hat off and put in on his knee.

Mr. Parker sat down heavily in his chair and scratched at the side of his nose. He folded his hands beneath his chin and looked at us for a long minute.

"I'm sorry this has happened," he said. "We did the best we could. If I thought for half a second that I could get Maryanne or Sky to say anything different about Carl, I would already be preparing the paperwork for another trial. I think you know that isn't going to happen. If they are never going to be truthful, then we have nothing else."

"All those people thought I was a liar. Why?" I just couldn't let it go.

"Because people are basically decent, and they find it hard to believe that someone would—could—harm their own child, much less cause his death. It is easier to pretend such a horrible thing couldn't happen. So, when given the idea that it did not happen on purpose, they cling to that, and it is hard to shake them. They honestly view Riley's death as a terrible accident."

"What now? Carl can do whatever he wants? Even move back into the canyon?" Father asked.

"Yes. He can do anything he wants. In fact, unless he and Maryanne sell that place, he probably will live there, at least for the time being. I don't suppose he has anywhere else to go, and he has no job, unless the tractor place will have him back." Mr. Parker looked at my father. "Norman, I know a little about you, enough to know you have a short fuse when it comes to certain things. I give you a friendly warning to behave yourself and not bring anything on your family you will be sorry for. You know what I mean?"

"I have a right to protect my family, don't I? What do you think our life will be like, living just up the road from a maniac like Carl? We have to go by that place every single day. Ain't nothin' can be done about that."

"Talk to Deputy Jay. Tell him your concerns and maybe he can keep an eye on things for a while. Meanwhile, we will hope Carl moves on."

"Sky said her mama would never live there again. She'll want to sell the place, I'm pretty sure." I remembered that conversation with Sky.

"Ain't nobody going to buy that piece of land," Father said. "They'd have to give it away and be damn lucky if they could do that. It's not worth anything." I knew how my father thought. If a fellow couldn't raise a cow on it, then property was worthless.

Everyone got quiet, and I felt like it was a sort of signal that it was time to leave. Mr. Parker shook hands with my parents, and he held onto mine for a second and gave it a little squeeze. He was a nice man, Mr. Parker was.

Twenty-Six

Christmas came and went without celebration. My parents were fighting again, and Father was drunk almost every night. Between his anger about life in general and Mama's depression, perpetuated by loneliness and a little red wine of her own, it was hard to be excited about Christmas. I already knew there was no Santa Claus. Actually, I had known for two years, but I went along with it so I could get more presents. I was warned in subtle ways that there wasn't going to be much for this Christmas.

"You know, Poppy, as we get older, we learn that Christmas isn't about getting presents," Mama kept saying. She'd say, "Don't expect too much. I don't think Santa will have much room in his sleigh."

By the time Christmas morning came, I didn't much care. The best part about it was that my brothers were there, and we ate supper together. Allen gave me books, and Tim gave me a pocketknife with a pretty pearl handle.

The worst part about Christmas was knowing I had to go back to school after the New Year. Thinking about it made me feel weak. Not weak-minded, but weak in the knees. Dread hung over me like a heavy blanket for two weeks. I tried to think of some way to get out of going back, but I couldn't come up with anything I thought would work. During a moment of desperation, I thought of saying it was because I couldn't bear to go past the mud house every day, and I couldn't stand to see the place where Carl drowned Riley. That is how I thought of it, Carl drowning Riley, because that is what he did. But when it got right down to it, I couldn't use Riley's death to keep me out of school, so I had to let that idea go.

Then, on New Year's Eve, Father came home and gave me a real reason for not wanting to go anywhere. Carl was back. His pickup was there at the gate. My father was reeling with anger, and he hadn't even started drinking yet. I think we had all convinced ourselves that Carl wasn't coming back, and then, there he was. Enough time had gone by since the trial that I had been able to quit thinking, every single day, about his return. On trips to town, I had looked toward the trailer and the mud house—sometimes long looks and sometimes glances, depending on how I was feeling. I saw enough to know that the place had an eerie, abandoned look. I couldn't pinpoint anything that had really changed a lot, but a strange feeling lay above the property, like some invisible cloud.

I had no idea how I was going to cope with Carl being just down the road again. What if I saw him by the bridge? What if our eyes met and I saw the same wild expression I saw the day he threw Sky out of the trailer? I thought about how, when spring weather came, I wouldn't be able to ride Nicky down the road for fear of passing by and seeing Carl. I felt breathless, smothered by his being there.

My father ranted and raved the entire New Year's Day. He drank until his tongue was purple and the whites of his eyes were brilliant red. He staggered against tables and doorways and eventually down the hallway to the bathroom where I could hear him, plain as day, heaving into the toilet. My mother, who had valiantly started out trying to keep up with his refills, glass for glass, had given up early on and gone to bed. It was still only late afternoon.

I pulled my coat on and went out to do the chores. I tossed the horses' hay over the fence to them and added extra because it was New Year's Day. I stood and watched them push and prod one another until they were all in a place that made them happy. I hung there on a fencepost in the cold of the early evening and breathed in the air that smelled like horses and hay and felt myself relax a little. I scattered feed for the few chickens we had that were on their way to roost for the night and fed the cats who stretched and purred around my legs. Goldie trotted along next to me, happy as can be, and I thought how easy life would be if I were a dog.

After I was back at our yard, I couldn't make myself go inside the house. It felt like a dungeon to me, like a prison. There was not a single smidgen of happiness in that house. I sat at the red picnic table in the cold and let the dark settle around me. I wasn't scared or nervous. In fact, I wasn't anything. All I knew was it was better sitting there than being in that dreary house.

Goldie snuggled against me inside my coat, and I sat for so long my backside became numb and my legs were cold to touch. But, I stayed there even longer. An idea was forming in my head, and I wondered why I hadn't thought of it before. It would be so easy on a day like this one. No one would even know until after I was gone for a whole day. Maybe they wouldn't even look for me.

The bus came lumbering to pick me up on the day I had to go back to school. Mr. George was so nice to me and seemed happy to see me. Loretta wasn't at her stop, and I wondered how she had been since she was in court for Mr. Parker that day. It was odd to drive right on by the mud house without hearing the gears shift down so we could stop and pick up Sky. I looked over toward the trailer, practically against my will, but I didn't see Carl. As I faced front, I met Mr. George's gaze in the wide mirror above the big windshield. I saw little crinkles appear at the corners of his eyes, letting me know his lips were smiling.

The mood felt the same as it had the first day of school, only worse. At each stop, the kids who climbed up the steps gave me a quick sideways look and went on down the aisle. No one said "Hi, how you doing?" or anything at all. There was a lot of laughter in the back as the seats filled, and I assumed it was about me. By the time we pulled up in front of school, my jaws ached from clamping my teeth together so hard. The back of my neck and my skull hurt from the tension. I walked to my classroom and stood inside the door for a minute to see if I was supposed to sit in the same desk. The other kids trooped past me, taking their seats, and eventually, my old desk was the only one left. I sat and opened the desktop to deposit the books I'd brought from home.

There was a sheet of paper, folded neatly in half, lying right there. I hesitated to pick it up, and when I finally did, my hand was trembling. I knew, as sure as anything, that whatever was written inside would be something hateful one of the other kids had written about me. I dumped my books and closed the top, holding the paper in one hand. I laid it on top of the desk, careful not to let it unfold, and clasped my hands together on top of it. I looked around to see if anyone appeared to be waiting for me to read it. I caught some glances, but no one was snickering or looking like they were waiting on me to unfold the sheet of paper.

Mrs. Gardner came into the classroom and put some papers down on her desk and took her coat off. When she finally looked up and saw me, she flashed a nice smile at me. She clapped her hands together to get the kid's attention and waited on them to settle down.

"Class, look who is back this morning," she said in a high, happy voice. "Poppy, welcome back. We have missed you. What do you say, class?"

Of course I knew they didn't miss me at all. In fact, I was darn sure they had forgotten who Poppy Wade even was.

They chimed in unison, "Welcome back, Poppy," and I felt my face flush at the attention and the falseness of the welcome. We started the first lesson, and I folded the notepaper a couple more times and slipped it into my coat pocket. I was on guard for the rest of the morning but, except for a couple of looks, no one paid much attention to me. When lunch recess came around, I pulled my coat on and headed for the girls' bathroom.

I was the first inside the concrete and block restroom and hurried into a stall and latched the door. I took the note out of my pocket and sat down on the toilet seat. I just held the paper in my hand for a few minutes, thinking I was preparing myself for whatever mean thing was written inside. I even ventured, for just a moment, to think maybe I was wrong and that there was something nice written inside. Maybe someone wanted to say they knew about what had happened to Riley and were sorry about it happening.

My fingers were cold, and I noticed my nails had thin lines of grime underneath them as I watched them slowly unfold the paper. I saw lines of neat, smooth cursive in dark pencil down in the center of the page. The light in the stall was dim, but I had no trouble reading the words: *We the jury find Poppy Wade guilty of killing off retard Riley Hogan by drowning him in the creek. Since it is not a real crime to kill off retards, we set you free from going to prison. Good move trying to blame his own dad. Ha ha.*

There was one more line, but I was so blinded with rage I couldn't see the writing clearly. I bent over my lap and closed my eyes and tried to breathe. My insides felt like somebody set them on fire. I raised up, held the page up to the light, and read the last line. In a different handwriting, another person had scribbled with an ink pen: *Send Poppy Wade to the gas chamber for murder, ha ha, signed, Perry Mason.*

I sat there on the toilet for the rest of the lunch hour recess. Girls came and went, loud and chattering, slamming stall doors and running water into sinks. The bathroom noise echoed off the block walls, making every sound piercing, and when I placed my hands over my ears, I could hear my heart thumping inside my skull.

I heard the first bell ring, which meant we had ten minutes until we had to be at our desks or get a tardy slip. I knew I wasn't going back into that classroom that day, or maybe ever. I refolded the note and put it in my pocket and stood on legs that had fallen asleep on the edge of the toilet seat. When I was able, I left the bathroom and made my way to the school nurse's office, which was right next to the principal's office. Nurse Ruth looked up as I walked through her door, and she jumped right up from her chair.

"Good land, girl. You look like you saw a ghost. Here, come over here and sit."

Nurse Ruth was a really nice lady who took her job seriously. Before I could sit in the chair she'd pointed to, she had a thermometer in her hand and was shaking the heck out of it. She had the thing under my tongue and was checking my pulse before I had time to say anything.

"Hmm," she said about my pulse. "Let me listen." She stuck her stethoscope in her ears and laid the cold metal disk on my skin inside my shirt. She moved it here and there, pulled the ends from her ears, and said, "When did you start feeling so bad?"

"Just a little while ago, during recess."

"Hmm. Do you feel sick at your stomach, like you might vomit? Does your head hurt?"

"A little bit."

"Which?"

"Both." It was true.

"Hmm."

She made me lie on the cot in the corner of the room. It had a cold, stiff sheet on it and a scratchy blanket. The pillow was hard and held my head up way too high. She sat me up and punched the fluff out of it a couple of times, but it didn't help much. My right hand stayed in my coat pocket and held onto the notepaper that was, by then, scrunched into a ball. Nurse Ruth said to stay still, and she bustled out of the door to go to the principal's office.

I lay there and closed my eyes, and all I could see were the words in the note that I gripped in my hand. I guess it was the last straw, as they say. I knew I was finished with everybody. It wouldn't matter much, anyway. I didn't have friends and, even if they were my parents, my father and Mama weren't any help to me at all. I had Goldie and Nicky, and that was about it. I didn't even care what happened to me. Nurse Ruth came back in. She said my father would pick me up in about an hour or so, and I should just rest. I just said, "Okay," and that was that.

Twenty-Seven

At three o'clock, the last bell of the day rang, and Nurse Ruth walked me out in front of the school and clucked around me like a mother hen until my father pulled up to the curb. He didn't get out, just leaned across and shoved the door open. Nurse Ruth took a step back from the cloud of cigarette smoke that came billowing at us, and I climbed onto the seat.

"She's feeling pretty puny, Mr. Wade. I'd keep an eye on her. Mrs. Gardner knows she may stay home tomorrow." She closed the door and gave me a wiggly-fingers wave.

"What's the matter?" Father said as we drove away.

"I don't know. I just got sick."

"You can't play sick to stay outta school, Poppy. You're back half a day and this crap happens. I don't know about that." I knew he thought I was lying, and I didn't care one bit. Not one single bit. I didn't even care when he reached under the seat and drug out his wine bottle in the crinkled-up paper sack. He unscrewed the cap and took a few deep swallows and screwed it back on, wiped his sleeve across his mouth, and lit up a cigarette. I opened my wind wing and pushed it all the way out. Inside, I was silently daring him to tell me to close the window, but he didn't say that.

Instead, he said, "What do you think your mother is going to say about this?"

I shrugged. "Don't know." I said it with a little sass.

"Don't get smart, you hear me?"

I looked square at him and didn't say a word. He looked back but turned away to watch the road. He dragged the bottle out two more times before we were home.

Mama hurried out onto the porch when we drove up. She looked surprised to see my father was home so early in the day, and when she saw me, her eyes grew wide, and she hurried down the porch step.

"What's going on?" she called before we even got to the yard gate.

"Ah, she says she's sick."

Mama gave me that narrowed look she used when she's second-guessing. "You sick, Poppy?"

"Yes, ma'am. I been feeling sick since lunchtime." It was the truth.

"What's the matter with you? Stomachache, headache?"

"Yeah." My voice sounded pitiful, even to myself.

"Which?"

"Both."

"Well, get on into bed. I'll get the Pepto."

I saw her look at my father with a question. I knew she didn't really believe me, either. I still didn't care. I planned to just go ahead and play it all the way. I didn't feel wrong for doing it, either.

In my room, I took the wadded-up note out of my pocket and put it under my socks in one of the deep dresser drawers. I flopped on my bed and stared up at the ceiling until Mama came in with the medicine and a soupspoon. I went ahead and took it, even though my insides weren't feeling as bad as they did earlier. In fact, I felt kind of like I didn't have any insides much.

Nobody woke me for school the next morning, and that made me wonder what was going on. I thought I would have to fight the devil to stay home. In fact, I thought I might have to fight every morning for years to stay home from school. What else could I do? I wasn't going back there again. They could do whatever they wanted, is how I felt.

Put me in a foster home, take my parents off to jail, I wasn't going to school anymore.

It didn't matter how much I decided not to care about anything anymore, I still got hungry. After my father went to work, I sneaked out to the kitchen and poured a bowl of cereal. I was headed back into my room when I heard Mama.

"Poppy, what are you doing?"

"I got some cereal."

"Come in to the table with it. I want to talk to you." She poured herself a cup of coffee, and we sat.

I stirred my cereal around in the milk and watched the flakes go limp. I felt myself tensing up, getting ready for what was to come. I never looked up.

"Poppy, I don't know what to do." She huffed out an exasperated breath. "I know you've had a real bad time, but you have to get over this behavior. You're not grown up, you know. You're only ten years old. There are certain things ten-year-olds have to do. I told you before, you have to go to school. It's time you started to learn how to behave like a young lady. You can't keep acting like a wild Indian." She sipped her coffee and lit a cigarette.

"I'm not going back to school." I kept stirring my soggy cereal.

"Yes, you are. You know what happens if you don't. We've said all this before."

"I don't care. I'm not going."

"Why, Poppy? Why do you hate it so bad? What can be so hard about going to school in the third grade?" Another sip and a deep drag off her smoke.

"Because I'm different. I am not like the rest of those kids, and they don't like me, and I don't like them. I'm not going."

"Why do you think you are so different from any other ten-year-old girl?"

I just couldn't believe she had to ask me that question. How could she not see that for herself? Because she never paid any attention, that's why. I was getting mad again, and I couldn't hold back my words.

"Mama, I've always been different. I don't like people. They're mean, and they say things that hurt each other. They're mean to me. They laugh if they don't think I notice. They say how dirty I am and that I lie. The only real friend I ever had was Sky, and now I don't even have her. She even turned against me." I think I saw Mama wince a little bit, and I thought, *good, you're hearing the truth now.*

"What if you tried to change some of those things? What if you paid more attention to your own care and did your hair nice and wore clothes that went together? What if you were nicer to those kids, Poppy, so nice they would feel like they should try being nice back? Do you think that would help make a difference?" She said all that fast, and it sort of ran together.

"No. Kids aren't like that. It wouldn't matter, Mama. They'd still treat me the same, only maybe worse because then I'd be acting like a baby. 'Oh, like me . . . please, please like me. Look, I curled my hair.' I'm not going to do that, Mama. I'm just not."

"You know what can happen to your father and me if you don't go to school."

"Well, you said they could put you in jail."

"And you don't care if that happens?"

I didn't answer her.

"Poppy, you mean to tell me you wouldn't care if your own parents went to jail just because you didn't feel like going to school?"

I stood up and put my bowl of sloppy cereal on the counter next to the sink. I turned and looked at Mama, and I felt a tiny bit sad, but not as much as I would have in the past. Before everything.

"I can't go back there," I said and went to get dressed so I could go outside.

I started prowling again. The minute the weather was decent, I was out of the door as soon as I could be each morning. For a while, Mama tried to stop me. She hollered and threatened, said things about how I was making her go crazy, and if she did, I better remember it was my fault. One time she even stood in front of the door so I couldn't get out. I wasn't dim-witted. I knew she couldn't stand there all day, so I just sat on the end of the couch and waited.

My father gave up on me right away. He worked and drank and picked at Mama, like he always had. He ignored me like I was a ghost, and I didn't care. Being invisible made life easier. I would dream up ideas about leaving, but I didn't have any money except what was in my piggy bank, and I never could think of where I would go. And there was Goldie. How could I take Goldie?

I knew the school was calling Mama all the time, and I would hear her trying to explain that our family was having some trouble and that she would see that I was back in school soon as things got straightened out. I don't know if they believed that, whomever she talked to, but I guess that held them off a few days at a time. I was sorry, in a way, that she had to deal with that, but not sorry enough to go back to school.

I still hung out with the horses and clung to Nicky's warmth if it was cold out, letting her blow her breath on me to warm me up. She loved me back. She quit running off and instead nickered for attention when she saw me. She would meet me and turn her itchiest part to me for a scratch. Sometimes it was an ear and other times it was her big, round rump. I still sat on her back when she was dry. I'd have horsehair stuck to the butt and legs of my pants from her thick winter coat.

The creek was still the biggest part of my life, though. It ran steadily, rising up to its muddy torrent when it rained a lot and dropping to a sweet, giggling stream when the rain stopped. It became a familiar friend. I hiked way up into the canyon and was astonished to find that it was actually two creeks that came together below a big culvert that brought one of the streams under the canyon road. The spot was so wild and perfect in that place, where the trees and brush made a little room as the streams joined.

I found I could bend low and make my way over to a rock, where I could sit right above the water. It reminded me of the big rock Sky and I sat on at the mud house. The creek fell over the tree roots, and there was nothing I liked more than the sight and sound of those baby waterfalls. Oh, except maybe me and Mama's spring tubs. I went there all the time. I couldn't actually go sit by one because the creek was running over them, but I would sit on the bank and wonder if I would be there when summer came. I wondered if my mama would ever walk there with me again, sit by the clear water, and eat honey sandwiches, but I doubted it.

The times I followed the creek downstream, I only went as far as the end of the horse pasture, where it flowed under the short bridge and onto land belonging to Loretta's family. There, it skirted along the foot of a steep tree and brush-covered hill in such a way that placed the canyon road and a meadow between it and the hill Loretta's house sat on.

On a sunny day, one warmer than most had been, I decided to go onto their property and on down the creek. Sneaking was easy with all the sycamore and oak trees that grew along there to hide myself in.

Twenty-Eight

Now, as I tell this, I think I knew the whole time what I was doing. Each time I wandered downstream, I went a little bit farther. I would make up goals—like the sharp bend in the creek or where the sycamore limb hung down to the ground or a certain curve in the road—and those goals became a challenge. Not once did I say to myself: *Today I will go to the willows by the mud house or the bridge that Carl built.* But I knew, deep down, that was where I was headed.

Each time I drew closer to the place of my best and worst memories, I would become more eager to go farther. My heart would pound hard, and I didn't know if it was because I was scared or because I was going to get a look at the whole story close up. Twice I chickened out and turned back, and when I did, I felt so sad, as if I'd lost something there again.

The perfect thing that could have happened was to get as far as the willows and see that Carl wasn't home—see that his old, junky pickup wasn't sitting by the crossing where he always left it. Then I could get a look at the place, maybe even sit on the rock for just a minute or two. I could take some time to remember how Sky and I sat there in the sun and shared things we would never, ever share with anybody else. That's what I thought then.

It only took a week or two of thinking about it until I became obsessed with the idea.

Mama asked me one day if I'd been going down by Sky's house. That's what she called it. Sky's house. I lied and said, "No. No way would I want to do that." Lying came easy by then. I'd learned to say whatever I thought Mama and my father would want to hear. I doubt that they always believed me, but it made things easier for all of us if they pretended they did.

I knew that the school was really on Mama about me not showing up. They had warned her that they were going to send a welfare worker out. Mama told me that, and I just said, "That's okay. Once they see me, they'll know why I'm not going."

The first time I walked as far as the willows, I got down and crawled along the creek bank like a blue-bellied lizard, being careful not to shake the limber branches. My heart was beating so loudly in my ears, I was sure, if I got too close and Carl was outside, he would be able to hear it, too. I would wiggle along a foot or two and then lie still and try to hear over my heart. When I saw him bent over his brick-making form, I swear I almost yelped because of the startling jolt that ran through my body. If I'd been a turtle, I would have jerked myself into my shell so fast. I watched him then. Watched him using his shovel to push that mud down into the forms and smooth off the top. I can't explain it right, but I think I felt willful and fearless, watching him without him even knowing I was there. I stayed a long time that first day I saw him. Then I came up with another idea.

It came to me that night. If I could climb up on the clay cliff, I would be able to look down on most of the property and see everything. I would be able to see the trailer and the rock and the bridge . . . all of it. I didn't sleep the rest of that night, I became so excited, thinking about being up high and looking down on Carl. Or maybe he wouldn't even be there, and I could scoot down somehow and get to walk around the tree where I'd tied Nicky and where I'd first met Riley. I had the plan all worked out in my head, and I lived the scene over and over.

It was easy as pie. A deer trail led me right up the back side of the hill that the clay cliff dropped off from. I could move up that trail like a deer, and I never made a speck of noise. I swear, sometimes I thought I really was an animal, something quiet and quick like a deer or a cat. Anyway, I walked near the rim where I could look over and see the canyon road, and as I went closer to the edge of the cliff, I could see more and more of the property. I saw Carl, and I dropped down so fast and landed so hard on my stomach, I felt my breath leave. If he had looked up, he would have seen me, clear as day. I was learning things all the time about hiding out and spying. Maybe all that pretending I had done in the summer helped me become better at sneaking around. It wasn't so different than pretending to be an Indian creeping up on the cowboys.

My big idea to get to be right down there and sit on the rock or walk across the bridge was beginning to weaken as I became more interested in spying on Carl. I can't tell you why that became so important. I guess it was just because I could do it and get away with it, but it felt like more than that. I felt like I had some sort of power over him. I watched him go about his business and pretended I could control what he did. *Shovel more sand in the wheelbarrow, Carl. Now pack it down tighter. Now shovel more.* I knew he would be furious if he knew I watched him.

I quickly became bored and antsy if it was too cold or stormy for me to go down the creek. I was stuck in the house all day with nothing to do, same as Mama. She was so lonely on those dreary days that she even spent some time talking with me, if she didn't go off into her room. She watched two soap operas on the snowy TV screen each day, so I would sit and watch with her. She could tell me all about the characters on the program and what they did way back when, who cheated, and who lied. I could see how it was fun to get to know those people in the stories. They all lived in beautiful houses, and there were never any homely ladies. I think Mama wished she was one of them. I couldn't blame her for that.

Once in a blue moon, she would get a phone call from an old friend in the valley who she hadn't seen in a long while. They'd gossip a little and talk about her friend's kids and me. She always said, "Oh yeah, Poppy's doing just fine." She never told anyone I wasn't even going to school. I knew she would be embarrassed if they found out that I was staying home. If I let my guard down the least bit, I would feel sorry for Mama, being stuck with a kid like me.

Not much ever changed for my father. He just kept doing the same old things he always did. If he got rained out at work, he drove into town anyway and got the mail and a newspaper and a bottle of wine. He'd come home and drive around our place and look at his cows. Sometimes Mama would go with him, but I never did anymore. It was just hard to be around him, knowing he'd be mad at me about something before we got back to the house. All the kindness seemed to have been used up during the trial. His aloofness didn't happen all of a sudden like. He just changed a little, day by day, until he didn't seem to care much about me anymore.

We had lived there a few months short of a year, and I already felt like we were all different people than who we were on the day we first drove up the canyon road. It seemed like we had lived there for a hundred years.

Twenty-Nine

I'd climbed up the cliff hill exactly four times, so by the time the fifth hike up there came around, I was completely at ease with making my way up and down the steep trail. After reaching the hilltop, I would button my coat around me and lie right down on the weedy ground and wiggle my way over to the edge on my belly, like an army man in battle, and I'd stay for a long time. Carl looked small and less of an evil man down there and wasn't the least bit frightening from my viewpoint.

He'd done the same things every time I had been up there, usually mixing the adobe to make the bricks, digging the clay out of the cliff beneath me. It was noisy business—the pick striking the rock-solid soil of the cliff wall and the clanking of his tools and wheelbarrow. Sometimes he'd walk over to the willows for a bit and sit on an upturned bucket to rest. I saw that he was smoking, lighting up from a bright-red package of cigarettes using a shining silver lighter. The only time I became uneasy was when he sat and rested, doing nothing, because then it would be so quiet I knew, if I made one sound, he would hear me up above him. Seeing him sitting so still made me think of a hawk or an eagle, with his sharp face and small, dark eyes, and I imagined he would possess keen hearing like they did. It was crazy, I guess, but I began to feel thrilled at the excitement of taking that chance of him finding me out.

But on the day of my fifth time up the hill, I reached the top and Carl wasn't anywhere to be seen. I was darn disappointed, but I knew he must be inside the trailer because his old truck was parked in its regular place, so I decided I would wait a while and see if he came out. I must have been there about an hour, and my clothes were feeling clammy from me lying on the damp ground, and my arms ached because of the position they were in, folded under my chin. Besides, the excitement of spying on him was beginning to fade after waiting such a long time. I decided maybe he was resting or eating or maybe he was sick and couldn't come out.

Calling it quits, I found I needed to stand up and get my blood flowing again. I did a backward crab walk that I'd learned would get me out of sight before I stood up. Before I could get my legs under me, I felt a firm blow to my back between my shoulder blades, and I flailed forward, falling to my hands and knees. I felt the sting of the scrapes on my palms, and I struggled to get on my feet, fell again in my panic, and finally scrambled up. Whirling around, I came face-to-face with Carl.

Boy, I wish I could tell you that, when I saw that it was him, I wasn't a bit scared, but that would be a lie for sure because I knew I was in big trouble, and I was so scared I couldn't think, and my whole body began to tremble. We stood still, looking at each other. He wore that stone face of his and held the handle of his shovel in his right hand, with the spade end resting on its tip against the hard ground. He leaned on it, all at ease.

My instinct was to take off running down the deer trail, but it was plain to see that I couldn't get past Carl to get to the trailhead. He knew what I was thinking, anyway, which made his mouth turn up at the corners—not a smile but an *I dare you to try it* look.

"What are you doing up here, Poppy Wade?" That's all he said.

"Nothing."

I was so tense that, when I shook my head from side to side, it sort of twitched around on its own. In fact, my whole body had a funny, herky-jerky feeling.

"Nothing?" Big question. Big eyes. "I think you've been spying on me. You've been up here before. Don't lie to me because I know you were. You thought you were sneakin', but I saw you every time. What was it you thought you would see, Poppy?"

I honestly didn't know what to answer because I didn't have any notion about what I wanted to see. I don't know to this day what I could ever see Carl doing that would be important to me. What I'd been doing had been about the scheme of watching him when he didn't know that I was. That was the power of it all. That was what gave me that feeling of outsmarting him.

So I said, "I don't know," because I didn't.

"Maybe you wanted to see what I looked like after I lost everything. See if I looked sick or lonely. Did I disappoint you? Did you want to see me all broken down, crying and carrying on since my boy was dead and my wife and little girl left me?" He smiled a big pretend smile, and his eyebrows raised way up. "Or, hey, maybe you thought your old friends, Sky and Maryanne, might be back, and you could drop by on your nag and say hello."

"No, that's not true."

"No? Well then you tell me why I found you up here watching me."

"I honestly don't know." I was thinking, *Why? Why was I?* "I was trying to get back at you." I knew that sounded more like a question than I meant for it to. "Watching you in secret made me feel like I was getting back at you. It was a way to pay you back for what you did."

"Oh yes, you're talking about Riley now. What I did to poor, dim Riley. He wasn't made for this world, Poppy. That accident down there," he nodded in the direction of the creek, "that was pure luck for Riley."

I was shocked at how Carl was talking. It made me sick. "How can you say that about him? Your own boy?"

"He wasn't mine. He was always Maryanne's and Sky's. They pampered him, made him spoiled and more helpless than he ever should have been. Wouldn't let me teach him anything. Said I was mean to him." Carl looked away for a moment, and his eyes went flat and cold.

"I wanted him to be a man, and they made him a sissy. When we found out he wouldn't ever be normal, I told them girls that they better not spoil him. That, for his own sake, they better teach him how to live his life. Naw, they were never going to do that." He shook his head.

"You could have sent him away if you didn't want him. There are places for kids like Riley. You didn't have to let him die." My voice shook, and I couldn't stop it.

"You know what those places are like? No, you don't or you wouldn't say that. They're prisons. Stinking, dirty places where kids pee themselves and live in it for days, and where they eat slop and sleep cold. So, do you think he's better off where he is now or a place like that?" Carl's face was beginning to show more expression. He was working himself up to being real mad. "You didn't know nothing about us, me and Riley."

I must have looked shocked, my mouth dropping open. "You killed him. I saw you, Carl. I don't care what you say."

I was foolish for talking back. He was practically spitting hate at me. I still wanted to run, but I knew I couldn't get by him with that shovel in his hands, so I just kept trying to think of something to say. More than once, I almost broke down and cried for Mama.

"Didn't pay to be such a little smarty pants, did it, missy. A jury found me innocent of killing my own boy. Guess they didn't believe the story you told."

Carl was smirking. That same cocky look I had seen on him when he was cruel to Maryanne or Ri. He shifted his hold on his shovel so that he held it across his body with both hands. As he talked, I had begun to inch to my left, thinking maybe I could get a chance to run for it. He may have known that was my idea, and that was why he held the shovel ready to thrust in front of me if I ran. Or he would hit me with it.

"Let me go home now, Carl. I won't bother you anymore, I promise. I don't even know why I came up here. I don't. Please, just let me go home." I heard the begging in my shaky voice.

"Why? So you can run home and tell your drunkard daddy about this here happening? What's he going to do about it?" He lifted the shovel slightly to indicate what he meant was happening. "Or your mama, you could run and tell her, I guess."

"I won't tell anybody. I promise."

Carl took two steps toward me, and I backed up from him automatically.

"Watch out, now. Remember there's a big old cliff back there."

I glanced back to see how far away it was to the edge. God, I was so close.

Looking back, I would say that this is about the time Carl began to lose his mind. I mean, he went off the deep end and started talking about going to court and how I lied to the whole world. He said he wasn't going to have people *judge him* because he had a retarded son. I think that was when I knew what Carl was all about.

What had happened, all of it, didn't have much to do with anybody else. It was about Carl the entire time. He couldn't stand having a retarded son and a wife and daughter who ruled his life—treating Riley like a baby, never letting Carl make him a man. He was ashamed of Riley, embarrassed that he had a retarded kid.

"Maryanne was laid up sick in bed in that trailer down there." He motioned into the air with the tip of the shovel blade. "She kept calling me in and calling me in, asking me about Riley. Was he okay? What was he doing? Did he get something to eat? Just one thing after another. I finally told her to just shut her mouth up about it. She started in cryin' and hollering, like she always did when we fought about Riley."

Carl was talking faster and faster and louder, as if he was angry at Maryanne all over again.

"He threw one of his fits and fell down on the floor crying. I couldn't understand him, blubbering like he was. Maryanne, she got up, weak as a kitten with her ailment, and came to see about him. I wondered right then what would happen if she ever passed on and left me to take care of both them kids." Carl was looking toward me, but I don't think he was seeing me. He was seeing what happened in the trailer that day.

"They were driving me crazy. All that racket going on in that little trailer. Cryin' and hollerin.'" One hand came off the shovel, and Carl ran his fingers into his hair, pulling it up hard. "Then Riley, he gets up and gets the door open and falls down the steps and hollers even louder. I'm putting my hands on my ears, sayin' to shut up. Maryanne tried to get by me, and I shoved her hard. I did. She hit her head on the edge of the table, and I knew it was pretty bad 'cuz it started bleedin' right away, and she didn't even try to get back up. By the time I got out the door, Riley was to the edge of the creek."

Carl stopped talking, and the silence of the hill and the canyon below was so clear and clean.

Carl found me in his focus again, and his eyes burned a hole into mine.

"I took off down there to get Riley, and that is exactly what I meant to do. I ran, hollerin' at him to keep him away from the creek, but I was too late. Even after he threw himself in the water, I still thought I could get him out. And you, young lady," he pointed at me with a forefinger, "you just jumped right in there, and for just a second I thought, look at that girl. She's braver than me.

"I trotted along the creek bank, seein' the two of you bein' drug under and banged around on the rocks, and every time I could see Riley's face, he was white as a sheet. I thought, that's how he'll look when he dies. White as paper."

Carl's voice had gone deep and calm. His emotion would kind of die out until he would focus on me again, and he'd get that nasty snarl across his mouth. I was still trying to think of a way to get away, but as he talked, I watched his sinewy hands spin that shovel handle around and around, holding it crosswise in front of him. I started wondering if it would be worth taking a chance to run for it. Just do it. Maybe he wouldn't reach me with the shovel, or maybe he wouldn't be fast enough. Anything could happen, and just maybe I could make it down the trail.

I saw a tiny glint of light in Carl's flat-eyed look. His voice perked up. He was saying, "Then I thought about how, if Riley didn't make it out of the creek alive, I wouldn't end up an old man taking care of a slobberin' dim-wit. My problem would be solved, and it wouldn't be nobody's fault but his own. It all seemed so simple and purely the right thing to happen." He seemed to be beaming with pride at having thought of the idea, as if it was the first time. His eyes were practically throwing sparks. He looked wild and crazy-like. But those eyes found me again and bore in.

"You. You almost ruined it all. Thought you were so smart and everybody would believe whatever you said."

"I told the truth, Carl. You knew it was the truth. What did you expect me to do?"

"I expected you should mind your own business. I knew you couldn't. You had been into our business since the first time you came here. You didn't like the looks of how things were around here, and you got Sky all riled about it." He stopped to spit into the dirt between us, and I stared down at the foamy wet spot. "She was a pain in the ass after she got mixed up with you. Mouthy, like her mama, and hard to deal with."

It was time. It was time. I had to at least try because he was getting madder by the minute. I had been standing with my arms tight across my body, and when I dropped them by my side, that was Carl's first signal that I was going to do something. I bolted to my left and dug in to run past him. Carl couldn't get into position to swing the shovel at me, so he jammed it toward me like a spear. The nose of the shovel hit me at my hip, and the pain jolted through me. I fell hard, skidding in the dirt on hands and knees. It seemed like it took forever to get back up, and I kept expecting to get hit again, which I did, but this time Carl struck me from the front. The back of the shovel landed smack into my stomach. He yelled something at me, but I couldn't understand what he said. I went down again, gasping to get my breath. I was crying hard by then, I know that, and I think Carl was laughing. He let me stand up, and he put the nose of the shovel in my stomach and started pushing me backward, jabbing it into my ribs.

I knew it wasn't far to the edge, and I was taking baby steps, sliding the soles of my boots in the dirt. I could hear myself making sobbing sounds. Every couple of steps, Carl would say something I couldn't hear or understand over the roar in my head, and then he would laugh. I knew the edge of the cliff was too close, and I remember, clear as day, how it felt—taking that last step backward and there was nothing there. With only one boot on solid ground, I pushed my body forward and wrapped my fingers around the shovel. Fear crawled right up my backbone, and I sucked in a great gulp of air. My hands gripped that blade hard, and I held on for dear life.

If Carl had let go of the shovel handle, everything would have ended differently. I would have gone backward over that cliff, and maybe nobody would have ever known what happened up there on that hill. I'd probably be dead, and he would be living there in his adobe house. But he didn't let go, so as I fell to my knees, gripping that shovel blade, pulling it into my belly, he lost his balance. His body twisted to the right, and down he went, shoulder first, losing his own hold on the shovel's handle. The last thing I saw of him was his boots. Carl tumbled over the clay cliff headfirst.

I lay there on the cliff's edge with my boots extended out into midair. I was terrified to try to move. I'd sprawled, face down in the dirt, as Carl tumbled away. My jaws were in pain, and I had grit in my mouth. I could taste blood from my tongue or lips. My face lay in the dirt, and my fingers were dug into that hard ground like claws. Using the strength of my forearms, I wiggled my body forward inches at a time until I felt that my boot toes had reached solid ground. I rested for a while, I don't know how long, before I attempted to rise. I was trembling so violently, all I could do was push myself to my knees. I had awful pain in my chest and stomach, and my right side ached all down my ribs. I couldn't find the strength to get up, so I let myself back down on the ground.

Everything had all happened so fast, I wasn't able to make sense of it. That I had not fallen off the cliff seemed so amazing to me, my mind couldn't grasp reality. I kept thinking how irrational Carl had been. Mean crazy.

I managed to get to my hands and knees and crawled a ways toward the trail. My fingers were in horrible pain, and I took a closer look and saw that my fingernails had pulled away from my fingertips when I'd dug them into the dirt to keep from going over the cliff. I could see the dirt and blood packed underneath them. I swear, they hurt worse than any other part of my body right then. I couldn't even look at them after that. After I crawled on my bloody skinned hands and knees across the roughness of the ground to the trailhead, I lay flat out with my cheek in the dry dirt and rested for a long time.

Thirty

As my pounding heart had calmed down, my hearing had become sharp and clear in a way that I had never experienced before. The scolding of a blue jay was piercing. I was listening for any sound that could mean Carl was still after me. I pictured him landing in a sprawl, body thudding and hard-angled arms and legs flung out at the bottom of the clay cliff.

I don't recall deciding how to go about it, but the way I chose to get down that trail was by sliding on my butt. I used my boot heels and the palms of my hands to scoot myself along. Thank the Lord it was a steep downhill trail or I wouldn't have made the distance. After a while, the ends of my fingers began to go numb, and that helped to ease the pain. I had a place in my side that felt like the bones were grinding together, and I would gasp once in a while if I moved just wrong.

I heard a car going by out on the canyon road, and I started crying hard again. It was so frustrating to think someone was that close and didn't know I was right there. Realizing help could be that near gave me the gumption, though. I knew I *had* to get down the hill and close enough to the road so that, if someone passed by, maybe they could see me.

I was more than halfway down the trail when I heard a noise and saw the tops of the bushes quiver farther down the trail. I froze.

Couldn't move a muscle. I knew it was Carl coming to get me, and I couldn't escape this time. I was too hurt, and there was no place for me to go. I don't know how long I held my breath, but it could have been longer than any human being ever had without dying. I didn't want to see him come around the curve of the trail, but I couldn't tear my eyes away. Next thing I knew, I was looking into the liquid eyes of a doe. We stared at each other for a long time until she turned and bounded down the trail. I was so relieved, I wanted to giggle. In fact, I felt a strange, giddy laughter trying to reach up into my throat, and I had to swallow it down.

Once I'd managed to get to the bottom of the trail, I felt a shot of relief for a moment before I realized I had another decision to make. If I knew anything, it was that I didn't want to pass too near Carl to get to the road. If he was by the clay cliff, I wanted to stay as far away as I could.

At last, I managed to stand and was able to take a few steps before my ribs hurt so bad I went to my knees again. I made an attempt at crawling, and that was much easier since the pain in my hands and knees had numbed. So that's what I did—crawled and rested and crawled some more and rested again. It seemed to take an awfully long time, but I made my way past the place where the adobe frames were stacked and then behind the trailer, getting closer and closer to where Carl should be. I stared in that direction while I crawled along, watching for any sign of him, any movement or sound. The land began its gentle downward slope toward the creek, and that helped my pace go faster, easier. By that time, I couldn't feel my palms anymore, so I didn't have to think about pain in my hands at all. It was my sides and my hip that hurt so bad I had to grit my teeth sometimes so I wouldn't holler or start bawling again.

I reached the exact spot where I could look to my left and see where Carl should have landed when he fell. As I looked, he sat straight up from the ground. Just like that, rose up and sat there. I screamed bloody murder. He looked like a monster. His head was split open from his right eye, across his forehead, and over his skull. He was gruesome and blood-washed, and his eye looked like it could pop out of its socket. I didn't know if he could see out of his other eye or not, but he made some deep, throaty sounds, as if he was trying to talk.

I couldn't quit staring in his direction. I swear, my whole body was waiting to see what would happen next. I think I expected him to spring up and lumber toward me with his arms out. That's when I saw that one of his wheelbarrows lay on its side with most of the clay dirt dumped out of it. I knew then that Carl had landed on the edge of that wheelbarrow and split his head open. He had struck the rim of it hard enough to overturn the heavy load.

I did cry more then and kept heading for the bridge. I prayed, too. "Please God, don't let Carl get me." I kept saying the little prayer over and over. Each time I had to stop moving to catch my breath, I could hear him making odd grunting sounds, but I didn't look at him anymore. When I got to the step where I could crawl up onto the bridge, I wanted water so much I could hardly stand it. I thought how good it would feel to lie down on my belly and put my face in the creek water and drink and drink. The desire became so strong, I chose that direction in my dull mind, but that spine-prickling terror of having Carl behind me drove me right up onto the bridge. That was when I decided that I would keep going as long as I could, instead of waiting on the bridge for a car to come. If I could reach the canyon road, I wouldn't have to worry about somebody driving past without seeing me.

I reached the gatepost and realized that was as far as I could go. I wouldn't be going any farther, Carl or no Carl. I leaned my back against the broad post and closed my eyes. By then, I was feeling little pain. Most of all, I felt that I could sleep for days leaning against the gatepost. I thought I was dreaming when I heard the sound of a car's engine swim through my heavy brain.

As the sound of the car came close, I realized it wasn't a dream at all, and my eyes flew open. I saw the front of the car with its big, grinning grill come around the curve, and it rattled right past me, raising dust and chucking gravel at me. I thought I might die from disappointment; the feeling was so intense it made my heart ache in my chest, and a heavy sadness crushed me into the ground.

But, nope, I heard it slow down, and I heard a women scream something, and next thing I knew, there was Loretta, looking at me with moon-pie eyes. She kept saying, "Oh my God, oh my God," and I didn't say a word. But then Mr. Jamison—Ward—ran up, and he was so nice and kind. He sat down right next to me and started to hold my hand until he saw my fingers had been bleeding, so he just laid my grimy, bloody hand in his big, clean palm all careful, like it was a baby bird or something. He told Loretta to run and tell her mama to go call my folks.

I told him that Carl was over by the cliff and hurt really bad. I watched him squint across the creek for a while. Then he said not to worry about that. They would check on him after I was seen to. He asked me questions, like how long had I been there and, you know, how did I get hurt so bad. I remember thinking it was too much to say right then, and I couldn't get my mind organized so that I could tell Ward how things happened. I closed my eyes.

Father and Mama came in a short time, as I remember. Mama cried and cried and sat down by me in the dirt. I think my father was more concerned right away about how bad I was hurt. He squatted there by Mama and asked me to move my arms and my legs. I did, and he said he didn't believe anything was broken.

I was exhausted, I s'pose because I felt safe and started to relax. I also hurt again. My hip was killing me. Mama seemed more concerned about my hands, but I know it was because they looked as if someone whacked them with a hammer. She looked so sad and so scared that I began to feel awful about everything. I knew that none of it would have happened if I hadn't gone spying on Carl. Her worry was my fault. I started saying over and over that I was so sorry. So sorry.

They picked me up and took me home. Mama and Janelle and Loretta helped me undress and sat me on my bed and looked at all my bruises and places that hurt.

Loretta was quiet, but Janelle, she was beside herself. She said we needed to go to the hospital, and she would drive us there. My father had called the sheriff's office and headed back down the road to see what to do about Carl. Mama said yes, we would go in to the doctor, but she wanted to wait for my father to come back first.

She went to the kitchen and filled her big soup pot with warm water and started washing me off with a soft cloth so we could get a look at what was under all the dirt and dried blood. We could see the bright-red outline of where Carl had hit me in my hip with the shovel, and the skin around the mark was already dark blue. My knees were skinned up and had dirt and pebbles stuck in the wounds and stung like a batch of bee stings whenever Mama tried to wash them off. I screeched like an owl if she touched my fingers. God, they looked so grisly. It took a long time but, little by little, I lowered my hands down in that warm water and let them soak a bit. Mama put a towel across my lap, and in a while, I just laid my hands there and let them dry by themselves. Janelle or Loretta, one of them, said they looked better when they were covered with dirt, and we tried to laugh a little.

They pulled a nightgown over my head and didn't even make me get dressed. Father came back home, and he and Mama helped me out of the house and into the pickup, and we headed into town.

I came right out and asked if Carl was dead, and my father said we would find out how he was when we passed by the place. Said Deputy Jay was there when he left to come get me. On our way to the hospital, I saw that Ward was still there, and he and Deputy Jay were standing by the bridge. They were kicking their boots around in the dirt there, looking down and just talking. I knew that Carl was dead or they would be with him. I was glad.

Thirty-One

Dr. Morse took care of me again. He had a different nurse than the one who had been there after Riley drowned, and this one wasn't so nice. She frowned and pursed her lips and kept poking around on all my sore places longer than I felt she needed to. She put my hands in a plastic bowl of green, sudsy water, and I yowled like a tomcat. Didn't bother her none at all.

The doctor was so kind to me, just as he was before. He sent me for x-rays and found I had three cracked ribs and my hip was bruised clear into the bone. He and the nurse wrapped my middle up with a bandage that was so tight it was squeezing me, but it made my side feel better. They dabbed ointment on my fingers and palms and wrapped my hands in gauze. I could use my thumbs and the tips of my first two fingers like crab claws, so at least I would be able to pick up things, feed myself. All I wanted to do when we got home was sleep. I did, for a long time.

Life changed all around again. Because I had to have help to do everyday things, I lost the stubborn independence I'd been living off for a while. I hobbled in misery from one spot to another until I fell asleep somewhere. My body ached, and it was going to take a while for my hands to heal.

Mr. Parker called to say he'd heard about what had happened and wanted to help me get through the inquest of Carl's death. Once again,

I would need to give a statement about what had happened. He was sure the coroner would state that Carl died an accidental death, but still, it all had to be done.

I didn't have to go into the beginning of the long story about why I was spying on Carl, thank goodness, because that was a hard answer to explain, but I did have to tell what happened up above the clay cliff. Telling about what took place on that day was nowhere near as hard for me as explaining about the day Riley drowned, but it was still awful. I didn't fear for my own life when I tried to save Ri. But telling about what happened with Carl brought back every tiny detail, made crystal clear because the scene was so charged with cold, harsh fear. Telling the story made my jaws clench with tension so that it was hard to speak. I would become nearly as traumatized as I had been when everything was happening. Seeing the tragedy unfold in my mind brought me to tears and exhausted me again. Mama held my wrist above my wrapped hand, and Mr. Parker and my father sat close by.

I was glad Carl was dead, plain and simple, and I didn't care that he died in such a horrible way, either. Good riddance. I felt smug about my feelings, as if I had the right to condemn him to death. That is, until I saw Sky.

We stepped out onto the sidewalk from the lawyers' offices where I'd given my statement and came face-to-face with Sky and Maryanne. Seeing her there in front of me took the breath out of me. We stared into each other's eyes for a minute—two young girls, each trying to grasp what the other was thinking. Sky spoke first.

"Hi, Poppy."

"Hi." *What to say? What to say?* "You okay?"

She shook her head no. "I'm sorry my father hurt you." She was looking at my bandaged hands.

"That's okay." I felt so stupid for saying that, but what else was I going to say to her? It was there on that sidewalk, for just a moment, I felt a true heavy sadness for the girl who had been my friend. She would never have a father again.

Tears filled her eyes, making them glisten. It was hard for me to look at her.

"Well, he's gone now. He won't hurt anybody else ever again," she said.

Maryanne was digging through her purse and pulled out a wad of tissue and handed some to Sky, keeping some to dab her own tears.

"Sky wanted to say goodbye to you, Poppy. We'll be moving away in a few days."

My heart broke a little again. I had still clung to the childish idea that maybe, someday, we could be best friends, like before. I have no idea how I thought that could happen, but I hadn't given it up. Not yet.

"Will you ever come back?"

"Maybe." Sky looked to her Mama. "Maybe we will be back to visit Auntie."

Maryanne nodded in agreement.

"Well, okay then," I said. "So maybe I will see you again."

Sky nodded a gloomy nod and turned away to leave. Maryanne spoke to me before she walked away.

"Poppy, I know that you did what you had to do, and you must never, ever feel bad about the way things turned out. You just go on and have a good, young life, okay?" I nodded, but I couldn't think of anything to say back. She was a nice lady who thought I had guilty feelings about Carl being dead. I wasn't going to say any different.

I was glad that day was over with and we could go back home. All I wanted was to get well, not have anything hurt anymore. It was a long time before I could really use my hands and touch things with my fingers. My nails were stubby and crooked, and the skin around them was bright pink and tender for what seemed like forever. Mama dug out a fancy pair of gloves she had and gave them to me to wear when I went outside. She didn't trust me to keep my hands clean. She was right. I'd pet Goldie and Nicky and play out in the saddle shed. I would sit astride my saddle for hours, pretending it was on Nicky's back and that we were really going somewhere.

I worried a lot about having to go back to school. One day, Mama said she'd had another phone call from the school and someone was going to come to the house and talk to us about me catching up my schoolwork. I started to throw a fit, and right away, my father put a stop to that.

"Don't even start that stuff, Poppy. I've had it with this school crap. We already let you get away with too much as it is. Hurt or not, you can't just decide how things will be when you're ten years old. Some things are going to change around here."

"But, what about my hands?"

"If you can run around outside and play all day, you can get your schooling. And don't run to your mother about it when I ain't here, either."

Belinda was the happiest lady I had ever seen in my life. She laughed about everything. I liked her, even if she was the enemy. Mama settled her on the couch and fixed her a glass of tea. She took the first sip and smacked her lips.

"Mmm mm," she said. "This here's the best tea I've had in a long time." Then she laughed a big old laugh.

Belinda shuffled some papers around and asked me how I was doing. She said she knew we had been through some "hardships" and hoped we were "coming through" all right. Then she became serious, looked from me to Mama, and asked what our plans were for getting me back into school. Poor Mama, she looked like she had a mouthful of sour milk. I spoke up and said I didn't want to go to school no more, and I didn't see how that was my parents' fault. Belinda laughed that rumbling laugh and said, "Well, suga' baby, I hate to tell ya this, but it doesn't matter one teensy bit what you think. You have to go to school, anyway."

She didn't beat around the bush with my mama, either.

"Mizz Wade," she said, "I don't know how things go around your house, but you surely know that no child ought to be telling her mama and daddy that she isn't goin' to school and them just let her stay at home. You got to know that isn't right."

Poor Mama. She finally said, "Well, of course we know it isn't right, but you have to understand the circumstances." She didn't get to finish because Belinda spoke right up.

"I've read all the paperwork about what's happened around here, and it sounds real bad, but Poppy still has to be schooled, unless she is excused because she is mentally disabled." She looked at Mama, waiting.

"My father taught me when I didn't go before." I wanted to be helpful and was feeling bad for Mama. "He helped me do my work and stay up with my class."

"Well, why aren't you doing that now?" Belinda asked.

"Well, he doesn't have time now." That was true, but it sounded lame.

Mama jumped right in, like she'd already made a plan I knew nothing about. "What if we found a real tutor for Poppy to finish out this year, and then she could get back to regular school for her fourth grade? She could do her work as long as it takes into summer and be ready to go on."

I stared a hole through Mama. Sounded like summer in hell to me.

"Do you know someone that would tutor Poppy, Mizz Wade? Someone capable and willin' to teach the curriculum?"

"As a matter of fact, I think I do. Her name is Loretta Jamison. She's a neighbor down the road." She didn't even glance my way.

I was flabbergasted. I sat in a stunned silence while they discussed Loretta and the possibility of her tutoring me.

It had been Janelle who had brought the idea up to Mama. I never had heard a word about it. Janelle and Loretta had come to see me a couple of times, and Loretta had been really nice to me, but she sure never said anything about teaching me my schoolwork.

Belinda said she would have to look into that happening and be sure that Loretta was capable of taking on the job. Mama gave her the Jamison's phone number, and Belinda gathered up all her papers and stood to leave. At the front screen, she stopped and looked square at me.

"Listen to me now, young lady. You are one smart little girl, and you could go a long way in this ol' world if you mind your Ps an' Qs. Youngsters like you spend all your time usin' those smart brains of yours manipulatin' life 'cuz you think you know best. Don't be one a them, sweetie-pie. You use those brains of yours to learn all you can about everything, you hear me?"

All I could do was nod.

Loretta turned out to be a good tutor and a real friend. We got together three times a week for her to teach me an arithmetic or reading lesson, and once I found out that I could ask her about most anything I wanted to know, I looked forward to those days. If the weather was good, we sat outside at the red table, but the times I liked the best were when I got to go to Loretta's house. The Jamison's house was bigger than ours, but what I liked most about it was that it was open and light. The place was neat as could be, and Janelle liked to bake something special when she knew I was coming to do lessons. The kitchen had an old woodstove in the corner, and the feeling in there was always warm and homey.

Ward and Janelle were so polite to me, always offering me something to drink or eat soon as I was in the door. What I saw the most was that they were so polite to each other, and they laughed. Ward's laugh was a deep, chuckling kind, and Janelle's laugh, big as the room. Sometimes, when I'd see Ward give Janelle a little kiss on her cheek while she was standing over the sink, I'd feel embarrassed. They hugged and patted on one another as they moved around their house. Out-and-out affection like that made me feel uncomfortable until I became used to seeing it.

One day I told Loretta I wished my parents were like hers. "They're so nice to each other and don't fight, like mine do."

"Oh! That isn't true," she said. "They argue over the dumbest things sometimes. One time Mama threw a spoon at Daddy because he said her soup tasted funny."

I couldn't imagine them like that and told her so. Loretta was the one who talked to me about my parents' behavior and tried to help me understand why they acted the way they did. She said that people end up being who they are for all different reasons. She didn't think their reasons had anything to do with me.

By July, I had caught up all of my third grade work, and Belinda came back out to see me and check that everything was up to par. She was so tickled that I had finished my work, she put her big arms around me and gave me a hug that just about broke my ribs again. She was laughing up a storm as she went to get back in her car. Belinda sure got a kick out of life.

The days were hot, but not like the summer before. No records would be set during that summer. The mercury seldom climbed to the one hundred mark, and the nights were cool enough to sleep as long as the windows were all open wide. I was content to have my own time back. I walked the creek every day, checking on the tadpoles and tiny frogs.

One day I came across my first rattlesnake down by the crossing and yelled my lungs out for my father to come see it. When he heard me, he grabbed a shovel and hurried down to where I was. We watched the snake coil up, and it started buzzing its rattles. Warning us to stay away, my father said. As he chopped at the snake with the shovel, I had a flashback to Carl chopping at me with *his* shovel on the clay cliff. The vision was so clear and happened so fast, I gasped and tried to run backward, falling down on my back in the dirt and rocks. I yelled "No! No!" and started crying hysterically. My father threw the shovel down and grabbed me up, carrying me part way up the driveway. He told Mama later that he saw pure terror on my face. He held me and hugged me like he hadn't in a long time. I had almost forgotten that warm, happy feeling of how safe and secure I felt in my father's strong arms.

Epilogue

Over three years have passed since Riley died. I'll be fourteen soon. I know this: nothing stays the same for long. Nothing.

Some things about the creek change each winter. A new tadpole pond will appear when a spring opens up, and an old one will wash away, fill in with sand. A bank will give up and tumble when the water is high, making a bend where it had flowed straight and neat for years. Fallen tree trunks make mossy, gurgling waterfalls. But the spring tubs are always there, always full of warm, summer water by June.

Going there is a ritual for me. Mama joins me sometimes, but I go alone most often, and I cherish the time. I lie on the warm rock, let my feet dangle in the water, and look to the sky. It is a place where I try to reason with the past and wonder about the future. I still secretly undress and slip into the deepest pool and float in the liquid softness. Sometimes I think that, if Mother Nature was a person, she would be my true mother. I know her madness firsthand, but I also know her beauty and kindness. She offers a safe place when I need it most.

I love the creek when it is a raging demon just as much as I do when it is nothing but tadpole ponds. Riley wasn't taken away by the cruelty of nature; he was taken by people who did him wrong. Even the ones who loved him. Someone—one of us—didn't do something we should have to make the difference in Ri's life.

I think about death too much. I remember when I was a little kid and I thought death just meant that people lay down and closed their eyes, and the angels came and made it sadly beautiful. The idea of dying terrifies me now.

And animals . . . I can't bear it when animals have to die. About a year ago, Mama came into my room one evening, where I was reading a book on my bed, and I knew something was wrong the minute I saw how her lips were set in a straight, narrow line and her eyes were squinty. She'd come to tell me that my father had found Nicky down between the creek and the canyon road fence. She was dead. Even though I knew she was old, and that old animals die like old people, I just couldn't take it. I wanted to die right then, too. I stayed in my bed and cried for maybe three days.

As far as Carl goes, well, even though he's gone, I still have to work on not being so full of hate toward him. I still picture him, sitting up, over by the clay cliff, with his head split open and his eye bulging, and that's when I hope he is still sizzling in hell. I swear, I will never forgive him, but Belinda says I will have to someday.

Until a person starts knowing me, they would probably think I'm just an ordinary thirteen-year-old country girl. But I'm not. Odd, different, weird, peculiar—I know all those words are used to describe me. I'm good at sticking my chin out like it doesn't matter, but those words make my insides hurt. I am who I am because of how I was raised. Loretta told me that when she was my tutor, and it makes sense. She said Mama and my father couldn't help it.

I don't know that they are any better at being my parents, but they are nicer to each other than they used to be, and that right there makes me love them in a different kind of way. Kids forgive their mamas and fathers for worse things than mine ever put on me. I have mostly forgiven mine.

Mama and Janelle are pretty good friends nowadays. Janelle is helping my mama to learn to drive and not be so nervous about it. I went with them down the road in Janelle's car once, and we laughed so hard at dumb stuff—like Mama hitting the brake pedal and throwing us forward—that she had to pull over to the side of the road until she could control herself. Mama says she wants to get some kind of job in town, at a store or something. My father doesn't want her to, but I don't think she's going to let that stop her. Makes me feel proud of her. She says he'll get used to it, and besides, they will have a little extra money coming in. Maybe that will be the change that fills up Mama's life.

My brothers live in town now. They come out on weekends, and Mama cooks up a big meal for them like they hadn't eaten all week. They help my father with his cows and fixing fences, things like that. They don't like me being a teenager. They boss me around and try to tell me how to act. They warn me about staying away from some of the town kids who have bad reputations. I swear, they know everybody.

My father is happy to see them come. I guess we seem more like a normal family than we used to. At least it feels that way.

These days, when I pass the mud house place, I don't look really hard over across the creek. Somebody hauled the little trailer full of awfulness away, and besides that, all the brush and weeds have grown up so much you really can't even tell where some things were. Father likes to mention that the adobe walls have turned to piles of mud, just like he knew they would. Makes me mad when he says it, I guess because it was supposed to be Sky's home, and now everything is gone. Every once in a while, I get a notion to walk across the bridge and sit on the boulder where Sky and I spent such good times together. I guess it would make me too sad or I would have done it by now.

The worst thing is my nightmares. They don't happen often anymore, but if I do have one, it's a doozy. Carl is always in them, doing something mean to me or Sky. He usually carries something in his hands—a club or stick or even the awful shovel he used on me. And if Maryanne is part of a bad dream, she is just a shadow in the background. I think of her as the ghost in my dreams because she is a blue wisp of a lady with long, dark hair. Most times, before I can make myself wake up, I dream I am in the muddy water, floating fast, and I can't see a thing—can't see Riley right there beside me because I can't force my eyes to open. I wake in a mud-brown fog and struggle to understand what has happened. Sometimes I call out for Mama like a little kid. Makes me wish I was just a regular girl.

I can't imagine living anywhere else but here in the canyon house. I never want to leave the creek and the Indian cave. I don't play silly pretend games anymore, but I remember how much fun they were, how I spent my time when we first came to the canyon. I still go up the hill and sit in the cave. It feels good to be there. I've lain out on the warm stone floor and fallen asleep.

People are always asking me what I want to be when I grow up. Mama and Belinda tell me all the time that I can be what I want to be, but I just don't know. Once, I told Belinda I wanted to raise horses and be a veterinarian.

"Well, suga," she said, "then you better get this thing you have about school straightened out in your little head. You will have to get good grades from now on if you want to be a veterinarian."

Belinda always encourages me to be a good person. She says I am too smart for my own good. I heard her tell Mama that I have an old woman's mind. Well, I don't know about that. No matter what, I'm just a kid.

The End

About the Author

Janice Gilbertson hails from the Santa Lucia Mountains in Western California where she lives with her husband and an assortment of critters. Only one or two crow-flown miles to the west lies the ranch where she was raised. Growing up in the '50s, a shy little girl with two older brothers, Janice learned how to entertain herself and developed a grand imagination. She was a conjurer of characters long before she began to put them on paper. Her love for all things Western, including the ranching lifestyle and eventually Cowboy and Western Poetry and story writing, have strongly influenced the stories of *The Canyon House* and her first novel, *Summer of '58*.

Special Bonus!

Here is a free sample of Janice's novel, *Summer of '58*, available at Pen-L.com, online, and in bookstores.

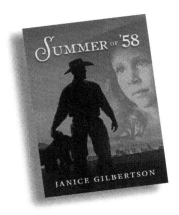

How long can you keep a secret to protect someone you love? Forever? That's what Angela Garrett promised the man in the dark.

"This is one of the best books I have read in a long time. It's one of those 'hard-to-put-down' books!"
— Yvonne K. Hollenbeck

"An exciting book about a young girl's desire to spend time with her father who happens to be a bronc rider. They take off in the summer of '58, both wanting to renew their relationship, even if it means being on the road and hitting all the top rodeos, sleeping in the car at times, and eating fast food. But for young Angela, it becomes a life-changing summer when she's caught between keeping her father alive and holding on to a secret of the worst kind. Gilbertson writes horror scenes with a gentle hand, not explicit, but enough to get the idea across."
— Carmen Peone

Angela watched the clock on the wall tick the minutes away, counting the seconds of them inside her head. Ten minutes until . . . five minutes until . . . and at six o'clock exactly, she heard his car pull up. Her stomach quivered, and her mind played a startling trick on her—maybe she shouldn't go with him after all. She didn't want to hurt her mother's feelings, and she knew her mom was worried. So worried. But then, there he came, clomping up the porch steps and peeking through the screen door like a boy coming to play.

"Hey, kid!" his voice filled up the living room. "You ready? Where's your ma?"

"I'm right here, Lanny Ray. You don't need to wake the whole neighborhood."

"This here's all you got, Ang? This ain't much for a long trip." He saw the questioning look on Angela's face and quickly shrugged his own comment away, "Ah, don't matter. We have to do our washin' along the way anyhow." He picked up Angela's suitcase and the box and headed out to the car, carrying them effortlessly as if they weighed nothing. Angela followed, and Arlene came behind, tightening the belt of her robe and twisting the soft sash in her fingers. Lanny Ray unlocked the vast cave of a trunk and put Angela's things beside his own large suitcase, his chaps neatly laid on top, and back in the corner, his saddle bronc rig.

Suddenly, Arlene felt as though she had so much to say to her girl. Too much. Words came spewing out.

"Call me. Promise. Anytime. Well, not mid-day but, you know, after work. After five. Unless, of course, it's an emergency then call anytime, okay? Promise me."

FIND IT AT
www.Pen-L.com/SummerOf58

If you'd like to hear more about Janice's upcoming books and other great Pen-L authors, sign up for our Pals of Pen-L Newsletter here!

34131925R00155

Made in the USA
San Bernardino, CA
19 May 2016